'Extraordinary' *Simon Mayo*

'Melvin Burgess is one of the founding fathers of
modern teen fiction' *Juno Dawson*

'A dark, deep tale of magic and manipulation' *Deirdre Sullivan*

'The godfather of young adult fiction' *BBC Front Row*

'Rich, twisty storytelling . . . Written with observation and skill'
Sunday Times

'Burgess is a master storyteller'
'Children's Book of the Week' *The Times*

'Melvin Burgess is an original, experimental voice . . . draws
on the rich tradition of British fantasy rooted in landscape
and folklore' *Observer*

'[An] arresting coming-of-age tale' *Guardian*

'Tackles issues of control, identity, personal freedom and trust
through the medium of folklore and magic . . . An arresting,
high-octane adventure' *Daily Mail*

'A nuanced and thrilling tale of magic, seduction and coercion'
Irish Times

'A powerful tale about witchcraft with a truly arresting opening
which sucks you in and doesn't let go' *Irish Independent*

'Addressing the subjects of family, inheritance, friendship and
politics, this is a compelling and exciting tale for teens'

Other books by Melvin Burgess

An Angel for May
The Baby and Fly Pie
Bloodsong
Bloodtide
Burning Issy
The Cry of the Wolf
Doing It
Junk
Lady: My Life as a Bitch
Nicholas Dane
Sara's Face

The Lost Witch

MELVIN BURGESS

ANDERSEN PRESS

2 4 6 8 10 9 7 5 3 1

First published in hardback in 2018 by Andersen Press

The right of Melvin Burgess to be identified as the author of this work
has been asserted by him in accordance with the Copyright,
Designs and Patents Act, 1988.

British Library Cataloguing in Publication Data available.

ISBN 978 1 78344 835 7

Typeset by Palimpsest Book Production Ltd, Falkirk, Stirlingshire

Printed and bound in Great Britain by Clays Ltd, Elcograf S.p.A.

To Charlie, for her patience, her relentlessness, her eagle eyes and of course, for her unbounded enthusiasm for killing off female characters.

Part One

The Second World

1

It was tipping it down. It had been for weeks but today the weather was savage. The wind heaved at the car, shoving it across the road and flinging rain like gunshot against the windows. There was water everywhere, pouring out of the air, flooding the black fields, flowing across the windscreen. It sprang in torrents from the walls and ran in rivers down the road.

The Wilder family were all furious after spending two weeks' holiday trapped by the rain in a farmhouse on the North Yorkshire moors. Bea in particular was outraged. Her friends had been to Italy, Spain, France – even Florida in one case. She'd been to a swamp in North Yorkshire. Her mum and dad had been bickering the whole way home while baby Michael grizzled next to her in his car seat. All any of them wanted to do was get back home. They weren't far off, either, only twenty minutes away on the high moors when it all began. A set of lights appeared, bouncing across the fields in the darkness above them. Someone was driving headlong down the hill. In this weather!

'Look at that,' said Bea's mum. 'Off-road. Bloody dangerous. He's going far too fast.'

'Must be a farmer on a quad,' muttered her dad, clutching

the steering wheel like it was a life jacket. 'Must have lost a sheep or something.'

'It'd take more than sheep to get me out in this,' said her mum. Then . . . 'Look, Jamie. There's more of them. And over there.'

Bea peered out. All around them people were charging down to the road, some on quads, some on foot, some on motocross bikes. More came into sight as they watched: running, slipping and skidding over the sodden black fields. Some of them were already climbing over the stone walls and pushing open the gates to the road. There were dogs too, running fast towards them.

'What on earth is going on?' demanded Bea's mum. 'What is it? Some kind of hunt?'

Even as she spoke, Bea's eye was caught by a movement down by the side of the car. A hare. No, two. No – three! Three hares, sodden-furred, muddy-legged, wet to their bones, loping along in the road beside the car, exhausted.

'Hares!' she exclaimed.

Her dad braked. Bea pressed down the electric window and leaned out to get a better view. One of the hares, a great, gaunt beast with grey on its muzzle, had only one eye. This was when Bea's life changed, when it ceased to be just hers and her family's and became something beyond that. She regretted that moment many times, but she never forgot the shiver of excitement that ran up and down her spine and raised the hairs on her arms and neck.

The hare turned its head sideways to look up at her. Bea looked straight into its eye and she saw . . .

Worlds upon worlds within worlds. Millions of them, some like this one, some impossibly different. They fitted inside one another like Russian dolls – more worlds than there are stars in the sky or atoms in your eye.

Bea recoiled, shocked at the size and magnificence of the universe she lived in. And at that same moment the quads and bikes burst upon them. Engines roared, sudden headlamps shone in and blinded them.

But that wasn't all.

Suddenly the whole hillside was lit up. There were no shadows; the light was everywhere – in the car, under the car, above the car. The bikes and quads, the people and dogs were as brightly lit from below as they were from above. It was as if the air itself shone around them.

Two of the hares, including old one-eye, dropped down under the car, but the remaining animal spooked. It jumped sideways, twisted in mid-air, caught its powerful hind legs against the roadside wall and bounded back – right at Bea. It shot in through the car window as neat as a bolt going home and landed with a bruising, sodden thump right in her lap.

'It's come in, it's come in,' yelled her mum, twisting about in her seat in a panic. Baby Michael let out a scream, then clapped his hand over his mouth in a curiously adult gesture, and stared goggle-eyed at the hare next to him. The hare scrabbled briefly and painfully against Bea's legs with its sharp claws, then crouched down into her and stilled. It was bigger than she thought a hare would be, as big as a small dog, so heavy on her bruised thighs, so muddy and cold and wet. In another moment the heat of its body warmed through to her skin. It became utterly still. Nothing moved; but the heart inside it beat furiously.

Bea understood at once that whatever else she did she had to give sanctuary to this wild creature.

'What's it doing, what's it doing?' yelled her mum.

The hare flinched. Bea glanced sideways at Michael, who was staring spellbound. She smiled at him to reassure him and Michael smiled back. The brilliant light shining from everywhere made everything crystal clear. Every drop of water, every hair on her arm and on the hare's back was microscopically vivid. The wind and the pelting rain blew in through the open window, but Bea didn't dare move. She stilled herself, just as the hare had done. She knew without looking that Michael was doing the same. She pressed her elbows and her legs together, made herself small and quiet. She was terrified and delighted in one go. Who would ever imagine such a thing? And it was happening to *her*.

Unlike her mum, Bea's dad was calm – he always was. He was staring over his shoulder at her.

'You OK, Bea?'

Bea glanced up. She could see every detail of him in that light – every fleck and stubble on his chin, every line of colour in his grey eyes. She gave him a little nod, and he nodded back.

'Calm down, Kelsey, it's just a hare. Bea's hiding it from them, aren't you, Bea?' Bea nodded again, gratefully.

Her mum put her hand on her chest. 'What kind of beast does such a thing? Look at it. It must be riddled with fleas!'

The hare lay on Bea's lap, its outside so still, its heart inside so frantic. It was huge. Any idea you had that hares were just big rabbits was gone. This beast could kick you to the ground if it caught you right. It could break your nose. Her mum was staring at it with her eyes bulging. Baby Michael reached out a pudgy hand and laid it gently on the hare's back. The creature flinched briefly again, and wriggled deeper into Bea's lap. Michael looked up at Bea and beamed at her, his mouth open in pure delight.

'It's a hunt. We're saving the hare from those bastards, OK?' said their dad.

There was a pause while they all took this in.

'You never see hares around here,' said their mum. They were whispering now. 'And they want to hunt down and kill the ones we have!'

'Sick!' hissed Bea. And that was it; they were united. The Wilder family had their moments, at one another's throats like everyone else. But once they got an idea in their heads they were rock-solid. Nothing was going to get between them on this.

Outside, the hunt was closing in. Bea's dad wound the window up and gently put the car back into gear, but before he could pull away a Land Rover came hurtling out of the field above them. It tore into the road in a slew of mud and skidded to a halt right in front of them. The wipers smeared mud over the glass, and Bea peered through it to see if they could squeeze past. A big man in a waterproof cape was getting out, black against the headlights. But before he got to them there was a commotion outside. A dog had shoved its great wide head under their car, growling and baying, and one of the hares sheltering there ran out – straight into the jaws of a dog on the other side.

There was a loud snap as the dog's teeth bit the air. The hare had bounded up at Bea's window just as the first had; but now the window was closed. It banged heavily against the glass and fell to the ground, but was up in an instant – a great arcing leap high into the air, right up on top of the car. They heard it landing above them with a loud bang, then the sound of its claws scrabbling for purchase.

In Bea's lap, the first hare raised its eyes, its mouth open. Above them, the hare on the roof slipped. It fell down the windscreen, its coat leaving a muddy trail behind it. It slithered briefly on the bonnet, and fell to the ground.

The dogs were on it in a second. The family stared in horror through the headlamp-spangled rain as the hare was flung into the air. The injured animal spun before them and came down with a bang on the bonnet. It tried to leap off, but it was half-stunned and dazzled by the light. It slipped and fell again to the ground.

The dogs rushed in. One of them seized it by the back legs and began to thrash it from side to side, like a heavy wet rag. Through the noise of dogs and people, the shouting, barking and yelling, they could hear the hare's voice, a thin scream of terror and pain as the dog thrashed it to and fro. Amazingly, from beneath their car, the old one-eyed hare emerged. It stood on its hind legs and started to box at the dog's face, tempting it to drop its victim and go for it instead, but the other dogs lunged at it, and it had to run back under the car or die itself.

The hare on Bea's lap stood up to look out of the window, front paws resting on the door handle. It turned its gaze on her – as if she could do anything! – and her heart broke with pity for the beast. She put her arms around its chest and wept.

The hare struggled to be free. 'Let me out,' it cried.

Yes! She would do anything to help. Bea pressed the window control, the wind and rain blew in again – but when she looked back, the hare was staring at her with astonishment, its jaw hanging open. Bea gasped, because . . . she had understood! She had understood! She saw the hare shake its head, then it turned and leaped out of the car window. It hit the wall and fell on its side on the ground with a jarring thud but gathered itself and bounded directly at the dog that held the other hare in its jaws.

It was such a hopeless thing, the hare's attack on the dog. In the car it had seemed surprisingly big, but next to the huge dogs, full of the lust for blood, it was frail and small. The two animals' desperate attempt to save their family – Bea was certain they were a family – struck right at her heart. And in her heart, something magical opened; a door which could never be closed again. She felt something rushing up towards her from deep in the earth. It was a force she could not resist.

She leaned out of the window, opened her mouth and a voice sprang into her throat:

'I SUMMON YOU, YOU CROWNED RUNNERS,' she cried. 'I SUMMON YOU FROM SLEEP. I SUMMON AND COMMAND!' This was not a voice that came from inside her. It came from deep, deep down – so deep it felt to her as if the earth beneath her had spoken those words, not her at all.

'Bea!' exclaimed her mum. You never heard such a noise from such a small throat. Her father looked at her strangely. 'Was that *words*?' he said, and Bea understood at once that no one there had any idea what she had said.

Everything changed – the light, the night, the rain. Shadows appeared all around them. Bea peered through the rain trying to make them out. So big! They were – deer? Yes, deer! But not the small roes you saw around here from time to time. Big ones – red deer, stags with huge antlers above their heads like crowns. They came pouring over the fence and out of the gates. One of them lowered its head and gored a dog, tossing it high into the air. The dog yelped, twisting as it hit the ground, and crawled off on its belly to hide under the Land Rover in front of them. People were shouting, yelling, slithering, falling in the mud as the deer barged into them, legs kicking out, great heads down among them, harrying them, chasing them away.

It lasted just a few minutes, then it was done. The deer, gone. The hares, gone. The supernatural light that had surrounded them died. The huntsmen and women floundered on their backs in the mud in the headlamps. A herd of huge deer! What a chance! Everything had been saved.

The wind gusted in on Bea through the open window, the rain fell in sheets from heaven. All around them, people picked themselves up from the ground where they had fallen or been brushed aside. The quads and bikes stood stalled or overturned on the road. It was unbelievable. There had been no red deer here for years – the last of them had been killed decades ago.

Bea's dad eased the car forward. There was just room if he took it slowly, but before he could drive off the tall man from the Land Rover in front of them came up to the car and rapped on the window. Her dad wound it down. The man bent to speak to him.

'If you'd just step outside the vehicle, sir.'

Her dad looked up in alarm. The big man had lost his hood and his brown curly hair was plastered down his forehead with the rain. He had a half-smile on his face, but his tone was commanding. There was a brief pause, and her dad moved to unbuckle his seat belt. But her mum, who always took charge of this sort of situation, put her hand on his leg and leaned across.

'We haven't done anything, have we?' she said.

'Just a routine check, madam.'

'Are you a policeman?' she asked him.

'We do have policemen here, if that's what it takes . . .' The man straightened briefly and called out – 'Ask Charles to come over. This lady needs the police to speak to them.'

He bent down to the window again, his hand gripping the window edge, and looked inside at Bea – right into her eyes. Bea stared back, but his gaze went so deep that she had to look away.

Bea's mum suddenly leaned across and slapped at his hand.

'How dare you, who do you think you are, get your hands off – off!' she yelped. The man let go and stood up in surprise. 'In this rain? You plonker. Is this Peterborough? Your giraffes are all over the car park. Go, go, go.'

Bewildered, the man looked around; Bea's dad took his

chance, revved the engine, put it into gear and shot off. He swerved, grazing the car against the stones of the wall, but just managed to squeeze through the gap between the Land Rover and the wall – and away! Behind them, the tall man lifted his arm to his face to protect himself from the spray of their wheels.

'The Wilders do it again!' roared her mum. Cheering loudly, they drove downhill towards home. It wasn't the first time Bea's mum's famous confuse-a-cop act had got her and Dad off the hook. Bea had heard all about it before, but she'd never seen it in action.

'That man! His face! Did you see it?' Even her dad, who was always so calm, was grinning, his grey eyes sparkling behind his spectacles.

'He looked like he'd just seen a ghost,' bellowed her mum.

Yes, thought Bea – or heard a hare speak.

'Did you hear it?' she demanded. It couldn't be true – could it? 'The hare? Did you?'

'What a noise you made!' said her mum. 'I thought you were throwing up or something.'

'Dreadful noise,' agreed her dad. Bea looked up at something in his voice and saw his eyes on her in the mirror, frowning. She looked away. Hares can't talk, she thought. But it had seemed so real! Could she have just imagined it?

She must have.

They drove on down the hill, marvelling at what had happened on the moors that evening. The deer! Where had they come from? The hunt! No one had ever talked about a hunt around here. So many of them out in such filthy weather, as if catching those hares was all that mattered. And that man, trying to stop them and get them out of the car. Who on earth was he?

Beside Bea, baby Michael reached out to pull at her arm. 'Wabbit,' he said. 'Wabbit, Bea.'

'No. A hare, Michael. It was a hare.'

'Hare,' he said.

Bea looked over to him. Had he heard it speak too? Michael nodded and looked back over his shoulder anxiously. She reached across and held his hand, still muddy from the hare's fur.

What a night it had been! Already she had lost any sense of what exactly was real and what was imagined. Talking hares. Voices from the earth. Such crazy things . . .

And then they were in the town, winding through the wet streets. Even now, in the rain and wind, there were people out and about, in the cafés, blowing down the streets, peering out from the bright windows of the pub on the corner.

The car turned up the hill towards home. Her mum sometimes said that the best thing about holidays was getting back home, but this time, thought Bea, the best bit had happened before they got there. But what did it mean? Such thoughts, such feelings – such events!

In bed that night, Bea thought about the hare that spoke and the voice which had visited her from the underground, which had grabbed hold of the night and turned it into living things, for a brief time. What's wrong with me? she thought. She'd been like a child at the theatre, believing everything she saw. But her family were rebels – atheists, republicans, realists. She knew magic did not and could not exist. It was a shame, but there it was.

She turned over to go to sleep. She had already started to disbelieve.

2

The next day Bea awoke exhausted. She sat up to look out of her window, wishing that the world had changed, but it was the same old view – same rain, same trees, same old Bea. Her phone pinged – a friend asking if she was back. But she was too tired, so she flopped down onto her bed and went back to sleep. She didn't get downstairs until early afternoon, when the smell of bacon called to her.

Her parents were in the kitchen with cups of tea and bacon butties. Michael in his high chair waved a soggy rusk at her when she came in, offering her a bite, which she took – just a small piece off a dry corner.

'Crikey, it's the living dead,' said her mum. 'Are you OK?' she asked, getting up to pass her hand over Bea's forehead.

Bea leaned into her. 'Just tired,' she said. She put her arms around her mum for a moment, then pulled away, grabbed a butty from the plate in the centre of the table and went over to the window. The sun was flinging a few glistening beams of light down between the clouds onto the wet trees and the road outside.

She got out her phone and started messaging her friends.

'I wonder if you should have a day in,' said her mum.

'Mum! I've been a virtual prisoner for two weeks!'

'You look so pale. And why are you so tired? You haven't *done* anything.'

'Exactly.'

'You could help in the shop,' said her dad, glancing up. 'I've got loads to do. I could do with a hand.'

Bea's dad was a jeweller, a neat, small man who made pieces out of gold and silver and tiny polished stones that would break your heart, they were that pretty. Bea was always amazed that her quiet dad – he was pretty ugly to tell the truth – was the creator of such charming little things.

'Not today, Dad. I want to see my friends,' she begged.

He shrugged assent, despite her mum's pout of disapproval, and Bea went back to her phone. She arranged to meet some friends down the park, reassured her mum by devouring a slice of cake and a banana on top of her butty – no sick person could stomach that lot – before putting on her wellies and raincoat and setting off down the hill.

The river was high, rubbing its back on the underside of the bridges as she walked down into town. She paused by the weir to watch it hurtling past, enjoying the thunderous rush of brown water and foam. For a moment, she imagined not water rushing past but a stampede of horses storming into town, glistening and shiny with wet, rushing and shoving their way past, full gallop . . .

Ridiculous! She was annoying herself now. Stop it, Bea, she thought, and hurried on to meet her friends and salvage what was left of the summer.

* * *

There wasn't much going on. Everything was wet and muddy. There was a puddle as big as a small lake on the football pitch. A few kids were out on the skateboard park showing off their tricks while Bea and her friends stood about swapping holiday stories and watching the skaters go through their paces.

There was a new boy on the ramps a few years older than them. Lars, he was called. He'd fixed some fiery red and orange lights to the underside of his battered old board, which was a cheap trick – but that boy knew how to skate. The board spun and glittered beneath him like an advertisement. He wore shorts and a T-shirt, arms and legs bare despite his dare-devil moves, with his red hair up in an Alice band. A total poser, thought Bea. Even so, you couldn't take your eyes off him. He flew. He made Bea want to fly too.

The girls were all over him. When he started to offer rides to her friends, they were queuing up. He stood with his feet straddling the board and had them stand between his legs. Then he pushed off, weaving in and out and around the slopes, the chosen girl leaning back into him, squealing and laughing while the older girls stood wryly watching. Bea stood with them, arms folded tightly across her chest. Ridiculous. Pathetic! But when he offered her a go, there she was, grinning like an idiot, running up for her turn.

Lars got her to step backwards onto the board, then put his arms around her. 'Use me,' he whispered. 'Lean back. I'll guide you.'

Bea giggled.

'Ready?'

'Yes, yes!'

He pushed off. Bea swayed for a moment in surprise, then relaxed back and pressed into him as he rocked behind her, swerving smoothly around the slopes. And – it was easy! The other girls had been falling all over the place, but Bea was with him on every curve. She was a natural. When it was done she stepped lightly off – the only one who had stayed on till the end.

The boy grinned. 'Good girl!' he said, and turned to the next.

'Like it?' asked one of the older girls dryly.

Embarrassed, Bea tossed her head and stalked off. 'It wasn't him, it was the board,' she told her friends. But it had been such fun! Suddenly she was hatching an urge to make a skateboard fly under her feet just as this one did for him.

Back at home, Bea nagged her parents to get her a skateboard of her own and a couple of days later she was setting out self-consciously with her new toy under her arm and, knee and elbow protectors in place, off to practise in the park. She was as proud as a prince – but when she put it on the ground and jumped up on it, that glimpse of magic she'd had with Lars had vanished. She wobbled, shook and fell to the ground like a leg of lamb.

She got straight back on, but it was no good. As soon as the board moved, she fell. To make it worse the red-headed boy turned up to watch her. After ten minutes, bruised and humiliated, she was ready to give up. But Lars the poser didn't sneer or tease.

'You're actually doing really well,' he said. 'It's the board that's bad. This thing' – he flicked his fingers against her shiny new skateboard – 'it's sketchy. It talks the talk but it don't walk the walk. My old thing might look as if it's seen better days, but it's got balance. Maybe I've got something at home you could try out. Here, look – practise on mine. I'll pop back home and see what I can find.'

He was as good as his word. Bea balanced and fell, balanced and flew, balanced and fell for an hour on the borrowed board, and then he was back with his easy smile and his pretty face, and a really ancient old board, even more battered and scratched than his.

'I learned on this,' he said. 'Maybe you can too.'

Every morning for the next few days Bea woke up covered with scrapes and bruises, aching from head to foot. She didn't care. Lars had taken her under his wing. The rest of the world seemed to fade away. Her mum and dad, her home, her friends all began to feel like events from someone else's life. And the hares on the moor, that glimpse of another world? Even though she'd thought at the time she would remember it for ever, that faded too. All she wanted to do was skate. She swooped up and down the ramps, spun and jumped and fell again and again, until she knew every tilt and groove in the park.

Her friends teased her. How she adored Lars! How much time she spent with him! They made her blush red from top to toe. Look at Bea! She's in love with him already!

'It's the skating,' she insisted. That was all. But in bed at night she squeezed her pillow with delight and grinned into the darkness. Life was sweet, she told herself. Oh yes, life is sweet, life is *so* sweet! But not because of Lars. Of course not!

Her mum saw what was going on and worried about her spending so much time with an older boy.

'You're not his girlfriend, are you?' she asked, which drove Bea crazy. As if you can't have a friendship between a boy and a girl that isn't like that! As if she didn't know he was far too old for her.

As if she cared.

3

It was mid-week, just ten days before school started. The sun shone in between fluffy white clouds – summer had begun just in time for autumn and Bea was making the most of it. She was practising a move – down one ramp, up the other – twist at the top. Down that side and up the other – twist at the top. Her record so far was five.

For the tenth time that day she took a fall and ended up rolling on her back in the gully between the ramps. She looked up to the sky and saw something that could not be.

A man was riding horseback among the clouds.

She lay still for a second or two, trying to make sense of it. Her eyes spun in her head, her stomach clenched. It was impossible! But when her breath returned, the vision was still there. 'What's that?' she cried, and everyone turned to look.

'What?' someone asked, and Bea knew in that moment that this was in her eyes only. For the first time in days came a memory . . . a hare with a single eye through which she had seen the universe. Another that had begged her – 'Let me out!'

She got up and went to sit on the grass away from the others, as if she were just taking a break. When she was sure no one was watching she tipped her head back and sneaked another look up towards the sky.

It was still there. The man was wearing old-time clothes, she wasn't sure from what period. The horse was a great heavy beast with feathery hair around his feet, and although his hooves were treading down on thin air the weight of him seemed to thump around her. It was unmissable – but everyone else was missing it. Bea ran her gaze across the park to see if anyone else had caught her looking, and at once her eye fell on a girl, about ten or eleven, standing over by the tennis courts. She too was gazing up at the rider. As Bea stared, the girl dropped her gaze to look directly at Bea, and pointed up.

Bea turned away at once, terrified. How could a thing be seen by some people and not by others? Either it was there or it wasn't. She waited a bit, then glanced back. The girl was staring at her intently. Bea got up abruptly and walked away. If she was going mad, she wanted to do it where no one else could see.

Out of sight of the skaters she broke into a trot. Past the café on the old bowling green, over the canal into the memorial gardens, where she found a bench. She went the whole way without looking up once, but all the time she was fearfully aware of the events unfolding high over her head. She sat down, cast a wary look each way to make sure no one was watching, then again raised her eyes to the skies.

The rider had turned his horse round and was trotting towards her now. Closer he came, down from the sky as if he was riding a stairway from heaven. But it wasn't Bea he was after. Suddenly he stooped low, put an arm out and plucked someone from the air. It was a girl, about four or five years old. She shrieked with excitement as he swung her up and plonked her on the horse in front of him, where she clutched hold of the coarse hair of its mane. Then she turned and looked up into his face, and she beamed, just beamed with pleasure.

'She's losing them one by one. It's getting faster, I think,' said a voice. Bea looked down with a jerk. It was the girl she had just seen in the park – the one who had looked up to the sky and pointed.

At once Bea got up and began to move off. She didn't want this. But the girl grabbed her arm.

'I know who you are,' she said urgently. 'I saw you looking.' She pointed up at the sky. Bea's neck muscles twitched, but she kept her gaze low. She wasn't going to admit to anything. She tried to push her way past again but the girl stood her ground. 'Wear this,' she demanded. She thrust something into Bea's hand. 'The Hunt knows you're here. It'll protect you. *Please!*' she begged, seeing the doubt in Bea's face. 'It *was* you on the moors that day, wasn't it?' she added.

Bea hid her shock by looking into her hand at the object the girl had given her. It fitted her palm nicely, but it was a dreadful thing, ugly as mud. It had a long, twisted face, with little blue stones for eyes, a row of tiny wee browny orange stones for teeth, and a sliver of bone for a nose. There was a piece of mirror in the forehead. The whole thing was made out of some kind of dirt. There were feathers and tiny bones rolled up in it. And yet . . .

. . . and yet the blue eyes stared up at her from the palm

of her hand, and the crooked orange teeth glinted in the light. It was dreadful, but Bea felt at once that it was on her side.

She was so surprised that she wanted such an ugly thing that she raised her head and took a good look at the girl for the first time. She was poor and skinny – poor clothes, poor face, bony from head to foot. She wore tatty old trainers, worn old trackie bottoms and a cheap pink cardigan. Everything about her said *poor*.

'My grandfather made it for you,' said the girl. She paused, as if unsure she had the right person. 'The dogs, the quads. The Hunt. You're a witch, right? You called the deer – you saved our lives! My grandfather wants to talk to you. We're past the station, on the waste ground, in the old caravan.' She nodded across to the wasteland on the other side of the park, eager to get Bea to agree.

Bea nodded, as much to stop the conversation as in agreement, and as she did, the face wriggled slightly in her hand. She squealed and dropped it, and before she had time to think she'd crouched to pick it up. She looked at it again and it winked at her. Bea jumped, but managed not to drop it again.

The girl grinned. 'It's a beauty, innit?' she said. 'That'll scare 'em off!'

'Thank you,' said Bea. She thrust the strange little idol into her pocket, slapped her board down on the ground at her feet, jumped on and skated off fast, down the sloping path towards the exit before anything else happened. When she reached the street she got off her board and turned back to look.

The girl stood watching her. 'Don't show it to anyone!' she

shouted urgently. She lifted a hand and waved. Bea turned
without waving back and scooted off.

'*You're a witch!*' the girl had said. She had seen the visions
in the sky too. But that was impossible. Everyone knew that
such things simply didn't exist. Everyone knew that people
who saw things were crazies . . .

Bea let out a sudden cry of bewilderment. What was
happening to her? A woman going past with her two kids
looked at her curiously and she turned and ran away from the
woman, away from the man on the horse, away from going
mad, away from the girl, away from everything impossible.
She got out of the park and was halfway home, before her
breath gave out on the narrow road that sided the river. There
she paused to look up again.

There was nothing there. Just clouds and sky and jackdaws
flying overhead. It had all been an illusion after all. She had
been hallucinating. Because if it wasn't a hallucination – what
on earth was it?

4

Bea came crashing in the back door and ran upstairs to her room, practically knocking her mum over as she came out of the kitchen.

'Careful!' her mum called, but Bea ran up without replying, slamming the door behind her. In her room she flung herself on her bed, hid her head and wished it all away.

Later, when she came down to dinner, she mumbled an apology to her mum for barging her out the way earlier.

'That's OK,' her mum said. 'Let's face it, you're at that age. It's probably just your hormones.'

Bea rolled her eyes.

'I was hoping it wouldn't include a bad temper, though.'

Bea was outraged. 'Why do you think everything I say has to do with *hormones?*' she demanded. 'Don't you ever think I might just be annoyed about something?'

Her mum wagged her head and smirked at her dad. Bea jumped to her feet. 'You never take me seriously!' she yelled.

Fearing tears, she rushed out of the room, but paused behind the door. All she was doing was proving her mum right. She was about to go back in, but then she heard her father say . . .

'That wasn't very clever, Kels.'

'It feels like she's going to have a difficult adolescence,' her mum sighed. 'I wonder if it's got anything to do with that boy she's hanging out with at the park. He's too old, and Bea is so naïve . . .'

'Bloody know-all!' screamed Bea from behind the door.

'That's enough of that!' yelled her mum. But Bea was off – out the door and down the steps before another word could be said.

When she was little, Bea's mum and dad used to take her for walks in the woods, but although she lived only a few hundred metres away, she never went there any more. Even so, for some reason, when she ran out of her house that day into the gloomy late afternoon she turned up the hill towards the woods rather than taking her usual route down into town. There was a rock by the river among the beech trees she wanted to see. When she was little she used to love to hang over the edge, watching the water stream by. Perhaps she wanted to recapture those still moments when she was small and life was simpler?

She was confused, upset and exhilarated all at once. What if she was going mad? Surely she was! Didn't mad people see things that no one else did? They listened to the voices and did as they were told . . .

'*Let me out!*' the hare had said. And she had.

The rock was wet, but she sat on it anyway. The water ran by, just the same; it was Bea who had changed. Nervously she peeped up at the sky breaking blue above the leaves and at the water running below her. All she saw was sky and clouds and trees and water, yet she felt a presence. Eyes in the shadows out of sight, faces hiding in the rocks, green arms and twiggy fingers shifting in the foliage just beyond her gaze. Watching her. Waiting for her . . .

It was her imagination of course, but it spooked her, and as twilight began to fall, Bea jumped suddenly up and ran home. She tore through the woods, paused outside on the street so that she wouldn't go in out of breath and then crept in as quietly as she could. But her mum was listening for her, and came up ten minutes later to make peace and lure her down to eat.

She sat on the bed and gave Bea a big hug. 'I'm sorry, I know I can be insensitive,' she said. 'Trouble is, I only realise it after I've opened my big mouth.'

Bea smiled and hugged her back.

'Your dad gave me a right telling-off. He said you should be allowed to get cross without me assuming it's something to do with hormones. But it's only cos I care. You know that, don't you?'

Bea allowed herself to be led downstairs where a great pile of cottage pie had been put aside for her. She was ravenous.

'I'm a silly sod sometimes,' her mum said. 'But you know I love you, don't you?'

Bea nodded and gave her mum another hug. They were forever squabbling, but they always made it up in the end.

'And the boy thing,' her mum added.

'Mum!' groaned Bea.

'I know, I know. But it's my *job*. I'm your mum. This lad, Lars. If he was fourteen or fifteen that would be different. But he's not, is he? How old is he, do you know?'

Bea thought about it. 'Too old for me,' she said. And that made her shed a tear or two as well. Her mum was right; she did fancy him after all. She blew her nose and her mum pulled her to her.

'Heartbreak hotel, isn't it?' she said. 'You know, Bea, it takes a while to get it right, but when you do . . . oh boy, Bea! Oh boy!'

Bea hugged her hard, laughed and shook the tears out of her eyes.

'So is that what was upsetting you earlier?' her mum asked.

Bea shrugged and got back to the pie. She ate for a little bit, then . . . 'When you got your hormones,' she asked, keeping busy shovelling cottage pie in her mouth, 'did you ever see things?'

'See what?' asked her mum.

'Stuff. In the sky. People, maybe. You know.'

Her mum thought for a moment. 'I never did, personally,' she said. 'Why, Bea, have you?'

'No,' said Bea quickly. 'The girls were talking about it.'

Her mum nodded. 'I expect they were teasing you,' she suggested.

'I expect that's it,' said Bea. She finished her plate and began to pick at the crusty bits on the edge of the dish.

Her mum leaned across suddenly and gripped her arm. 'Don't pay them any attention,' she murmured. But Bea knew her mum well enough to know that she had alerted her, which made her even more unwilling to admit what was really going on.

5

Over the next few days, Bea continued to catch glimpses of things that weren't there – faces in the brambles, feathers in the wind, leafy green women playing among the broccoli plants her dad planted in the garden. One day she saw a brown and silver boy running over the surface of the river. She called to him, and he turned his head but then disappeared in a cloud of spray by the weir. From time to time, another vision would float across the sky – an old-time car, a group of people talking, sheep in a field or sometimes just a landscape she'd never seen before. A funeral floated by her window, and once she saw a handsome young man with a broad hat and only one eye, smiling down at her. She wasn't sure if he really saw her or just happened to be looking that way.

All these things made her sick with fear. Bea closed her mind to them all, walked with her head down and let her eyes slide past anything she didn't understand. She didn't think about them; she simply refused them. Once or twice she saw the strange girl who had given her the amulet, who seemed to want to talk more with her. But that was the last thing Bea wanted. As soon as she saw her, she fled. Anything rather than engage with things that could not be.

She left the amulet in the pocket of her combats and

managed to forget all about it for hours on end, until she'd suddenly come across it. Then she'd slap a hand on it, think – oh yeah! – she should throw it away. But somehow she never got round to it.

All these mind games worked too – up to a point. Hours passed without her noticing anything strange. She edited her visions out of her mind, the way you edit your dreams from the day, or the cast that floats in your eyes, or the bird that sits in the hedge every morning as you walk past, and yet you never notice that it's singing only for you.

Boarding was all she thought about. Rain or shine, she was out in the park ignoring the carnival in the sky. Inside her, a web of fear and hope trembled and shook. She spent so much time on the slopes that even Lars found it odd. 'Don't you have a life?' he teased. 'A boyfriend somewhere . . . ?'

Bea blushed like a firework. She was so angry she tried to kick him, but he just slid out of the way, laughing.

'OK! Just asking.'

Lars loved to tease but Bea hated it. Even though she knew she was too young for him, her heart still sank when she saw him flirting with the older girls. He cared for her, she was certain of that. He spent hours with her, watching her, advising her on her technique. If she fell and hurt herself, there he was, kneeling at her feet dressing a wound on her leg with some antiseptic and a plaster from the first-aid gear he kept in his bag. When Bea looked down at him tending her and smiled, Lars smiled back.

If only he wasn't so old! If only she wasn't so young . . .

* * *

One hideous day her mum came down with a friend to the skateboard park. They sat themselves on a bench not far from the ramps to watch her, which made her horribly self-conscious. After ten minutes or so, she was called over. Bea sulked across. Her mum and her friend were full of compliments. How good she looked, how much she'd grown. Chit-chat, chit-chat. How well she was getting on with the board . . .

'And that's Lars, is it, with the red hair? He's been teaching Bea skateboarding,' her mum added to her friend, before turning back to Bea. 'He's a looker, isn't he? I'd like to meet him. Call him over, will you?'

Horrified, Bea froze to the spot and blushed red to the nape of her neck. Her mum was here to check him out. No way! No way was she going to introduce her to Lars.

She turned on her heel and trudged back to the slopes, ignoring her mum, her mum's friend and Lars. She just wanted it all to go away. It didn't. Lars swung up on his board to meet her at the top of the ramp.

'Is that your mum? I'll go and say hello.'

'No,' said Bea.

But he was off down the slope, flicking his board up into his hands as he hit the grass and casually walking over to them. Bea watched out of the corner of her eye until he turned and waved her across.

Her mum was already charmed. Lars sang Bea's praises. How talented she was! – a natural athlete. He was surprised they hadn't picked it up at school. He had a sister about Bea's age, he'd been trying to teach her for ages but she was nowhere near as good. He even managed to get a wink in to Bea, as if to say – I know what's going on here. What a laugh!

When her mum said how pleased she was to meet him, since he was so much older than Bea, he got it totally. His mum was the same. He was always being sent out to keep an eye on his sister too.

'Bea – she's just about the age, isn't she?' he smirked – the traitor! Bea stood there dying. She didn't know who to hate the most – her mum for making her feel like a child or Lars for helping her. Then at the end, as if on cue, one of the girls he hung out with turned up.

'Hey, here's my girlfriend – gotta go, Mrs Wilder. See you later, Bea.' Lars sauntered off, arm round the girl's shoulders. Bea's mum left, reassured. Bea took herself to the woods with gritted teeth and wept.

When she got back, Lars was still away, and she drove herself like a fool on the slopes until she took half the skin off her leg and had to limp ignominiously back home.

On the way back, the strange amulet the girl in the park had given her was rubbing against her skinned thigh. Irritably, she took it out and looked at it, grinning at her with its little orange teeth in the palm of her hand. She'd been wondering whether or not to show it to Lars – he was the only one she could imagine showing it to. Maybe they'd have a laugh about the crazy girl, or perhaps he'd think it was really a magical thing after all.

Well, he'd blown that today. It was all stupid anyway – just a load of superstitious nonsense. It didn't mean anything. That day, Bea had been particularly successful at keeping the visions out of her mind. She shrugged, dumped the amulet in the nearest bin and headed on home.

6

The next morning dawned cloudy and damp. Bea left the house as usual, her board under her arm, and right there at the end of her road the girl who had given her the amulet was waiting for her.

Bea tried to slide past, but the girl dashed forward and grabbed her arm. 'You threw it away,' she said.

'What?'

'The fetish I gave you. You threw it away.'

'You mean that face-thing? How do you know that?' Frightened, Bea tried to shake her off, but the girl hung on.

'I *know* it's you. I jumped in your car and hid on your lap. You saved my life! Now I'm trying to save yours.' She pointed up at the sky. 'You can see it too, I know you can,' she insisted. 'Look, look!'

But Bea wasn't having it.

'I don't know what you're talking about,' she hissed. She pushed the girl away roughly, and ran past. After a few steps she turned to check if the girl was following her. She wasn't. She stood in the same place, still pointing up at the sky.

'Look!' she commanded. And despite herself, all her practice, all her tricks, Bea's eyes were drawn irresistibly upwards.

Sailing on high above them in the lifting mist were a

group of people sitting around a dining table. Bea knew at once it was a big family gathering. There was a bird, not a turkey, something smaller – too small for the eight or nine people gathered there, Bea thought. It was Christmas, although she didn't know how or why she knew that, as there were no crackers or paper hats. Inside her, at the same time as that bolt of fear that always comes from seeing impossible things, she felt a surge of Christmas – happiness, excitement, everyone together. It made for a very strange set of feelings.

Yes, Christmas. A family having Christmas dinner in the sky. Bea could hear the distant rattle of cutlery and the laughter drifting down to her on the wind.

'Christmas dinner,' said the girl.

That was enough. Bea shoved the girl backwards, slammed her board to the ground, jumped on it and sped off down the hill.

'Come back, please come back,' shouted the girl behind her. 'They're after you. They're—'

Her words were lost in the wind as Bea raced downhill, rattling and splashing over the concrete ridges in the road. Straight down she went, faster than she had ever dared before. She hurtled right down to the bottom and across the T-junction, before she dug her heels down, spun the board to a halt and jumped off.

Without thinking she looked back up the hill towards the sky. Perhaps she thought she'd gone so fast she'd left it all behind, but no. Above her the Christmas dinner was still going on. A glass clinked. She could hear it clearly. It wasn't as real as the ground beneath her feet or the board she rode on, but it was more real than dreams. More real than wishes. Real enough for that girl to see it too.

Bea sighed. She tucked the board under her arm and trudged back up the hill to confront her.

'You came back,' said the girl. 'I think you're wonderful,' she added shyly.

Bea stood and watched, and waited.

'You have to hide,' the girl said.

'Who from?'

The girl blinked. 'You don't know *anything*, do you? The Hunt! You saw them on the road that night. They know you're here. We think they don't know who you are yet, but they will. My grandfather'll explain. Come on . . .' The girl smiled encouragingly and tried to lead her back down the hill, but Bea dug her heels in.

'No way.'

The girl scowled. 'You *have* to speak to my grandfather. You threw away the fetish – that's crazy! Any one of them only has to look at you to know. Granddad'll tell you everything. Please, Bea. Please. Come on. Come,' she urged. The girl caught at her sleeve and pulled.

Bea pulled away. 'I'm not going with you to see some old man I don't know.' She glanced up at the sky. The vision of the Christmas diners had blurred slightly, like coloured dust blown in the wind, or the aftermath of fireworks. 'What is that? Why can no one else see it?' she demanded – then paused, uncertain despite what had happened that the girl could see it too.

The girl looked up. 'Memories,' she said. 'Memories from before we were born. Look – candles.'

There were indeed candles on the table. Above the diners, an oil lamp burned. The scene, which was encased in skylight, was itself shrouded in darkness, lit dimly from within by pools of light from the candles and lamps. The diners were wearing old-fashioned clothes. It was as timeless as a Christmas card.

'When a witch dies, we lose our memories,' said the girl. 'It's my grandmother. You saved my life that day, but the dog got her. Remember?'

Bea felt the flesh creep on her bones. 'You . . .' she began, but the words wouldn't form on her lips. Clouds were one thing, but that hare had been flesh and blood.

'In spirit we can enter into the body of another living thing but when you come back, the marks of the day are on you. Look.' The girl pulled her tracksuit bottoms down on one side to reveal the purple remains of an old bruise. 'When I jumped out of the car, I fell. Remember?'

Bea shook her head. 'That hare was real!' she blurted, the words forcing themselves out of her lips.

'So's the spirit,' said the girl. She spoke as if she was stating the obvious, but then she looked oddly at Bea. 'You summoned those deer and you don't even know about the spirit world?' she said.

'I don't know what you're talking about,' said Bea coldly. All she wanted was to get on with her life – ride her skateboard, hang out with Lars. Grow up. She turned away, but the girl seized her arm in a panic.

'*Please* come with me,' she pleaded. 'They're getting so close. You threw away your fetish. You don't have *time* for this!'

Bea was stubborn and shook her head. 'You tell me,' she said.

The girl winced and looked around her. 'I'm trying to. But not here,' she said.

Bea paused. She didn't want to be seen with this oddity, this skinny girl who believed she was a witch, in her stupid pink cardigan, with her blonde hair pulled back off her face so tightly. She belonged to a different tribe altogether.

'We could go to the woods,' suggested the girl.

Bea shrugged. Her last trip there hadn't left her wanting to repeat it, but it was better than being seen downtown with this girl and having to explain to people why.

'OK.' She turned and marched up the hill towards the footpath that led that way, the girl hurrying behind.

The path to the woods cut across the hillside through an overgrown meadow and a hamlet of scattered houses before emerging among the trees on the valley side. Bea strode on ahead so the girl had to hurry to keep up. She took her down a narrow footpath descending towards the old mill. The path here was rocky and wet, lined in places with stones trodden to curves by the mill workers in their iron-shod clogs, maybe two hundred years before, as they tramped to and fro during their long days of work.

As they got lower, an old mill chimney came into sight above the tree tops. The mill was just ruins now, one chimney still standing, another fallen sideways like a felled giant . . . a few foundations, some odd bits of stonework. It was set right at the bottom of this narrow valley where the sun never shone. No one went there much. So dark and damp – why would you?

Bea was already furious with the girl, as if it was her fault that things went bump in the night, that dinners took place in the sky with diners who turned to mist. The ground got wetter as they got further down towards the valley floor and Bea, in her trainers, was soon slipping and sliding in the soft mud, while the girl, who was wearing solid-looking boots, was keeping her feet much better. That just made Bea crosser. Even so, she waited until they were right down on the sticky mud at the bottom of the valley miles from anyone, before she turned to confront her.

'Right,' she said. 'Tell me what's going on. What's your name?'

'Silvis,' said the girl. She rubbed her arms and looked anxiously around. 'I wish you'd come to see my granddad. He'd *show* you what I'm talking about,' she complained.

Bea shook her head. 'How do you . . . *why* do you think I threw that thing away anyway?'

'Granddad told me. He knows everything.'

'That's crap. This is all crap.'

'You saw for yourself on the moor,' insisted the girl.

'I didn't see anything!' Bea hissed back. 'Why are you following me? What do you want?'

40

Silvis crept closer to her, her hands clenched under her chin. 'You don't know how dangerous this is! You're like a baby!'

Bea was furious – being told off by a ten-year-old! 'Shall I call the Hunt to me then? Shall I?'

'Don't be stupid!'

'Hello, Hunt! Over here . . . here I am. Come and get me!'

'Stop it!'

'Over here! I made the deer come!' bawled Bea. Silvis ran to her and grabbed her face, but Bea pushed her easily away.

'You crowned runners, I summon you!' she yelled. But it was in her own voice, not that deep, resonant cry that had come from beneath her feet.

Silvis, who had slipped and fallen to the ground, leaped up at her like a fox.

'You don't know what you're doing,' she hissed. 'You're going to kill us both!'

For a moment the two girls tussled together, sliding in the wet mud. Then for the second time, Bea felt it. It began as before, deep under her feet, welling up from far below. Before it had been made of pity and love; now it was made of fear and rage. The words were in her mouth before she had time to think:

'I SUMMON YOU, YOU THORNED ROPES, YOU THAT BIND AND TEAR. I SUMMON AND COMMAND . . .'

Silvis staggered back with a cry. Something seemed to have lassoed her. It was a briar – a great thick briar, with jagged thorns running up and down it like the claws on a giant cat.

It had Silvis around the waist and seemed to be dragging her down. No plant could attack like that – but this one was. Before Bea's eyes a whole thicket of briars grew up around Silvis – great, thick, clawing things, lashing at the slight girl, wrapping around her arms and legs. The blood was already running freely.

Silvis screamed in pain and fright; but she couldn't have been more scared than Bea. What had happened? Had she done this?

'Stop!' she yelled. She bent and pulled at the briars to help free the girl, ignoring the scratches on her own hands and arms. A voice shouted, and Bea saw – to her horror – a woman's face glaring out of the middle of the brambles. But it was not a human face. It was a face made of green leaves and red stems. The woman grinned; her teeth were thorns. She lunged forward and snapped her jaws at Bea, who jumped back; and then the face was gone, and there was only poor Silvis, rolling and screaming in the middle of a thrashing bed of angry brambles.

Overcome with fear and confusion, Bea turned and fled, her only thought to leave this mess behind. She half ran, half fell, slipping on the dark mud, but she had gone no more than twenty or thirty metres before she stopped. What was she doing? The girl needed help. She was on her way back when she heard Silvis shout.

'Run! Run, Bea! They're here. Run!'

What was here? She paused – and then she heard it. An engine. A motor of some kind? A bike. Motocross? Or a quad . . .

Bea froze. There were no roads near here; the rider was in the woods. And another – up on the hill behind her, heading down. And another ahead. And . . . dogs. Dogs barking. And then the light came on again – the same light that had suddenly lit up the moors a week before. The dark woods were ablaze – the trees, the leaves, the mud under her feet. You could see everything. Every crack in the bark of every tree, every crevice, every stone was illuminated from all sides. This time, she knew what it was for. The light left nowhere to hide.

Bea was terrified, but she couldn't leave Silvis. Hadn't everything she said been true? Hadn't Bea herself led the other girl into this danger?

She began to run back the way she'd come, but a noise to her right attracted her. It was a dog, galloping full pelt parallel to her on the other side of the valley, glancing all the time across at her. They'd found her! There was a beck in between her and it, but the huge beast, as clever as a man, was running to intercept her where the stream formed a narrow gorge. Bea turned and ran the other way, but the creature changed direction at once and came at a charge directly down the side of the valley towards her, tearing over the little cliffs of earth and ivy, over the stones of the old mill, over roots and fallen trees. Its eyes were fixed on Bea, its mouth agape. With one huge leap it cleared the river.

It was already only metres away and as fast as a machine. Bea stood no chance. Its hot breath was behind her, its rapid, thudding feet. It touched her foot with its paw, and she went sprawling forward into the muddy leaf litter. Then it was on her. It bent its huge head – it was as big as a calf – and took her in its jaws by the waist.

The giant dog didn't bite down on her – not yet. It held her firmly in its great blunt teeth and pressed her into the ground with an immovable strength, growling dismally in its throat, warning her to keep still.

Above, higher up the valley, she heard shouts. The bikes and quads revved up and headed down towards her.

But before they could reach her, Silvis came – scratched from head to foot, her clothes shredded, bleeding from her arms, her legs and neck, but she didn't hesitate. She flung herself at the dog, grabbed it by the ears and heaved with all her might. For a second she struggled and tugged in the unnatural light, but the dog just shook Bea in its jaws and bit down harder. Bea screamed again, then clamped her mouth shut as the dog bit down harder yet.

That seemed to bring Silvis to her senses. She stamped her foot and yelled at the dog, more in rage than fear. Then she reached into her cardigan pocket and took out a fetish, much like the one Bea had thrown away, made of dirt and mud, feathers and bones.

She held it in her two hands in front of her like a shield and thrust it close to the dog's face. Twisting over, Bea could see the beast looking sideways at it, its eye showing white as it rolled round in the socket to see. The dog growled deep in its throat. Silvis said some words – Bea didn't understand the language – and then, with a peculiar gliding motion, pushed the mask into the air and let go. The mask sagged slightly to one side, as if unsure of itself, but then righted itself and floated, upright, turning to face the dog.

'Yessss!' hissed Silvis, as if she had managed something merely hard, rather than impossible.

The beast snorted down its nose, its eyes fixed on the mask. As the mask came closer, it shook its head – not hard, as a terrier shakes a rat, but in confusion. It growled again, low in its barrel throat, but not at Bea now – at the mask.

Closer came the mask, closer. Gradually the huge jaws relaxed their hold on Bea's waist, then it let go of her completely. The dog stepped back away from the mask, which was creeping closer and closer to it. The mask opened its black mouth and began to whisper to the dog in a voice like dry leaves. Bea didn't hear the words, but its tone conveyed terrible, terrible things. The dog whined, crouched down, the mask rearing up over it. It began to crawl backwards a few metres, then turned with a yelp like a puppy and ran, tail down, fast across the forest floor.

The mask reared up into the air and let out a derisive hoot of triumph.

Bea lay frozen, in fear of the mask as well as the dog. The light around them was still bright, still shining from everywhere at once. Silvis stayed still too. Not until the beast was out of sight did she pluck the mask out of the air, take Bea's hand and lead her quietly away, the pair of them tiptoeing like foxes through the leaf litter. Once a stick snapped underfoot and they paused again; but the dog did not reappear. The brilliant light began to dull, slowly at first, then rapidly. The bikes and shouts and barking began to fade. They got further away, out of sight . . . further, further away . . . Then with a sudden little yelp Silvis broke into a run. Bea was after her in a trice.

Run as fast as you can! Under the trees, over the rocks and the roots, uphill, panting and gasping for breath, clawing and slipping on the muddy slopes.

They paused in the trees by the road to be sure there were no quads waiting for them. Then onto the tarmac . . . along the valley side, down the hill, fast as they could, completely out of breath . . . until they reached the houses.

The two of them doubled over, gasping for air. As soon as she was able to breathe Silvis reached out and took her arm.

'*Now* come and see my grandfather,' she said.

Bea looked at her, the girl who had rescued her, covered from top to toe in vicious scratches. She nodded. Silvis grinned at her – a bright grin of triumph. She shot off, and Bea shot off after her.

7

Silvis led the way across town to the park, past the railway station and into the waste ground beyond. After a few minutes' walk, they cut across through the wet grasses towards an old caravan, crooked with age and up to its wheel arches in the long grass. Silvis ran up a set of steps into it while Bea hovered anxiously outside.

'I got her, Granddad. She's outside. She called up brambles. They shot up out of the earth. She was— Oh!' Silvis suddenly leaned out of the caravan door. 'You're fantastic!' she yelled.

Bea looked up at the younger girl, covered in scratches from head to foot, and winced.

'Your eyes turned blue,' said Silvis. 'Even the whites. It was *amazing.*'

An old man appeared in the doorway. He was so tall he had to bend down to get out of the door – a giant of a man, but bent and stooped with age. His long jaw was white with stubble, his white, shoulder-length hair hung untidily under a wide-brimmed, faded leather hat. His skin was brown and wrinkled with age and he had only one eye.

He looked grimly down at Bea, then pulled Silvis into view. 'You did this to my granddaughter,' he said in a gravelly voice.

'I'm sorry,' said Bea. 'I didn't mean it.'

47

The old man nodded. 'You don't make a life your own by saving it. You know that, don't you? Don't you?' he enquired, sounding suddenly doubtful of his own remarks.

Bea nodded, although she had no idea what he was talking about.

The old man sighed. He came down to shake her hand and introduce himself as Odi, then invited her up into the caravan.

'There are things you need to know.'

Bea climbed the steps into the carriage. Inside was arranged like some kind of workshop. There was a calor gas bottle connected to a single gas ring, a workbench, shelves on all four walls with various Tupperware boxes stacked up on them, and a baggy little sofa and an old armchair at the far end. All over the shelves and from the ceiling hung rows of little masks like the one Silvis had given her – like the one she'd used to scare away the dog.

'Fetishes,' said the old man, watching her. 'The only way any of us can be safe around here. Hebden is infested with the Hunt.'

Bea licked her lips, which had gone as dry as stone, but said nothing.

The old man tapped his lip. 'Now then, where are we?' he muttered to himself.

'Granddad – it's now! It's here!' said Silvis impatiently, sitting herself down on the little brown settee.

'None of that helps,' he told her.

Silvis frowned and stuck out a lip. 'He lives in all possible worlds,' she told Bea. 'He knows everything, but he gets confused.'

'The question isn't so much when or where – it's which,' Odi said. He turned to the shelves and selected a few Tupperware boxes, from which he added some herbs to a basin of warm water on the gas ring. He swished them around a bit, then got to his knees at Silvis's feet. Very gently and tenderly, he began to wash her wounds. Poor Silvis was literally criss-crossed with deep bloody scratches. She winced and scowled and tried not to cry; it stung.

'But I got her, Granddad,' she said.

'You're a heroine,' he told her. He turned to look at Bea with his one, soft, smoky-blue eye. She couldn't meet it and dropped her gaze. 'But you, Bea Wilder – you're a danger. A danger to Silvis, a danger to us all. But most of all a danger to yourself. I would put the chances of your surviving without our help very low indeed. The Hunt is everywhere – you've seen that. You don't know yourself and if you don't know yourself, how can you control yourself? Every time you summon, you give yourself away. Only we can help you. But how can I ever convince you of it?'

'I don't know,' said Bea; and that was the truth.

The old man nodded and turned back to his work, dabbing and wiping softly at Silvis's scratches.

'She has to believe us!' exclaimed Silvis. 'She's seen it with her own eyes, haven't you, Bea?'

'She doesn't just have to believe in new things – she has to disbelieve all the old ones too. How easy do you think that is?' he demanded of Silvis, who shook her head. 'Maybe she will choose to perish rather than do that. If you do decide to perish, Bea,' he added, 'we will respect your wish, even though you could be of great use to us. But we would rather save you.' He got painfully to his feet, and sat himself down sideways at the workbench. 'How can I make you believe? Seeing is not believing. Hearing is not believing. Thinking is not believing. Believing itself is mostly just made up.'

'But then . . . how do we know anything?' asked Bea.

The old man smiled and touched the rim of his hat to her. 'Good question!' he said. 'Maybe you will become one of us after all. Now then. You threw away the fetish I made you.'

'Yes.'

'I'll make you another. Now that one of their dogs has held you in its jaws, maybe you'll take better care of it.' He turned to his bench and gathered some of the Tupperware boxes in front of him. Inside them were little collections of stuff – dirt, clay, a dish of little bones, shards of mirror, feathers, seeds – and began to mould her another little mask. As he worked, the masks arranged around the ceiling and shelves began to mutter. Bea sighed. Already she was getting used to masks that talked. What next?

She watched the old man at work a while. 'The Hunt,' she said suddenly.

He turned to look at her. 'The Hunt,' he agreed.

'Who are they?'

'Another good question.' The old man considered. 'The leaders – we're not sure any more. Powerful people. Business people, politicians. People with power.'

'Tell her about the Huntsman,' said Silvis.

'Yes, the Huntsman. You met him,' he said, working deftly at the filthy clay with his big fingers. 'The big man who tried to get you out of the car that time. If you'd done what he wanted, you wouldn't be here now.'

'Who is he?'

'The question is, *what* is he? He's a golem. Most of the Hunt that you actually get to see, the ones who chase us down, they're nearly all golems – people who've had their spirits stolen and replaced with something else. Sometimes it's the spirit of another person but more often an animal, a dog usually, since they're so easy to train. They can do it with clay too.'

'Not just clay,' said Silvis. 'They use resin and plastics these days. You can't tell it's not a human being until you touch them.'

Odi nodded. 'Have you ever heard of Matthew Hopkins?' he asked Bea. She hadn't. 'He was a witch-finder from long ago. We think the Huntsman houses his spirit. His body died long ago but the Hunt has found ways of passing his spirit on to other people, or into clay or resin golems over the years. He can track us, you see. He can sniff out our spirits. Hard to hide from.'

'If he can track witches, isn't that like being a witch himself?' asked Bea.

'Exactly,' said Odi, smiling at her. 'He thinks it's a gift from God,' he added, and shrugged. 'When people learn to hate, it's often themselves they hate most of all. He's dangerous. But not the real leader, we think.'

'But who is?'

'No one person probably.' He raised his hands in the air. 'They remain hidden.'

Bea shook her head irritably. Was there no clearer answer than that?

'I'm afraid not,' said Odi.

For a little while he worked at his fetish in silence. Bea looked across at Silvis, who was half dozing on the old sofa at one end of the caravan. The medicine he had bathed her in was making her dopey. Already her scratches were fading. That was good. Bea had hated herself for hurting her.

'But what do they want?' Bea asked.

'They used to kill us when they first started,' said Odi quietly. 'These days, they don't like us to go to waste. These days, they harvest us for our spirits.'

Bea pulled a face. 'I don't even believe in spirits,' she said.

'Every living thing has a spirit,' the old man told her. 'Everything, no matter how tiny. Each ant, each germ, each egg, each fleck of life, every man, woman and child. The spirit is what gives us life. You could say it is life itself. Even the woods and the rivers have a spirit – but not you, apparently.' He turned to look at her again. 'For most people it's a hidden world, but we witches have a connection with it. Do you doubt it?' he asked. 'How can you when you've seen it with your own eyes?'

Bea thought of the brown and silver boy running down the river, of the faces in the bushes, the tiny children at play in her father's vegetable garden. She thought of the wicked woman of brambles who had attacked poor Silvis.

'Why do they want your spirits then?'

Odi shrugged. 'The usual suspects: power and wealth. Some people will do anything to win it, to hang onto it and to keep it from others. If you capture a witch's spirit, you capture their witch gift as well. That's what they're after. They can power their weapons with our gifts, fight their wars, manage their businesses. How do you think those quads on the moors crossed the fields in the dark so easily? Where do you suppose the light in the air came from that night? Those gifts were powers once held by living witches. Now their spirits are kept enslaved inside machines and golems. Some witch gifts can change what you think and feel. With the right gifts they can manipulate who you vote for, what you buy, what you think. They can re-make the world as they want it.

'And you, Bea . . . you are not just any witch. You are a summoner. It's been many generations since someone with your gift was among us. You can call up spirits from the past and no doubt from the living too, if you learned how. The Hunt wants your summoner's spirit. At the moment they have to use a machine to steal our spirits, one at a time. It's slow. If that machine had a summoner's spirit gift inside it, their power would increase a thousand times.'

He looked steadily at her. 'The Hunt cannot tolerate any power that's not in their hands. They will do everything they can to make yours theirs.'

'You have to come home with us,' demanded Silvis.

Bea glanced at the door. What if these two were dangerous? Look at all the crazy things they believed in!

Odi frowned. 'If you want to run to your own destruction, I won't stop you. I can't answer for Silvis, though.'

'I won't let her,' said Silvis. She grinned fiercely at Bea, who smiled warily. She wasn't sure if this was a joke or not.

Odi smiled sadly at her. 'It's hard to discover that you are not who you thought you were, and that the world is not what you thought it was. But, Bea, is it so surprising that there's more to the world than you ever dreamed? Isn't that only to be expected? Don't you think?'

Bea shrugged. She thought that *maybe* what he said was true, and that *maybe* she would agree with him at some point in her life. Only perhaps not just now . . .

'If it's only the things we understand that are true, what a small place the world would be,' said Odi.

As he spoke, the old man was putting the finishing touches to the little fetish he was making her. He'd made it with eyes of blue and teeth of yellow, and it looked as ugly as sin itself. He reached over suddenly, looped his finger around a few strands of Bea's hair and tugged.

'Ouch!' yelled Bea.

Silvis burst into a peal of laughter. 'He always does that,' she said.

'Sorry,' said Odi. He worked the hairs into the back of the face. 'It's better with something of you in it,' he explained. He smoothed the surface down with his finger, held it up to inspect it, and nodded. Then he breathed on it slowly. The mask pursed its lips and began chattering quietly to itself. Odi stood up and hung it up among the others above his head.

'It needs to cure with its friends for a little while,' he said. 'It'll be better than the other one. Half an hour or so, it'll be done.'

Above his head the masks murmured to one another. Another moment and they began to chant softly.

'It will hide you from the Hunt and protect you from harmful spirits,' Odi continued, 'but only so long as you wear it at all times – at all times, Bea! You understand? Your life depends on it.'

Bea nodded. Odi leaned over and took Bea's hand in his. She pulled away quickly. He sighed.

'This is hard, so hard, I know,' he said. 'But you have very little time. The Hunt is on your tail.'

Bea nodded, even though she had no idea what to believe.

'And now I must tell you the hardest thing of all. If you want to be yourself, you *must* join us. You must put away everything you know, everyone you love, and you must follow us.'

'What about my family?' said Bea.

'You must leave them.'

Bea backed off. Crazy talk – dangerous talk! 'I won't leave my family,' she said firmly.

'But you must!' wailed Silvis. 'Don't you see? The Hunt will come again, Bea. They will get you.'

'Of course you're loyal,' said the old man. 'I would expect nothing else. But you must understand that you're a greater danger to your family if you stay. When I say you must leave them, it's not just for your own good. The Hunt will take them too, once they find out who you are.'

Bea was thirteen years old. She loved her family and they loved her. To throw them away just like that? It was impossible! Even if she believed every word he said, it was still impossible. That much she knew for certain.

She looked towards the door.

Odi sighed. 'On the moor that day, Bea, you looked into my eye. Now look again. I want to show you the world as it really is.'

The old man tapped under his one remaining eye. Bea followed his command and gazed into it. It was watery, as pale as ash, but bright with light. He leaned down, so that his face was on a level with hers. Her gaze, against her will, was drawn into that eye. And she saw . . .

Worlds within worlds upon worlds . . . worlds without end. More worlds than there are stars in the sky or atoms in your eye . . .

Bea had seen those worlds before, by the side of the road on the high moors, looking up at her through the eye of a hare. She turned away; it was time to leave. This was crazy. She took two steps out of the door – and was confronted with a world she had never imagined existed.

8

The air had changed, that was the first thing. From head to foot, Bea could feel countless tiny movements against her skin, as if every hair on her body was stirring. She lifted up her arms to see what was causing it – and a moment later it all came into focus. She became suddenly aware of *everything*.

Life! It was here in its legions. She hadn't realised before but the grasses and hedges were teeming with life. Thousands of tiny spiders, a million ants. All through the trees caterpillars were munching leaves, greenfly were stealing sap. In the air, gnats and flies moved about their business. Bea wasn't seeing their bodies; it was their lives shining – the spirit itself. The world was suddenly a-glow. It was these, the countless lives around her, that were causing so many flurries of air on her skin.

She forgot all about Odi and Silvis, all about being a witch, about the dog in the woods, about going mad. She walked slowly down the steps from the caravan so as to be in the middle of so much life.

The creatures were just the start of it. Each plant had a spirit too. The mosses, the grasses, the trees, the lichens. So much life! She had never dreamed the world was anything like this. There was a small spider hanging from a thread just before her eyes; Bea could see tiny drops of venom on its fangs. A ladybird trundled in miniature along a leaf by her shoulder. It came to the edge, flipped upside down and went back the other way. She could see the cells opening and closing on the leaves around her, like tiny mouths – she could even hear the soft noise they made as they moved. Her hearing had become so acute she heard the soft and sharp sounds of tiny creatures scurrying about on the floor, in the earth, in the air, each one so clear, so precise, so separate.

She walked slowly through the wet grass towards the trees, where she paused and looked up. Above her head, a billion tiny drops of water hung on the edges of the leaves, on twigs and buds, seeds and fruits. Her eye fixed on one drop in particular, and as she watched it, that little drop swelled, filled out, and fell. Down, down it came, Bea's eyes following its sparkling journey. She saw the colours of all the lives around it reflected and distorted in its curve until it struck her bare arm with a cool plop.

She looked down to where the tiny jewel glowed on her skin. Inside, a beautiful little creature, frilled as a piece of lace, swam into the surface of the water and bounced back, as if the droplet had a skin. The drop quivered, and all around it the water fractured the light . . . rays of it bouncing about inside, outside, everywhere. She looked closer and saw that the droplet was full of life – tiny creatures living their whole lives out in that tiny bauble of water.

Suddenly, so suddenly it made her jump, her skin began to glow. She looked down in time to see light escaping from her chest, pouring out like a streaming rainbow. A million tiny rays of light poured out, so bright she had to screw up her eyes. As they struck the water baubles in the leaves, in the air all around, they too lit up like Christmas lights.

This was *her* light – her spirit. It poured out of her, filling the glade she stood in with its rainbow beams.

A small shape flew into her light and Bea jumped into it. A blackbird. The little creature shook in surprise as her spirit joined its own; then they were one creature. She landed on a branch and waited till it calmed down – she only wanted to share. The blackbird sang, beautiful notes flowing out of her throat; then it took off, flying through the woodland leaves, then bursting out into the open air – two spirits tethered together as one, just as Silvis and Odi had tethered themselves to the hares that time.

They stayed together a while, riding the wind, higher and higher, until the blackbird was scared so far from cover. Bea left it to fly back to the woods while she rose up still higher into the upper air.

Below her, spread out at her feet, was the world she knew . . . the trees her body stood in, the wasteland by the railways, the canal, the park, the town. Beyond them were the valleys and the woods and the hills; some of them had spirits too. But Bea could not just see the landscape. She could see the life that inhabited it – the gnats and flies that filled the air around her, the mites, the seeds and wind-borne spores. Plankton in a pond far below, rootlets hosting fungal threads under the earth, trees, sleeping bulbs, swelling seeds, the bugs and the beasts, the birds and plants, the worms and snails. All of life was stretched out before her.

She had no idea how long she hovered there, but she slowly became aware that her spirit was lowering itself down through the air towards the girl who stood far beneath her in the wasteland by the railway track. Down through the trembling, light-ridden air, down through the trees – and home. Bea in herself.

As she hurried back home, she passed a blazing silver light waiting for her by a fence near the footpath: Silvis. Bea ran to her and the two girls hugged. She didn't try to talk about it. What she had seen was beyond words.

'Come with us now?' begged Silvis.

Bea shook her head.

Silvis pressed the fetish Odi had made for her into her hand. 'Your witch eye is wide open now. You *must* keep this on you at all times. They'll know you at once if you don't.'

Bea nodded.

'Promise me.'

'I promise.' She kissed Silvis impulsively and ran off back home.

Bea spent the evening in her room, claiming a headache. Before she went to bed, she peered out of her window at the night which was suddenly so full, so beautiful, and so dangerous. At once she knew that someone or something was out there. She ducked down and hid behind the curtains before peeking out again.

The figure of a huge man was standing under the apple tree at the edge of the lawn. For a moment she thought it might be the Huntsman, but the wide hat gave it away, and that one eye shining under it in the moonlight.

Odi turned and lifted a hand in greeting to her, then turned his back and looked out across the valley. That day her spirit had been opened up wide for the first time, and she was more vulnerable and visible to the Hunt than she had ever been. The old man was standing guard.

She woke up several times in the night and peered out of the window. A wet wind was blowing the mists away and dark clouds were on their way in over the hills; but Odi still stood there, stock-still in the rain and wind, under the apple tree. Come the morning he was gone. The apple tree was covered in little birds sitting quite still among the branches. They stayed there until her mum went out of the back door to empty the compost bucket, when they flew off across the valley like a string of little black beads.

Odi was with her that night. But if Bea supposed that the danger was past, she was entirely wrong.

9

The blinding vision had faded, but the spirits were still there. That morning, Bea was full of excitement – it was a new world! She rose early, had breakfast, then went out on her own to explore.

In the woods the trees smiled down at her and shook their branches. The brown and silver boy returned and sat next to her a while on a rock by the river. She looked away, and back, and he was gone, but the rock where he'd sat was wet. Who had known, she thought, that the river was alive? The grasses milled around her feet, the wild flowers danced for her as she passed. Truly, a second world was hidden behind this one.

Later she went into town to spy on the people. Their spirits shone with a golden yellow, shot through with colours, each one different. Her own spirit was similar – brighter, clearer, perhaps, with more colours hidden amongst the gold.

Bea wanted to see if she could spot more witches. She sat on a bench in the square and watched the people go by, but she saw nothing as bright as she and Silvis were. She headed off to the park instead; she had an idea that maybe Lars – exciting, beautiful Lars – might be a witch too. As usual, there he was on the slopes. His spirit was red-gold, as red as his hair. It sparkled with energy – but the colourful light of a witch was absent. He was a boy – a beautiful boy, but no more than that.

He came over as soon as he saw her. 'Where's your board?' he asked, pouting slightly as if she'd let him down – only half joking.

Bea blushed as he looked her up and down. She was in tight jeans and a T-shirt. She'd left the loose gear she wore for boarding behind and hadn't even noticed.

'I'll be back tomorrow,' she promised. 'I can have a few days off, can't I?'

'Course you can. It's a good idea having a break sometimes. Let things sink in.' He tucked his red hair behind his ear and scooted off to the ramps without a backwards glance.

Bea made her way home. She'd loved her time with Lars. It had been exciting. He'd been her first crush. But things were changing fast. Her life up to now had been of this world; now she had a foot elsewhere. A second world, a world that was all around, but which only she and others like her could see.

'I'm a witch,' she said to herself. For the first time, she understood that it was really true. She could see things that others couldn't see. She had gifts that they could never understand. She knew the world in a way that a non-witch never could. She paused by the side of the river with her eyes closed before turning right up the hill to home. She could feel it all around her – life, singing in the air, filling her veins. The river, the fish swimming in it, the air that blew on it, the gnats that danced above it.

She was a living breathing witch – the real thing. And all around her, worlds within worlds upon worlds full of the spirit life, that only she could call from sleep!

10

The next day Bea surfaced to find her mum standing by her bed.

'What?' she groaned.

'There's someone here to see you. A girl. She was waiting outside. She said you promised to teach her skateboarding?'

Silvis. It had to be. 'I'll get up,' said Bea.

'She's an odd little thing, isn't she?' her mum said, and paused to see if any more information was coming. It wasn't.

Of course she was odd, thought Bea. She was a witch! Inside, her heart swelled.

She flipped back the covers and hurried to get dressed.

Downstairs, Silvis was sitting on the sofa with baby Michael standing on her lap trying to suck her nose – a trick he'd learned a few days ago and tried on everyone he met.

Her mum was hovering. 'Ah, here's Bea. Silvis has been here for *ages*, haven't you, dear? She can't wait to learn skateboarding!'

Silvis gazed at Bea, her white face pleading. Michael, as if he sensed how anxious she was, put his arms around her neck and hugged her.

'Michael's really taken to you, Silvis,' her mum said. 'But

I have to separate you – he's going to the childminder today.'
She came to pull him off her, and he started to cry. Silvis
buried her face in his neck and blew a raspberry, so that he
squealed with laughter.

'You baby, you great big baby!' cried their mum, lifting him
in the air and shaking him gently. 'I could eat him up! And
you too, gorgeous,' she said, passing by Bea. She put her arm
around her and kissed her on the cheek. Bea, remembering
how the witches wanted her to leave home, hugged her mum
back. Yes, there was a new world waiting for her. Yes, she was
a witch. Even so, this was where she belonged – with the
people who loved her.

'You'll be wanting some breakfast first,' said her mum,
raising her voice over Michael's squeals. 'I expect you're hungry
too, aren't you?' she added, glancing at Silvis's skinny little
arms and legs.

'Not hungry, thank you,' said Silvis.

'Nonsense,' said Kelsey briskly. 'Anyway, Bea is. Bea, take
Silvis through and get something – eggs, cereal, whatever. I'm
off to the childminder. I've got a day off! I'm going to work
on my manuscript. Hurrah!' She tossed Michael joyfully into
the air. Bea's mum was having a few years' break from her
usual job as a script editor for TV while Michael was still so
little, but her true love was poetry. She'd had two collections
already published and was hoping to use her time off to prepare
the third. So far, she'd managed precious little.

She left the room, taking Michael and his wails of protest
with her. Silvis got up and came to Bea. 'Have you seen the
sky?' she whispered.

Bea looked to the window.

The sky was *alive*.

It wasn't just a single scene, it was a landscape. Above the sycamore trees beyond the window, a gallery passed by – trees, hills, seas, mountain ranges. The girl she had become familiar with over the past week was everywhere – at the seaside with her family, sitting on a bench doing her schoolwork, kneeling in the road crying. In another she was older, walking hand in hand with a man. In another she was making up her face. In another . . .

There were too many to count. The sky was teeming.

'She's dying,' said Silvis.

'Who is?'

'My grandmother! I told you. She wants to see you. *Please* come.'

Bea paused. A dying witch. She didn't feel at all comfortable about this. 'What does she want to see me for?'

'She was the third hare, the one the dogs got,' replied Silvis. 'Remember?' Her eyes suddenly filled with tears.

'I'll come,' said Bea.

'Come on, then,' said Silvis, pulling at her arm. Bea put her finger to her lips and led her to the front door. Her mum was still getting together the baby stuff. She slipped on her trainers and together they ran out – straight into her dad coming up the steps.

'Bea – just the girl I want to see.'

Oh God, she thought – just her luck. He was going to hijack her for the shop. 'I'm going out,' she snapped.

But it wasn't that. 'I have a present for you.' He was already fishing in his pocket. 'I just finished it this morning. I knew at once it was for you. Look.'

He held up a short necklace. It was a simple thing, just seven polished pebbles, green, yellow, brown and cream. So simple. And yet it was utterly lovely.

Bea held out her hand as he draped it over her fingers. She was shocked at how beautiful it was.

'Thank you,' she said. She glanced at Silvis who was staring at it spellbound, open-mouthed. 'Thank you,' she repeated. She wanted to say how much she loved it but she didn't have the words. Her father stood smiling at the necklace proudly. She always thought her dad wasn't much – but look what he could do!

Her mum came banging out of the front door and was stopped short by the necklace.

'Oh my God. Is that for Bea? It's *gorgeous*!'

'Yes,' said her dad. And they all looked at him. He almost never praised his own work. He beamed at them both, blinking through his glasses.

'What are the stones?' asked Silvis.

'Just river stones,' he said. 'Now the water's down I found them on the little beaches. Polished 'em up – and look.'

'My clever, clever man,' said Bea's mum, kissing him on the cheek and running her hand through his wiry hair. 'He's a wizard! Turns pebbles into jewels. Make sure you wear this one, Bea,' she warned – Bea had loads of gifts from her dad, but most of them lay unworn in her room. 'If you don't, I can promise it's going to vanish and reappear by magic – round my neck.'

Bea lifted up her arms and put the necklace on. The little stones sat in the hollow of her throat like kisses.

'Bugger, look at the time, I have to go.' Her mum scattered kisses to her family, waved at Silvis and ran off to the car.

'It had to be yours,' said her dad, smiling at the necklace.

'Thanks. I really, really like it,' said Bea.

Her dad nodded, still smiling his tight little smile. Then he turned and wandered back down the hill.

'Do you like it?' Bea asked Silvis.

'I've never seen anything like it. Maybe your dad really is a wizard. We'll show it to Odi. Come on – let's go!'

She grabbed Bea's elbow and led her away from town, up the hill.

Bea had no idea where they were going or how far, but it turned out to be a much shorter journey than she imagined – just twenty minutes' walk up the hill to the next village.

Heptonstall was an ancient little place of narrow cobbled streets, the houses tossed together like stones washed up by a stream. Silvis's grandparents lived at the end of a short row of houses on the corner, opposite the pub. Silvis pushed open one of the doors and led the way through a little parlour, down a winding stair to an arched stone-roofed basement, and then out the back to the kitchen. Like a lot of the houses there, this one was built on a hill and the back had an extra floor, lower than the front.

Sitting out in the little square garden were a man and a woman, shelling peas. Bea had seen both of them before around town.

The woman in particular was unmistakable.

She was short, just a little over five foot tall, dressed in dark clothes, trousers, short grey hair, cut like a man's. She was a stout, muscular woman with a permanent frown on her face. Extraordinarily, her hands were different sizes. The left was normal, but the right was huge and muscular, almost twice as big as the other.

The man was tall and dark skinned, silver-haired, very beautiful, perhaps a few years younger than the woman. He was wearing pale brown, almost beige clothes, and he had the most startling eyes of bright green. He stood up to greet them when they came in.

'The new one,' he said. 'You're so welcome!' He came over and embraced Bea warmly, then straightened up and beamed at her. Silvis introduced them as Frey and Tyra – 'Witches, like us,' she added proudly.

Tyra remained seated. 'Has she come to stay?' she demanded.

'Tyra,' complained Frey – affectionately, though he was chiding her for being rude.

'She hasn't said yes, yet,' said Silvis.

'She's a bloody idiot then,' said Tyra, and she bent her face back to shelling peas.

'She's come to see Nana,' Silvis said.

'Jenny's resting,' said Tyra.

'I wouldn't like to be the one to keep her from seeing Bea,' said Frey. 'Come on – I'll take you up.' Silvis took her hand and led her after him; but Frey paused. 'I think she'll want to see Bea alone the first time,' he said.

'What if it's the last time, though?' complained Silvis. But she stopped and let Bea follow the tall man up the stairs on her own.

Frey led her a winding way, up one set of stairs and down another, along two long corridors until they came to a short landing at the back of the house, where he paused.

'You know she's dying,' he said.

'Silvis told me.'

He nodded. 'She'll be happy to see you. You understand what's happening to her? When a witch dies, our memories escape.'

'Like forgetting?' asked Bea.

'More like sharing.' Frey looked out the window to one side of them. Beyond, a young woman was dancing on the air. Autumn leaves were falling on a clearing in a wood. The same woman was kissing, or being kissed perhaps. Her lover was so passionate Bea blushed and had to look away.

'It's her life being painted on the sky, for those that can see,' said Frey. He squeezed her shoulder. 'There are so few of us now,' he said. 'It's so good to see a new one! And a summoner! That's such a thing. You have no idea.' He looked anxiously down at her, before turning to tap lightly on the door in front of them.

'Her name's Jenny,' he said. 'She's been waiting for you.' He opened the door and stood aside to let her in.

Bea paused a moment on the threshold. The window was open and the fresh air was stirring, but she had never been so close to death before. She took a deep breath and went in.

* * *

The room was in shadow, dully lit only by a small nightlight at the side of the bed and a sliver of daylight coming in through a narrow parting in the curtains. But the shadows were alive. As her memories left the old witch, they moved around the room like ghosts – colours, blurs, half-sensed sounds and smells, as if they didn't know where they were or what they needed to do. Only when they reached the window did they come to life. They jumped up and flew out to paint the sky, as Frey had put it, in all the colours of her life. The curtain swayed slightly as they passed by.

Bea stood still a moment, waiting for her eyes to adjust. A king-sized bed filled the centre of the room with a chair on either side. There was a wardrobe, a chest of drawers and two tables with lamps by the sides of the bed – a very ordinary bedroom. An old, old lady wearing a felt hat lay there, propped up on pillows. Her head was turned and she was smiling weakly at Bea.

Bea sat down on the chair nearest to her. The old lady put out a hand, a bony claw, which Bea took.

'I wanted to say thank you right at the start,' the old woman said.

Bea nodded, trying not to be distracted by the sensation of Jenny's memories creeping around the room to the window.

'I'm sorry the dog got you,' she said.

Jenny smiled. 'I've had a long life, and a very full one. I can't complain,' she said. 'I just hope yours is as long and as good too.'

The old lady's skin was so thin you could see every bone in her body. Her eyes were sunken and dark, and all the crevices of her body, her shoulder bones and eye sockets, were set deep in shadow. So this is what dying looks like, thought Bea.

'Not long now,' said Jenny.

'What's it—' began Bea; then stopped short. She had been about to ask what it was like to die, but she'd remembered her manners at the last moment.

'I've had more fun than this, I can tell you that,' said Jenny, and she smiled weakly.

Bea felt a sudden pang of regret. If she had only acted sooner, maybe she could have saved Jenny as well.

'Not your fault,' Jenny said; she seemed to be able to read Bea's mind. 'Listen to me, now. Listen; you are important, Bea. Not just to yourself. To us all.'

'I was never important in my life,' Bea complained. She meant that she didn't want to be now.

'No one chooses their own fate,' said Jenny. 'Has it been fun, being a child? And now you find that you have a spirit as big as the whole world.'

'You don't know me,' said Bea. She knew what the old lady was going to say and she didn't want to hear it.

'I do. You know I do.'

Bea sighed. They hadn't even met! But so many things that were not possible before were possible now.

'Odi believes you will be at the end of this stage of our fight with the Hunt, one way or another. What your role will be, I have no idea – but you've saved the lives of my family once already and I'm so, so grateful for that.'

Bea's eyes were caught by a glimpse of bandages under the

covers. Jenny pulled the sheet closer to hide her injuries. 'I feel sorry for the hare,' she said. 'It died that day. That wouldn't have happened if I hadn't entered it.'

She fell silent and lay still. After a couple of minutes Bea wondered if she'd gone to sleep or even actually died, and tried to take her hand away, but the old lady squeezed her, so she let it be.

'We had run and run that day,' said Jenny at last. 'We were at the last of our strength when we ran into you. None of us dreamed that there was one of us so near until Odi saw you look into his eye. He knew you'd seen his soul.' She nodded her head slightly. 'Silvis knew too. She jumped into your lap. She loved you at once.'

Bea nodded. For a while Jenny lay still again, gathering her strength to speak.

'I thought I was as good as dead when the dog caught me, but you've given me the chance to die like this, in my own bed. Oh, Bea, I'm so glad to see you.' She paused a moment. 'It's a wonderful thing to have my life saved by a child!' she exclaimed. 'It's a wonderful thing to see a summoner amongst us again.'

There was another long pause before she went on. 'Terrible things have happened. Terrible things will happen again. But I'm so pleased you came. Here are my good wishes for you, darling. Thank you.'

What those good wishes were and how they worked Bea had no idea; but she felt them enter into her, warm and loving, and she knew they came from the heart. She loved Jenny straight back for that. The two of them sat there a while in the half-light, holding hands, until there was a soft knock at the door and Frey came in to take her back downstairs. But before they could leave, Jenny lifted her hand one more time.

'Your necklace . . . so lovely,' she whispered. 'Who gave it to you?'

'My dad made it. It's a present,' said Bea proudly.

Jenny turned her head on the pillow to look at her. Bea could see the whites of her eyes shining dully in the light from the door. 'Your father is a witch,' she said.

Bea was stunned. Her dad? Her neat, fiddly, fussy dad? 'How do you know?' she asked.

But Jenny lay exhausted, unable to do anything but look up at her.

Frey shook his head and held the door open while Bea slipped out. On the landing she turned at once to him.

'Why does she think that about my dad?' she whispered.

Frey bent and stared intently at the stones around her neck. 'I've no idea,' he said. 'Maybe Odi can tell us.'

He led the way back down to the kitchen, but Odi was out. Tyra and Silvis examined the stones carefully, but whatever it was Jenny had seen in them, none of the others could.

Bea was over the moon at the idea that she was not the only witch in the family. Perhaps now the witches would not try to make her leave them. Her family needed saving too. But she was going to have to wait to find out more.

11

Salem Row was a short terrace of three houses that had been run together with corridors and landings to form one big house. There were eight bedrooms all told – nine if you counted Odi's workshop on the first floor. The whole place was a maze of corridors and odd-sized rooms scattered about, including a sitting room as big as a small chapel with an inglenook fireplace you could have put a sofa or two in. Below ground was the dining room and kitchen, nestling under arched ceilings made from huge blocks of black stone.

Silvis lived in Odi and Jenny's house on the corner these days. She used to live with her family in the middle house, but her parents and brother and sister had been taken by the Hunt on a trip in the north visiting relatives some years ago. There had been a long chase across three counties before they were cornered and taken in the shadow of York Minster. Silvis had only been eighteen months old, too young to go with them. She couldn't remember anything about them, but the feelings she had for them remained. She confided to Bea that on her dark days she sometimes wished she had gone with her family. At least that way they would have been together.

'I always wish my big sister was alive, at least,' she added, glancing shyly at Bea. She showed her the unused bedrooms.

Books and toys and clothes on the shelves, photos and posters on the wall . . . everything was in its place, waiting, but the owners would never come home. The dust had settled and the damp had crept in because the heating was rarely on. The only signs of recent life were on the carpeted floor, where Silvis sometimes played with her brother and sister's toys, or sat on the floor of her parents' bedroom flicking through photo albums and wishing she could remember.

The third house, the smallest, last in the row, housed Tyra and Frey.

Salem Row had housed four or five families once upon a time. They used to have shared meals in a long room that stretched across the back of two of the houses, and in the evenings there would be musical entertainments and games in the big sitting room in Odi and Jenny's house. It was much quieter these days, courtesy of the Hunt. For the first time, in that oddly empty house, Bea began to understand just how ruthless the persecution had been.

There were two other witches: the Flint sisters – but they had given up their lives to be a part of a strange contraption kept below ground. The witches called it the Spook.

'You have to see it to believe it,' said Silvis. 'It's what hides us from the Hunt – they'd be on to us in a moment if it wasn't for the Spook. It's the only thing that's half-machine, half-spirit, half-person.'

'That's three halves,' laughed Bea.

'I told you – it's amazing!'

The witches had gardens too – not little plots behind the houses, but fields of orchards, vegetable plots, greenhouses and livestock. Although they lived on the cold Pennine hills, their gardens were incredibly fertile. It was almost autumn and everywhere else life was slowing down and ripening. Here, Frey was still planting seeds.

There were other wonders too. As they walked in the orchards, Silvis told Bea to look closely at one of the apple trees. At first, it just looked like all the others, with gold and pink apples ripening on the branches.

'Look with your witch eyes,' said Silvis.

Bea stared and stared at the tree – she knew enough by now to know that things were not always as they seemed. Suddenly her mind seemed to pop behind her eyes and saw them for what they truly were.

'Peaches!' she cried. Yes, peaches, growing outside, four hundred miles north from where they normally were. They picked one each to eat – heavy, sweet and soft, and warm to the mouth as if they had been plucked off a tree grown under a sun shining in southern France.

'We keep them in disguise,' said Silvis. 'The Hunt would be on us in a moment if they found peaches growing like this in Yorkshire!'

There were goats for milk, butter and cheese, chickens for eggs, ducks and geese fattening on the pastures. The spirits were more vivid than usual here, and sometimes they were so strong they overran their own bodies. At one point, Bea saw a little run of white, feathery fairies running across the grass towards a muddy pond. She gasped and turned to Silvis.

'Fairies! Fairies – look! They're real!'

They were the real thing right enough, with long gossamer

wings edged with soft white feathers, bare little legs and skirts made of flower petals. Silvis turned to look, and shrugged.

'Ducks,' she said. 'Listen.'

Bea focused her ears – and sure enough, her pretty fairies were quacking. Then her eyes adjusted and she saw them as they were – young ducks, still shedding their baby down, running for the shelter of the pond, where their fat mother floated and gurgled to herself.

Bea was disappointed. 'There're no fairies, then?' she asked.

'No, don't be daft! It's your eyes playing tricks on you. I once thought I saw an angel from Heaven come down to carry me away, I was terrified! But it was just a seagull trying to steal my sandwich.'

As they walked, Silvis told her more about the witches. Odi, who lived at once in all possible worlds, who knew everything that was and will be but could never remember which world he was actually in. Frey's gift was to make things grow – it was down to him that the garden was so fertile. And Tyra, whose giant right hand, Silvis claimed, had its own spirit and an unbreakable grip. Not just a physical grip either. She could put a spell on anything you cared to name, and it would become immovable.

She told her about her parents too. Her father William, who could shine. Not just his own body – he could light up a dark place even at a distance. It was his stolen gift, she said, that the Hunt had used to light up the moor that day when Bea had summoned the deer.

'At least it means his spirit is still in this world. But it's trapped,' Silvis said sadly. She had no idea whether the Hunt had allowed his body to live on as a golem with a borrowed spirit inside it, or if he was actually dead.

There was her aunt Helen, who could do the same thing with darkness. Her mum, who could ask the water for favours.

And others who had been lost. There were so many of them. Drue, who could travel to the Underworld, the dimension the dead went to first of all. Cherry, who had three shapes – a woman, a cat and a wren. Olwyn, who . . .

'Something to do with sex,' said Silvis.

There was Arthur, who knew how to induce sleep; Avis, who could make any living thing dance; Ambrose, who knew how to help living things survive and grow without food or drink. There were dark witches as well – witches who could cause death, or sickness, who could make the crops fail or break friendships, or cause people to fall out of love. Each had their own gift, some rarer than others. Most gifts involved some kind of relationship with certain sorts of spirits – cats, dogs, deer, birds of various sorts.

Odi had a brother, Lok, who could take on any shape he wished, but had no shape of his own. The only way you could ever tell it was him was because he had two faces – one in front, one behind. His spirit resided in the second face, and that part of him alone he could never change or look at. The spirit-face slid out of his sight rather than let him see it, as if it was ashamed of itself.

'It was him who invented the Spook,' Silvis said. 'But he turned traitor. There was a disagreement and he joined the Hunt.'

'So what happened to him?'

Silvis shrugged. 'They took him. They wanted his spirit and stole it. They always do, in the end.'

'Then why did he join them in the first place?'

'I never met him but they all say he was greedy. The Hunt probably made him some big promise they never kept. I don't think anyone understood what he was up to.'

'And what about you?' Bea asked. 'You're a witch. What's your gift?'

Silvis blushed red. 'I'm not much of a witch,' she confessed. 'I can see the Second World and I can pull off a few tricks, but that's about it.' She shrugged. 'I have a voice – not like yours. Just tricks, really.'

'What sort of voice?' asked Bea.

'It's nothing. It comes and goes,' said Silvis, blushing.

'Show me,' begged Bea.

Silvis took some persuading, but she agreed in the end. As they were walking back she took a little detour to a short row of cottages that backed onto the fields. In one, tucked next to a shed, was a rabbit hutch. Silvis and Bea hid behind the hedge, peeping through into the garden.

'Watch this,' Silvis whispered. She opened her mouth and let out the most extraordinary and beautiful cry, more like some kind of musical instrument than a human voice. It rose into the air and resonated all around them, in the trees, in the grass, in the air. The leaves in the hedge in front of them trembled in perfect sympathy with it. Even when she had closed her mouth, the note remained hanging in the air around them. So clear, so pure, so beautiful. But what was it doing?

As Bea watched, the door to the rabbit hutch popped open

and Peter Rabbit, beloved of the little boy who lived there, hopped out joyfully to help himself to Frey's lettuces.

Silvis giggled. 'The parents of the kid who owns that rabbit keep putting new locks on the hutch, and they can't understand how he keeps escaping.'

Bea laughed. Silvis had a wicked side!

'They don't look after him properly anyway,' said Silvis.

The rabbit spent his days sitting on a pile of his own poop and Silvis was always singing him free. Peter had a reputation as an escapologist in those parts.

'See?' she said. 'I can open rabbit hutches.' She said it in such a tone of disgust that Bea laughed.

'Can't you open other doors?' she asked.

'Not really,' growled Silvis. She led Bea off among the trees. 'I can't even sing with it, I only have one note,' she complained. 'Maybe when I'm older it'll come. Lots of people don't get their gifts until they get older. Odi says there's some power in it somewhere, but for some reason or other I can't reach it. But who knows? Odi says a lot of things.'

But Bea was entranced. 'Maybe just being beautiful is enough,' she said. Because it was, without doubt, the loveliest sound she'd ever heard.

Silvis turned and hugged her hard, pressing her little face close to Bea's. She was a funny thing, Bea thought, but she was wonderful with it. Already she had begun to love her back.

12

They returned to the house for lunch, which was served outside in the garden at the back. Odi was there, so Bea got him to look at her father's necklace.

He turned it over in his hand in silence a few times, then he broke into a smile.

'These stones don't eat or drink. They can't move or think or feel. And yet they live. It's hard to imagine that a stone can be alive, but these little pebbles are as alive as you and I. They have spirits. Stone spirits are very rare and hard to see. In all my life I've only seen two such things, yet your father has found seven of them in one little river. And they *let* him.' He gazed at the necklace with real love in his eyes. 'It would be better to say that they found him,' he murmured. 'Bea, this is a very precious thing.'

Bea stared at the necklace, so ordinary and yet so lovely. The stones were alive, Odi said – but it meant more than that. 'So he is a witch!' she exclaimed. 'It's not just me.'

Odi looked sympathetically at her. 'He must be. But don't be disappointed if he's unaware of it. 'It can be a terrifying experience to realise that there is another world side by side with the one we all know. He may have kept it stamped down deep inside him his whole life. It could be dangerous for him to awaken too quickly. He'll need time.'

'Then what's his gift?'

Odi held the stones up to the light. 'Beauty, I'd say. Wouldn't you?'

Bea was shocked. 'Is that all?'

The witches laughed. 'Isn't it enough?' asked Frey.

Odi gave her the necklace back. 'Our gifts as witches depend on what kind of relationship we have with the spirit world. The stones love your father. They can't move, they can't sing. All they can do is show him their true nature, and this they have done. How much more magic can there be?'

'Your father is a lucky man,' said Frey, getting up to fetch lunch. 'His gift is still honoured in the world. I wish that could be said for the rest of us.'

'We don't know the whole of it yet. The stones might bring favours of other kinds. Luck, perhaps. I've heard of such things. Time will tell. If you wear it, though, you must be more careful than ever to keep the fetish with you. If anyone from the Hunt spots it . . .' He shrugged.

Bea nodded. 'You'll rescue my dad as well, won't you?' she said. 'He'll need a fetish, won't he?'

Odi gazed at her thoughtfully. 'Not necessarily. The Hunt will see him only if he awakens. As for rescue . . . if he's ready, if he wants it, yes. But we will never force him, Bea. You must understand that.'

Bea nodded and put the necklace back round her neck. All through lunch she kept touching the stones. She trusted her dad. Certainly he would awaken. And then everything would be all right.

* * *

There was home-made bread and a light golden soup with all sorts of nibbles and bites in it. It was delicious, like an elixir, Bea thought. Perhaps it was. Before the meal, Frey insisted on saying a thank you to the plants and animals who had died to make their meal – a witch's Grace.

As they ate, the witches asked Bea about herself, her family, her friends, how things were at school, what she thought of the gardens she'd just seen. After the soup, there was fruit and cheese and biscuits to nibble. Tyra had a bottle of beer – three of them, in fact, by the end of the meal – and the witches told Bea something of their history.

The persecution had been going on for thousands of years, ever since the Christians first came to Europe with their ideas of one god.

'A jealous god,' said Tyra. 'We were never mean like that in our time.' She took a big swig of her beer, peering down the bottle at Bea.

The witches believed that all the spirits around them were a part of God themselves, but the Christian priests believed that all non-human spirits were devils, sprites, fallen angels – evil things, enemies of the one true god. People began to turn away from the Second World. Soon they came to think of those who dealt with it as evil them-selves.

As the Church increased its grip on belief, it drove the witches underground. Those able to see the spirits learned to keep their mouths shut. The alternative was imprisonment, torture and probable death. At its peak, the Hunt was murdering witches by the thousand every year.

'We were never numerous,' said Odi. 'Soon we became rare. Many gifts were lost – summoners among them,' he added, fixing Bea with his one eye. 'In the end, we became so few and learned to hide so well that people stopped believing in us altogether. It was as if we ceased to exist while we still walked the earth.'

'The Hunt never stopped believing in us,' said Tyra.

'They followed us underground and hunted us there,' said Odi. 'They hid in the government, in the army, in the police and the justice system. There was no more open persecution; witches simply disappeared. They died in police custody or car crashes, or drowned at sea. They were found murdered, or they were framed and sentenced for crimes they didn't commit. Even in a world where only our enemies believed in us, we were still diminishing. Until . . .'

'It's the Spook! Tell her about the Spook,' begged Silvis.

Tyra sniffed. 'A lot of good that did us,' she said, glancing at Odi. 'It was meant to keep us safe.'

'It does. It did,' said Frey. 'The Hunt were getting so close, Tyra. You know that.'

The Spook had been built during the Second World War by Odi and his brother Lok – clever, mercurial Lok, who had no shape of his own but could change his appearance in an eye blink. He had conceived the idea of trapping a living spirit in a machine. He had always loved devices – amulets, spells, curses, anything like that. But no one had ever thought of using spirits to power machines before him.

'To imprison a living spirit is a dark thing,' said Frey. 'In the past we sometimes trapped the spirits of wrongdoers in a tree, or a stone – a kind of prison. But only ever as a last resort. To use life itself as part of a machine – that was new. No one had considered that before.'

'Not just life,' said Tyra. '*Witches'* lives. He wanted to put the powers of a witch's spirit into a machine. I could never trust a man who has no shape of his own,' she added.

'None of us were keen, but we found a way round it,' Odi said. 'A way of using the spirit of a witch while they still lived – *if* they were willing. And two of us were willing to serve.'

'The Flint sisters,' cried Silvis.

'Idiots,' said Tyra.

'It's a great sacrifice,' insisted Frey. 'Even today it keeps us safe. You want them to come out? How long do you think we'd last?'

'At least we could fight instead of having to hide like weevils,' growled Tyra.

Odi and Lok built the device together all those years ago out of pieces of domestic machinery and early radio and TV equipment, together with amulets, fetishes, spells, blood, living tissue and the pure spirit of two living witches.

That was the Spook. They kept it deep underground, working day and night to keep the witches of Heptonstall hidden from the Hunt. It had been a wonder in its day, and even now, although it was old and failing, it still did its job.

'But how does it work?' asked Bea.

'The Flints are what we call sideways travellers,' said Frey. 'They can skip between dimensions. There are trillions of other worlds, you see. Some are so different to this one, they are unrecognisable. In some, for instance, the dead in this world are alive there, and those who are alive here are dead there.'

'The Underworld,' said Silvis.

'In another everything is fire. In another, everything is void,' said Frey. 'Others are simply what we call the future or the past. But many of them are so close to us here, you couldn't tell the difference. Even if you hunted for the difference, you might not find it in many lifetimes. The sisters can hop between these worlds, sideways, forwards and back. With the Spook, they can take us all with them. If anyone suspicious comes close, they are simply moved to a world only slightly different to this one.'

'How's it different?' asked Bea.

'We don't live there,' said Odi. 'See? Simple.'

The witches laughed. Simple – but so clever. And then, when the unwelcome visitor left the area, they went back to their own place.

It was a wonderful piece of technology. Soon other groups were asking Odi and Lok to build one for them too. But things never got that far. Wonderful though the Spook was, like all technology, it served no master. It wasn't long before the Hunt got their hands on the same idea of using spirits to power machines. They had always changed with the times. Now they changed again. In the age of religion, they had wanted to destroy the witches because they served other beliefs. In the age of commercialism, they were more straightforward. Now they simply wanted witches' powers for themselves.

'And Lok taught them how,' said Tyra. 'It wasn't enough for him to use the spirits of volunteers – he wanted to capture spirits for his own ends. Of course we wouldn't play, so he went to the Hunt instead. He betrayed us.'

'He paid the price for his betrayal,' said Odi sadly. It was his brother who'd died, after all.

Tyra, who was up opening herself another beer, shook her head. 'I won't believe he's gone until I see his corpse,' she said.

'No witch has survived inside the Hunt for long,' Odi said. 'In all the worlds anything like this one, there are none where Lok lives.'

'Lucky for him,' said Tyra. She held up her huge right fist and shook it in the air. 'If I got this round his throat, he'd be sorry.'

'No one here would be mourning him,' Frey agreed. 'But he's gone, thank God.'

Tyra checked that Bea was watching her, then reached out with that huge hand and sank her fingers into the wall. Bea thought it must be plasterboard at first, but soon saw it was solid brick and mortar. Without even blinking, Tyra tugged a brick right out of the wall and crushed it in her hand. Such strength! – it took Bea's breath away.

'The Grip,' said Silvis proudly.

'Tyra!' growled Frey. 'Look what you've done to that wall. You're such a show-off.'

13

After lunch, Bea was ready to go home. She did not get the reaction she expected.

'Home? Haven't you heard anything anyone has said?' Tyra demanded. 'You're a witch, you stupid girl. Here, in these houses on this street, is the only place the Hunt can't find you. Do you want to have your spirit stolen right out of you and put to work running a vacuum cleaner, or polishing the windows? Are you an idiot?'

Despite everything Bea had heard she was still astonished. 'But they're my family!' she said.

Tyra shrugged. 'You're nothing but a danger to them. Once the Hunt have you, they'll be next, top of the list,' she said. 'If you want to help them, leave them. It's that simple.'

But Bea was not ready for that. They were all she knew – her life, her start, her end. 'I can't leave them, they're in danger too. I have to convince them,' she said.

'You don't have time,' insisted Tyra.

'But my dad! He's a witch, isn't he?'

'And the baby,' said Silvis suddenly. Bea turned to her excitedly. 'I just thought,' Silvis said. 'The way he came to me when I was at your house. Like he already knew me.'

'We won't know for a few years yet,' Frey said. 'No child that young shows their gifts.'

'We could steal him from your parents if you like,' Tyra said.

Bea was shocked. Steal a baby? 'Do you do that?' she asked.

'We would,' said Tyra.

'We would certainly *not*,' said Frey.

'You *have* to come and live with us,' urged Silvis.

Bea shook her head. How could she desert her mum and dad, let alone baby Michael? 'I have the fetish,' she said, touching the little mask in her pocket that Odi had given her the day before. 'That'll keep me safe, won't it?'

'For a while,' agreed Odi. He raised a finger at Tyra, who was about to interrupt. 'Keep the fetish with you at all times. If you lose it, they *will* find you, and quickly. As for your people – you're right. We must try. We need a plan. Come to us tomorrow – we'll talk about it then. Maybe we can help your father open his witch eye.'

'If he really has one,' growled Tyra.

Odi ignored her. 'But we must be swift, Bea. That fetish won't hold the Hunt back for long.'

Bea nodded, relieved that she had permission to put off the dreadful decision.

'And remember – not a word to anyone,' urged Odi. 'Trust no one – not your parents, not your best friend. The Hunt can steal their spirit and you won't even know until they betray you. And it's not just your spirit at stake – it could be ours too.'

'I promise,' said Bea.

* * *

Outside the house, Bea turned on her phone and got a row of messages. Her mum was going crazy. Silvis coming to the house so early had set her off.

'They can tell, sometimes,' said Silvis, peering at the phone.

'About what?'

'About us. Witches.'

Bea smiled. She loved this! Silvis recognised her smile, and smiled back.

'Witch sisters.'

'Witch sisters,' said Bea.

Yes, it was wonderful – but Bea was still her family's girl. It was time for her to go back and show her face.

'See you at the park later?' she asked Silvis.

'But you haven't seen the Spook!' insisted Silvis.

Bea paused. 'Maybe later,' she said.

She set off for home. Silvis walked with her down the hill towards Hebden, but they hadn't even left the village when Silvis turned up a narrow alley between some houses.

'Where are we going?'

'You *have* to see it. Come on. It won't take long.'

Bea wanted to get home – all that talk had made her anxious about her family. But she was curious, always curious, so she followed Silvis through a back door into Salem Row, then through another door down to the cellars. At the bottom of a short row of steps was a brick-built spiral staircase that coiled down into the earth like a corkscrew sunk into the hill.

Silvis turned to her. 'There's spells of silence down here,' she said. 'It'll be quieter than anything you never heard. OK?'

Bea nodded and Silvis led the way down. Within three

steps they were plunged into a silence so deep it was as if sound itself had never been. The creaking of the house, the sound of her foot on the steps, the blood in her ears and the breath in her throat – all gone. Bea let out a gasp of astonishment – it truly was an experience not of this earth – but that too was swallowed up by the fathomless quiet. Silvis turned to look at her, grinned and stamped her foot. Nothing. Bea grinned back and clapped her hands. Nothing.

Magic! Silvis turned and spiralled down, and Bea followed her into the earth.

The way was lit by a pale, reddish glow that seemed to be seeping from the stones around them, shedding just enough light to see the step below. They trod on for an alarming amount of time into that deep, velvety silence. It seemed to get warmer as they left the sun behind.

They reached the bottom at last, and found themselves in a small lobby with a sofa to one side, a couple of dusty plastic bottles of water on a table beside it, and a narrow corridor leading off. Silvis turned to Bea and pointed to her ears, wincing, and then down the narrow corridor. Bea gathered that the noise was going to return, and that it was going to be loud. She nodded – understood.

Silvis set off again. Sound returned – it startled Bea, although at first it was just the usual sounds of her own body. But there was soon more. From out of the darkness before them came a heavy pulsing beat, like a heart. But no human heart ever beat so slowly, or with such strength. It must have been a whale's heart or that of some other huge beast – a dragon? wondered Bea – that was waiting ahead of them. Such a deep, dull beat; it came up through the stone around them as much as through the air.

As they walked on, the pulse grew louder and was joined by a distant muffled clashing, as if some far-off madman was flinging drawers of cutlery across the room. There was a rushing noise, like a torrent of water hurrying through a huge pipe; then a high-pitched throbbing cry, rising and falling. Voices – but were they singing or wailing? In ecstasy or pain? It was difficult to be sure.

They arrived at a heavy door in the corridor. Silvis turned to Bea, grinned and opened it. In the space of a heartbeat the muffled sounds turned into a full-on riot, a screaming, clashing, smashing torrent of a noise. Bea couldn't make any sense of it – it seemed so loud and chaotic – but as her ears tuned in she realised it had a shape to it, like some kind of fearful music. Above it all the voices – women's voices, she realised – soaring and wailing in a language so strange she couldn't be sure it even had words. But she wasn't alarmed – on the contrary, she was filled with excitement. She ran forward the last few steps to see the astonishing machine that made its own reality.

As Silvis had said, the Spook was like nothing she had ever seen. There was skin and bone, there were wires and valves, there was blood and brain. Pipes ran everywhere. Towers of circuit boards rose up into the mists that surrounded it and great blue sparks, like glowing reptiles, crawled all over it. The tremendous pumping that sounded so much like a leaky heart was exactly that – a heart as big as a small bathroom, sitting in the middle of the device in a huge hexagonal glass jar. With every pause the jar filled up with fluid, with every beat it emptied again and the whole machine shuddered under the pressure.

The oddest thing of all was half hidden among the shifting mists at the very centre of the machine. There amongst the tubes, the rising and falling columns, the batteries, the tubes, the organs and muscles and bones was a face – an ancient-looking face, gasping and panting to the rhythm of that great beating, bloody heart. One moment it appeared to be solid, the next it was a shape imagined in the clouds – part-real, part-dream, part-hallucination. Bea couldn't be sure if it was made out of steam or tin or flesh and bone or pure light. Its mouth was like a whistle where the steam came out, its eyes were like mirrors one moment, white of egg the next, and they cast desperately about, as if trying to find someone in a crowd.

'It has a spirit of its own – the only machine that does,' bawled Silvis above the racket. 'Isn't it marvellous?'

It *was* marvellous – but it was also sad. Everything about the Spook looked home-made, half-baked, ill-thought out. There were kooky repairs everywhere, pipes stuck into one another, bits of tape and string holding important-looking parts together.

'Bloody thing's on its last gasp,' yelled Silvis.

They walked around this incredible device, and at the back of it they came across the Flint sisters themselves – the old women whose spirits drove the whole thing. They looked even older and more worn out than the Spook itself. Their long hair was ratty and grey, hanging in greasy hanks on their shoulders. They were panting and gasping for breath even as they peered across to their visitors and smiled them a tired greeting. Bea thought it would be a mercy to take them out of there. They were strapped in, wired in, tubed up, connected with the Spook on every level; they were part of the machine and there was no way of knowing if it was keeping them alive or they it.

Silvis introduced them – Nora and Melissa. The old ladies, very polite, greeted Bea in between gasps of breath, and said how nice it was of her to come and visit. For a little while they chatted, Silvis relaying news from above ground, but before they got very far, Melissa seemed to have some sort of attack. Her head lolled on her chest, her eyes rolling up in their sockets. Bea thought she was having a stroke and glanced at Silvis. But her friend was watching proudly, as if this was something only to be expected. Melissa flung back her head, her mouth gaping open in a toothless oval, and burst out into that wordless, wailing, soaring song that Bea had heard as they approached. A moment later, Nora joined in and the two of them were lost in a strange, breathless opera, half-chant, half-song. It soared, reached a peak, began to die. The old ladies' eyes, which had rolled up in the tops of their skulls, came back down to look at Bea again. The rhythm of the machine changed and the mist and fog arranged around the Spook formed itself into distinct, if smoky shapes.

'That was a big one,' said Nora.

'Guilty,' said Melissa, looking directly at Bea. 'But never mind.'

Bea wasn't listening. There were visions. Out of the steam,

in the light, on the monitors that were perched here and there amongst the pipes and tubes, forms took shape. And Bea knew them.

She saw her father walk out of the machine and take a step towards her before he melted away into nothing. Elsewhere she saw her mum talking to someone in a white coat. Here was Lars and her skating in the park . . . there they were, kissing in a barn as he undid her blouse. There was a monster as tall as a tree chasing a small girl in the woods. A monster with three horns and an oddly familiar smile approached her as she sat in a hedge by the edge of a field. She saw herself trapped in a glass bar, stealing people's lives.

She shrank back. 'What's happening?' she begged.

'The sisters are sibyls,' said Silvis. 'They have visions of what might be.'

'They can tell the future?' Bea was amazed. 'Then why don't you just . . . find out what to do?'

'They don't always tell actual *events*,' said Silvis. 'And you never know which world they're talking about, or whether it will happen, or just might happen.' She thought about it a bit. 'Overall,' she said thoughtfully, 'it's usually better not to ask.'

'Can I ask them a question?' asked Bea.

Silvis looked anxiously at her. 'If you like. You won't find out anything useful, I expect. And . . .'

'What?'

'It's not usually much fun.'

But Bea wasn't going to let a chance like this slip by. She walked closer to the sisters, who looked up at her as she approached.

'Is it a question?' asked Melissa.

'Yes please.'

'Ask.' The old lady looked evenly at her.

'I just want to know . . . I just want to know how it will turn out for me? Being a witch, I mean,' said Bea.

The old woman tipped back her head. 'Your question has already been answered,' she said.

'But . . .'

'Your question has been answered,' she repeated. She gestured to the part of the machine that her sister had created in her passion just before.

Her with Lars . . . kissing him! Really?

Bea looked up at the old woman in alarm. 'But it doesn't say if it will work . . . if it will be good,' she stuttered. Melissa smiled grimly at her. 'Good and bad, they're never part of the truth of things,' she said.

Bea stared into the sister's watery eyes. All the things she had just seen would happen, or might happen, or perhaps had happened. But which was which?

How sad it was, Bea thought as she hurried down the hill for home, for the two lady witches to be trapped down there, so far underground. They had made a huge sacrifice to save their friends and family. The witches were a loyal crew, no doubt about it.

14

At home, her mum quizzed her about what she had done with Silvis that day. Bea paused. Was now the time to tell them the truth? But in the world of the blind, light was a lie. Speaking proved nothing. Somehow, she had to *show* them.

She decided to wait until she had spoken further with Odi. Instead, she told them a pack of lies about a day at the park with Silvis. They seemed to swallow it.

That night, Bea woke up in the wee hours to see the fetish hovering in her room. It faced the window, muttering to itself in a hoarse whisper. Then it floated slowly round to face her door, as if it was following some presence outside the house. It made two or three slow revolutions of the room, always facing outwards, before waiting a long, long time, looking downhill. Then it hooted softly to itself and came to lie on her pillow, close by her. It smelt of pee and rum and mud. The whole experience had such a strange, dreamlike quality that in the morning Bea wasn't sure if it had really happened or not.

By the time she got up, her mum and dad were drinking tea around the kitchen table. Bea had some breakfast and told them she was off down the park skating again – but they wanted to walk to town with her. Bea was disappointed – she had an appointment in Heptonstall. But there was no way out of it, so she went to put on her skater gear. Back in the kitchen, her dad noticed that she wasn't wearing the necklace he'd given her.

'Not when I'm boarding,' said Bea. 'It's too precious.' He looked so disappointed that she ran to put her arms around him. 'It really is my most precious thing,' she told him. 'I couldn't bear it if it fell off.'

'It's meant to be worn,' he told her.

'Go and put it on,' her mum told her.

Bea went to do as she was told. Odi had said to be careful, not that she absolutely couldn't wear it. It made her dad happy. He ran his fingers across the stones as they lay in the pit of her throat and smiled.

'You can't lose it,' he said.

'Don't tell her that!' exclaimed her mum. 'Poor thing'll be terrified. You can lose anything, especially when you're thirteen.'

'I didn't mean she wasn't *allowed* to lose it,' said her dad. Although what he did mean, he didn't say.

The whole family set out down the hill, her dad to the shop, her mum to the swings with Michael, and Bea, with her board under her arm, off to the skateboard park. Baby Michael babbled in his pushchair while Bea and her mum and dad talked about school – in just five days' time! Bea could hardly believe it.

But was she actually going to go? Her life was on a knife edge – everything could change at any moment.

They dropped her dad off at the shop and Bea left her mum in the park. She bent down to hug Michael.

'Are you a witch too, baby Michael?' she whispered. 'Is it you and me together?'

'Bea, Bea, Bea,' cooed Michael back. Bea stood up. Suddenly she felt like crying.

'What were you telling him?' her mum asked.

'Telling him I'm a witch,' said Bea. Her mum laughed at her, and went to find a free swing. Bea headed for the ramps.

It was mid-morning already. The skaters were all there, practising their tricks, Lars among them. Bea joined in, but her heart wasn't in it. He got cross about it. It was funny – he so much wanted her to be his follower.

'What's up with you?' he asked, pulling her up by the arm after yet another fall. He gazed into her eyes, scowling as if there was a secret hidden there. There was. Bea stared steadily back at him, daring him to see her true self. But of course he couldn't. Even had he been a witch, she wore the fetish Odi had given her in her pocket.

A little later her mum came to say she was going back. Bea gave her fifteen minutes before she made her way up the hill to be amongst her own kind.

She learned a lot more that day about the witches and the gifts they had. Tyra showed her more of the Grip – she set a spell on the front door so that they were all locked in for half an hour. Even throwing rocks at the glass didn't work – the stones just bounced off. Frey showed her how to tuck plants into the earth and gave her a spell so they would hold tight to their fruits until they were properly ripe.

Jenny was a little better that day and Bea was able to spend time sitting with her in her room. Her ability to read minds came through a spirit from one of the other worlds that was able to sit in people's brains and see what was in there. She conjured it up for Bea. It took the form of a Pakistani lady who sat on the end of the bed, and whenever a memory emerged that Jenny had forgotten, she reminded her of what it was. She stayed with them for maybe half an hour until Jenny fell asleep, when she hissed furiously at Bea, turned into a squirrel and jumped out of the window.

Odi came to join her for a while. He sat quietly until Bea left for the toilet. When she came back, she could hear him weeping by the bedside. She waited a while, popped her head through the door to say goodbye, and left him to it. He looked so tragic, sitting there holding his dying wife's hand. Unfairly, she was surprised that love could spring so strong in a heart as old as his.

She spent a very enjoyable hour or so with Silvis and her voice, trying to open locks. It didn't always work, though. Silvis could make the rabbit's hutch spring open pretty well every time, and sometimes she was able to pop the locks on Frey's chicken house and a few other things, but that was it. She put on a brave face, but Bea could see how disappointed she was.

'It'll get stronger as you get older,' said Bea.

Silvis shrugged. 'Odi says it may be because I lost my family so early. Either that or I'm just not very good. Someone has to be not very good, don't they?' she said sadly. Loyally, Bea refused to believe it.

Odi wanted to take another look at the fetish he had given her – he had some ideas of how to strengthen it, using a drop of her blood and some fragments of a mirror she had looked in. He had a little workshop at the back of the house lined with shelves where he kept all the things he needed. What Bea had seen in the caravan so long ago was just a mobile workshop – this was the full kit. He kept dried plant and animal material – human as well as beast's – from all over the world in Tupperware boxes on racks and shelves up and down the walls. Feathers, bits of mirror, even pieces of machinery all had their role to play.

As he worked, he talked to her about her family.

'You're right to think you can't explain things to them,' he said, holding the mirror above the smoke from the singed hairs from some kind of animal. 'The spirit world can't be explained, it can only be shown, and only a witch can see it.' He paused, watching the smoke drift across the surface of the fragments of mirror. 'Of course, it's your father we must consider first. We know that he has powers of some kind, however deeply buried they may be. The trouble is – how can we get him to recognise it?'

Odi finished his spells on the piece of mirror. He laid it flat on his worktop and tapped it with a stone so that it shattered. All around the room, the little fetishes he had hung up to cure jumped and shouted.

'But if he is a witch, he must be able to see, mustn't he?' Bea insisted.

'Not so,' said Odi. 'Most of us only ever see a fraction of what's there, and three quarters of the world isn't always there in the first place. Remember how much all this scared you? What if your father is afraid too? Grown-ups are often far more scared than children – they've just learned to hide it, even from themselves. Still – we must do our best with him. When do you think is a good time to get to him?'

They laid their plans, but first of all Bea would try to find out if he had seen or heard anything that night on the moors.

'It won't be easy for him,' Odi said. 'But if you get any idea at all that he knows what you're talking about, bring him to the caravan. I'll know you're there.'

15

Bea got home exhausted after her exciting day at Salem Row. She went to bed early and had a minor row with her mum, who barged in to pick up her clothes for the wash, cross that she was still having to do this sort of thing for her daughter.

Bea stayed in bed late the next day, dozing and reading – putting off what she had to do. By the time she got up, the morning was almost gone.

Her dad was at work. Bea was thinking she might try to grab him there at lunch time – she did that from time to time over the holidays. He was always pleased to see her and some-times took her out for coffee and cake or lunch, if he had time. But before she got out the door, her mum, still annoyed at her laziness, sent her to hang out the washing – she could do that at the very least.

As she opened the front door, Bea found on the stone step before her the muddy footprints of an enormous hound. There were more on the wet flags beyond, and in the shadow of the hedge was a large dry patch on the damp flags, as if some great beast had lain there while the rain fell. Old rotten leaves, half-turned into soil, were lying about. Leaves from the woods.

Bea ran in to ask about it. Yes, said her mum, she had seen

those paw prints too. And there had been something banging about the bins early this morning. A stray dog – a big one, to have left such prints.

The thought that the same huge dog which had seized her in its jaws had stood with its front paws on her doorstep in the night made Bea's heart falter inside her. Her mum saw her face and wanted to know what the problem was, but Bea shook her head. How could she explain what was frightening her to someone who couldn't ever see what it was?

But she had protection – the fetish Odi had given her. She slapped her pocket but it wasn't there. It must be in the pocket of her hoodie, still lying on her floor upstairs. She was about to run up and find it, but at the same moment realised her mum had come to pick up her washing last night.

'Where's my hoodie?' she demanded.

'In there, I expect,' said her mum, nodding at the wash basket Bea had carried to the door. Bea dived in, found the hoodie, felt in the pocket . . .

And the pocket was empty.

'Honestly, Bea,' said her mum, 'it looked like you were carrying a turd around with you. What on earth was that thing?'

'Where is it?' begged Bea.

'I threw it out – it was disgusting,' her mum said primly. 'Where did you get it? I can't imagine—'

'That was mine! You can't throw my things out . . .' But what was the point? 'Where is it?' she demanded.

'. . . why you have to carry something like that . . .'

'Where is it?' yelled Bea.

Her mum tutted. 'Down the tip, I would think. It's bin day. They went hours ago. Sorry, darling. I never thought . . .'

But Bea wasn't listening. Just a couple of hours without the fetish and the dogs had already been here. She had to get another. She turned to run up the road to Heptonstall, but her mum stopped her. 'No, Bea. Darling Bea,' she said firmly. 'I'm sorry. You're right. I should have asked you. But we've been worried. We need to have a talk.'

Her parents had been watching her all along. They had seen how she walked with her head down; seen her peering anxiously up at the sky when there was nothing there to see. They had seen her talking to herself, in her attempts to crowd out the voices and sights of the spirit world. They had seen how those conversations had changed, how she seemed now to be welcoming things that didn't exist. And then that ugly thing in her pocket; and now her obvious terror that it had gone.

'What was that thing?' her mum asked.

'You don't understand . . .'

'Well then, perhaps you'd better explain it to me.' Bea tried to make a bolt for it, but her mum caught her by the arm. This had gone far enough. She needed to know what was going on. What was it – something to do with the boy she'd been seeing in the park? Or that strange girl who'd called the other day? Drugs?

Bea pulled at her mother's hand and shook her head. 'Let me go!' But she did not let her go. Instead, she yanked her inside and locked the door. Bea was grounded. Then she called her father at the shop.

'He's on his way.' She turned to look at her terrified daughter. 'You have no idea how worried we've been. You've been scaring the life out of us. We need to know what's going on.'

So the questioning began. Bea held out, but not for long. She was scared and confused, and as soon as her dad arrived, out it all came. The visions in the sky, the sneaky faces among the vegetation. The dog in the woods. Silvis, Odi. The fetish, which she had kept in her pocket all day and slept with under her pillow every night. She confessed it all, but her eyes were on her dad. Surely, *surely* he would understand!

But her dad's face gave nothing away. He wore a slight frown and looked curiously at her, as you might look at a specimen of some kind. It made her scared to question him, but she did.

'You believe in witches, don't you, Dad?' she begged.

'No.' He sounded surprised she had ever thought it.

'But what if it's true?' demanded Bea. 'I could be a witch. So could you.'

'Oh, Bea, no, you can't, you know you can't,' her mum wailed.

'Why can't I? You don't know. I might be. Dad, please. That necklace you gave me. Only a witch could have made it, because . . .'

His eyebrows raised slightly. Because . . .

'Because the stones are alive!' she blurted. Even as she said it, she knew how ludicrous she sounded, how foolish – how mad.

Her dad let out a curious noise, a kind of groan.

'And on the moors that day when the deer came. *I* called them. They were spirit deer. And the hare spoke to me. You heard it, Dad, didn't you? I know you heard it . . .'

But her dad shook his head. 'I heard no such thing,' he said. 'Darling, how can you be a witch when we all know there's no such things? There's just the world. It's a wonderful, wonderful world. It doesn't need spirits and wizards and witches.'

'But I've seen them. I've *seen* them. I've seen the spirit world,' said Bea.

Her mum cast a horrified glance at her dad and lifted her hands to her face. Her dad shook his head, his lips pursed. He sat still and neat in the grey three-piece suit he wore at the shop, looking so ordinary. But he wasn't ordinary, was he? The stones loved him! What right had he to be ordinary? Then she remembered – her witch eyes! She could *see* if he was a witch.

She shook her head and tried to focus. It was hard, so hard when she was scared and confused with her parents on either side, nagging at her – but look! There! A dull light shining in his chest. Was that it?

But where were the colours?

This wasn't the spirit of a witch. But even then, she couldn't be sure. Hadn't Odi told her that a witch could bury his spirit too deep to see from sheer fear?

Suddenly, she was furious. 'You know it's true,' she insisted. 'You're a witch. You found those stones in the stream out of millions of others like no one else in the world can. You can't tell me you're not a witch. Dad. Bloody hell – Dad! *Please!*'

He reached out and grabbed her by the elbows. 'Bea, stop it!'

'You heard the hare speak . . .'

'Bea, stop it. You're being ridiculous!'

'You're lying!' she screamed in a froth of fright. 'You're just too scared. I know you heard it. Tell her – tell her you heard it too.'

Her mum wept. Her father gripped her arms as if she was about to fly away. 'No, Bea,' he said firmly. 'You know I didn't and neither did you.'

'Liar,' screamed Bea. 'You liar. You've seen them too, I know you have . . .'

Words left her. She tore herself out of his grip and ran for the front door, but her mum was in the way so she turned and fled upstairs to hide in her room instead.

They gave her a little time to calm down, and then the questions went on. How often had she seen these visions? What were they like? Did they speak back? Had they ever told her to do things – given her instructions of any kind? If so, had she obeyed them? They were very curious about Odi and Silvis. Where did they live, what had they said? Didn't she know she was not to talk to strangers in that kind of way – and certainly never to go into their homes!

Only one thing did Bea keep back, as Odi had asked her to – Salem Row. Instead, she told them about the caravan on the waste ground by the railway.

Her mum nodded. 'Right, then,' she said. 'We'd better go and have a look, hadn't we?'

They wasted no time. They got straight in the car, dropped Michael off with friend for an hour or so, and drove down to the railway station. Then, under the railway bridge, along the footpath to the waste ground . . .

Bea was filled with foreboding. What if it was all wrong? Suppose she really was mad? She didn't want to find out. She tugged back. 'I don't want to go,' she wept.

'You must,' her dad said grimly.

The caravan stood just where she had seen it, up to its wheels in long grass, the brambles tangled in the wheel arches. But it was different to how she remembered it. The windows were broken, the tyres flat. Algae grew on the paint and clouded the one remaining window. They pulled her through the grass up to the crooked carriage and made her look.

'Is this what you saw?' her mum asked.

Bea stared at the caravan in disbelief. It was a wreck. Her dad went up the steps and tugged the door open. A cloud of stinking air wafted out as they looked in.

Old newspapers, empty beer cans, crisp packets and crumpled fish and chip papers littered the floor. There was some used toilet paper covering a mess in one corner. It smelled of pee and shit. It was trashed. It had been trashed years since.

In horror, Bea turned and fled, tumbling down the steps and off through the long grass, but her dad was on her tail. He caught her in a few strides, swung her round and held her tight to him. Bea gasped for breath. The world was changing – first normal, then magic, then back again. But the world didn't change like that, did it? Only crazies thought that it could.

Mum ran up and hugged her from the other side. There they stood, one behind her, one before her, and they held her tight while she gasped and choked for air. When she could breathe, she cried out in panic.

'But it's magic, it's magic,' she yelled, struggling to get free. 'It isn't like you think. It's magic!'

Her parents held her firm, as parents should. They stroked her and loved her and blessed her until she had calmed down. Then they took her home.

Bea was grounded for her own safety. 'Just until we find out what's going on,' as her mum said. They made an appointment with the doctor for that same afternoon.

Now that the fear of madness had been said out loud, it seemed to Bea that they might be right after all. The sight of the derelict caravan had shaken her badly. Did the world really change so much, so far, so fast? Such crazy things she had seen! It had seemed so real! But didn't it make sense that crazy people believe crazy things?

Banned from leaving the house, she crept into the garden to spot spirits, but although yesterday they were all over, today there were none. Perhaps they were hiding from her? She remembered what Odi had said about what fear could do. She was certainly afraid now. She knew so little.

But the Spook! Poor dying Jenny and her memories in the sky. Bea looked up, but the sky was empty too. Just clouds and the sun and the birds flying over . . .

Tyra pulling out a stone from the wall and crushing it in her hand. Odi and the worlds hidden in his eye. How could such vivid memories be wrong? But how could such impossible things be real?

It had begun to drizzle. Bea sat on a rock at the edge of the vegetable plot and stared at the apple tree across the garden. Just yesterday she had been able to see the spirit of that tree – a plump housewife with her pinny full of little apple babies that wriggled as she polished them up, one after the other, and hung them from the branches of the tree. Today, there was just the tree, the branches bent down under their heavy loads. Leaves and bark and fruit – nothing that the eye couldn't see.

She was interrupted by her dad coming up the garden with her coat in his hand. He handed it to her with a little smile. 'Might as well stay dry, eh?' he said.

Bea put the coat on while he settled himself nearby on another rock.

Bea dared hope. 'Every living thing has a spirit,' she said. 'They must have. How else are they alive?'

Her dad nodded. 'Life's a mystery, I'll give you that,' he said lightly.

'A witch is just someone who can see the life inside things, that's all. I can see those things sometimes. Why can't I be a witch, Dad? It's possible, isn't it? I mean, we don't know everything, do we? Do we, Dad? Do we?' She began to babble in fear and hope. Her father turned and took her hands firmly in his own.

'Bea – no, listen, listen. Please listen. There's no such thing as witches. You know that and I know that. You're an impressionable and very imaginative girl. But . . . There are. No such things. As witches. Get it?' He smiled grimly at her.

'You did hear the hare speak, didn't you, Dad? Didn't you?' she begged.

Her dad looked devastated. All the colour had drained from his face.

At last he found his breath. 'Now then. That's enough of this nonsense. Of course not. Of course I didn't. That's why we're going to the doctor's later this afternoon. And it's all going to be OK. All right? I promise.'

Bea nodded. He came to sit next to her and put his arms around her, and she wept onto his chest. She wasn't sure she believed a word he'd told her, but she had no doubt that he wanted the best for her. He was her dad! You have to trust your parents at moments like this, don't you? And the Second World had disappeared from her eyes – didn't that mean it was never real? Crazy people believed their own hallucinations. Why else did they fight so hard against sanity itself?

She was no different from any of them.

16

The visit to the doctor that evening was quickly over. She listened carefully as Bea told her about the things she'd seen and heard. She didn't seem shocked or alarmed and felt sure there was help for this sort of condition. She prescribed some mild sedatives and something to take at night to help her sleep, and made her an appointment to see a specialist at the hospital.

It was oh so normal, but terrible to Bea. She'd thought she was gaining a world but instead it looked as if she was losing her mind. But how could she be sure? If only one person saw something, that was madness; but Odi and Silvis had seen the very same things she had. If two or three people saw it at the same time, how could it be madness then?

When she expressed these thoughts at home her mum sank to her knees in front of her and begged her to understand. 'Darling Bea, you have to face facts. Look at the caravan – it looks nothing like you saw it. Darling, you're ill, but you don't have to give in to it. In your heart, you know there are no such things as witches. Right?'

Her mum looked up into her face hopefully, but Bea refused to nod her head.

Her mum closed her eyes and sighed. 'We just want you to get well again.'

Bea hated this – the way they spoke to her, the way they looked at her. But wasn't their theory so much more likely than hers? The world they lived in was the world she had lived in, right up to just a few days ago. For a little while she had been convinced that she was someone special, someone different. Now, she was just mad.

And yet . . . and yet . . .

She had to be sure.

Bea knew that the medication she was given at bedtime was different from the medication she was given during the day. She acted like a good girl and took everything they gave her all the next day and the next, but at bedtime on the third night, when her mum gave her cocoa and pills, she hid the pills under her tongue and spat them out as soon as she was alone. She read a little, turned out the light and lay down.

Her parents stayed up late that night, watching an old movie. In bed Bea lay still, fighting sleep. She got up, read, played music loudly on her headphones, but it was no use. As soon as she lay down, sleep came whispering up to her.

She couldn't wait for the house to sleep. She had to go now. She had to *know*.

She got up, dressed, went to the door and listened. The TV was murmuring in the sitting room. Out onto the landing she crept, then down the stairs one at a time. She knew long ago which ones creaked and stepped over them, or hung on the bannisters to avoid their tell-tale voices. As she reached the bottom, her parents began to speak. She paused – but they were only talking about the film. She tiptoed towards the kitchen.

Sickness of the mind, she thought. If you had such a thing, what could you trust? Nothing you saw or heard or thought. But still, you had to try to understand, didn't you? Or else you were lost.

She let herself out of the back door, the furthest away from the room where her parents sat. It was late. The summer days were getting shorter, the nights cooler and darker. Bea ran up the steps behind the house to the garden, past the dark lawn and fruit bushes to the crumbling stone wall at the back. She scrambled over it onto the road behind her house, ran across to Moss Lane and up the hill towards Heptonstall.

The windows and doors to all the houses were shut, but a few lights were still on in front rooms and bedrooms where people read or watched TV before they went to sleep. No one noticed a young girl slipping in between the shadows. Like witches in so many past years, Bea moved in secret, in fear of what her neighbours would do if they knew her business.

As she went she tried to see the spirits of the Second World – they were there, she was sure of it! But although she peered into the shadows, half closed her eyes and tried to see beyond the surface of the world we live in, there was nothing. Why? Because of the medication she'd been given? Because she was beginning to doubt the reality of it all? Or because none of it had ever really existed in the first place?

How can the mad ever really know anything?

She reached the borders of Heptonstall and paused on the cobbled road. Which way to go? Up there, towards the church?

That way, that led to the meadows? Over there, by the pub? She had no idea.

'The Spook,' she muttered. The Flint sisters in their magical machine were keeping her away. Or was the explanation simpler – that she had never actually really been here . . .

But no. Odi had told her to go to the caravan! No wonder . . .

Down the hill she fled. Back onto Moss Lane, down into town. The park in darkness scared her silly, but she made it through to the ghostly station buildings on the other side. Under the railway bridge the air was as black as blindness. She scurried through it like a rat, fast as she could, but by the time she got to the waste ground she was totally spooked.

It was darker than ever there, away from the street lamps. Every cautious step seemed to take an age, but at last she saw a darker shadow ahead of her. She pushed her way through the tall meadow grasses, the dew wetting her legs, until she was able to lay her hands on the old caravan.

She wasn't going to give up. Not yet.

She climbed up the broken steps to peer inside. It was too dark to see anything, of course – even the moon was hiding behind the clouds. But the same stale stink wafted out – piss and shit and rubbish, and the slightly warm, rank smell of . . .

There was someone in there. Perhaps there was a certain warmth in the air, but she knew suddenly she was not alone. Quietly, she began to feel her way back down the steps – too late.

Suddenly there was movement inside, right in front of her. There was a shout. Bea screamed in alarm and fell backwards.

She landed flat on her back with a thud, knocking every breath of air out of her. The door flew open and a figure reared out above her – a frantic shape, with huge, scared-looking eyes and long, thick hanks of hair hanging around his shoulders. He stank to heaven. He shouted something at her and then launched himself into the air. He jumped right over her and ran off into the long grass.

Bea had seen him around town. A crazy – mentally ill, with no home, no family, no friends. A couple of times her mum had tried to talk to him and offer him help, but all he would ever accept was money. The old caravan must be one of his sleeping places.

Bea crawled onto all fours and hung there, gasping for breath. She tried to calm down and find the air, but it was over a minute before she could get to her feet and look around her.

The man had gone. The moon had emerged from behind the clouds and she could see the dull shape of the old caravan more clearly now, standing crookedly on its sinking wheels, mossy, broken, stinking and useless.

Bea turned for home, her heart still banging. See the danger her madness was putting her in! Her fate wasn't with witches, not even with ordinary people. She belonged in hospital. She was a mad girl, a crazy girl, someone who talked to people who didn't even exist.

But she had gone no more than a few steps when she heard the door open behind her. She paused, rigid with fear, hardly daring to turn around to look. Another crazy? Another vision . . . ?

She spun about and there, standing there on the steps of the caravan looking down at her, was Odi. He looked surprised to see her. 'You *are* here,' he complained.

Bea shook her head and stepped back. Could she trust this?

The old man looked over his shoulder back into the caravan. 'It's her,' he said. He looked back at Bea with a wry smile. 'Got worlds mixed up again. Thought you were somewhere else . . .'

As he spoke, Silvis burst out of the door, ducked under Odi's arm and ran to seize hold of her. 'What is it? What's happened? Are you OK?' she begged.

But Bea backed away. 'You are real, you are real, aren't you?' was all she could say.

'Yes, yes – this is real. I'm real, aren't I? And so are you!' said Silvis, and she hugged Bea so hard it hurt her bruised back.

Bea clung onto her friend. Yes, yes, she was real – she felt real, she sounded real, her kisses were real. But even then, even as she ascended the steps up into the caravan, in her heart of hearts she still didn't know what was true and what was an invention of her brain. Or if there was any difference between the two anyway.

Inside, it was all back. The jars, the shelves, Odi's workbench. It had all been gone a moment before, and now here it was again, just as it had been last time.

'Magic!' explained Silvis. 'Don't you just love magic?'

'Don't fill her head with nonsense,' said Odi. 'Not magic at all. Just the same place in another dimension.'

'But isn't that magic anyway?' asked Bea.

'There's no such thing as magic,' said Odi. 'Just more to the world than anyone knows.' He sat himself down on his old armchair and looked at her. 'Every time you decide to go left, another world exists where you turned right. Every time you eat a mouthful of potato on your plate there is another world where you ate cabbage, or meat, or nothing at all. Every second, a billion new worlds come into existence.'

'And he's in all of them,' explained Silvis, settling herself on the arm of his chair and putting an arm round his huge shoulders. Odi was so big and she was so small, they looked like something out of a circus together. 'That's why he gets so confused.'

Bea thought about it. 'You can't be everywhere – you can't be in all of them.'

'All the ones I know about anyway,' said Odi.

'Billions?' asked Bea.

'Trillions,' said Odi. 'Fortunately, I can concentrate on just a few at a time. Even so, it's hard to work out which one I'm actually in. At the moment, I reckon this is one of only several thousand, which is helpful for me, but not for you. If only I could work it out exactly,' he added, 'I'd know what was going to happen next.'

'But you never can,' said Silvis.

'So when I came here with my mum . . .'

'While we were away I took this caravan into a different world and swapped it for that old one in another.'

'You came here with your mum?' asked Silvis. 'And we missed her!' she said, looking accusingly at Odi.

'Sorry. That world seemed so unlikely. You can only play the odds,' said Odi. 'So then, Bea, what's been going on?'

Bea felt her heart fall as she remembered her troubles.

'Come and sit here,' said Silvis, patting the other arm of the chair. Bea was shy of Odi, but went anyway, and perched there, side by side with Silvis – like two pet birds, she thought.

She took a deep breath and tried to explain what was going on.

'So now the Hunt knows who you are,' said Odi. He looked at her curiously. 'It's getting increasingly unlikely that we get to save you,' he said.

'Granddad!' exclaimed Silvis. She batted at his head with her little hand. 'Why do you think they know?' she asked him. 'Are you sure?'

Odi shrugged. 'She's been to a doctor and told her everything. It's not rocket science, is it? The Hunt is all over the NHS,' he told her. 'Always on the watch for a new witch.'

'You see? Now you *have* to come to live with us,' Silvis said.

Bea looked from one to the other. Leave her family? It seemed so wrong. Her bones told her it was wrong, even though her head was screaming at her – go! Go!

'It's your only hope,' said Silvis. 'You *have* to, Bea. Doesn't she, Granddad?'

'We must become your family now,' said Odi.

Without thinking, Bea shook her head.

Silvis was furious. 'You're crazy, Bea,' she said.

Bea almost laughed. Yes! However you looked at it, she was

crazy. 'If they know it's me, they'll take my parents too, won't they?' she asked. 'We have to bring them too, don't we? My dad . . .' Her voice trailed away.

Silvis began a passionate argument with her grandfather. As they talked, Bea realised with a shock that there was nothing they could say which would make her run away from home. Yes, it seemed that it was true that there was another world of which her parents could see nothing. Yes, she was a witch. Yes, she was being hunted. It was all true – but it was simply beyond her power to desert her family. She lacked the conviction, or the courage, or perhaps part of her spirit believed that no matter what, her parents would never allow her to come to harm.

This realisation astonished her. She really would rather be given the spirit of a frog or a cat than leave her parents. Amazing. In a few years she would be begging to leave them. But not yet.

If she went, she'd be like those girls you hear about on the news who vanish one day and are never seen again. Their desperate families weep on TV and beg them to come home, beg whoever has taken them to let them know their beloved child is safe. They never do. It left a terrible hole in those families' lives that never healed. She simply was not able to do that to her mum and dad, or say goodbye to her baby brother. It was beyond her. She had no idea whether it was loyalty, stupidity or bravery; she only knew it was true.

'She doesn't really believe in us yet,' said Odi.

Bea came back to earth with a slight start. She was standing in the old caravan, now pooled with lamplight. She had slid off the arm of Odi's chair and gone to gaze out the window at the darkness outside. Odi and Silvis had been watching her think.

'She does believe us!' said Silvis. She jumped down and came to hold Bea's hands. 'You *do* believe in us, don't you? The spirit world, Bea! You can't let anyone take that away from you now, can you? Not even your mum and dad?'

Bea licked her lips. All her life she'd loved the idea of being different, of being extraordinary. Now it had turned out that she really was, and she didn't want it. Being extraordinary wasn't all that different to being mad, it seemed. Right then, at that moment, all she wanted was to be ordinary again. An ordinary life. School, career, job. Love. Babies. A family of her own.

What was it her dad had said? '*It's a wonderful, wonderful world. It doesn't need spirits and wizards and witches.*'

Was the world not enough for her? Yes, it was enough. At that moment it was enough.

'I'll never run away from them,' she said; and at the same time she took a step towards the door, half believing that they would kidnap her rather than let her go to her appointment at the hospital.

Silvis flung herself at Bea, seized hold of her and tried to drag her deeper into the caravan. Bea pulled away, but Odi stopped the fight.

'Enough!' He was on his feet; his voice froze them both. 'It's Bea's choice. If she wishes to lose her witch-self, we have no right to stop her. Now – sit. Calm down.'

He plonked Silvis down on a chair, and she sank her head

onto the table and wept bitter tears. Bea stood and watched her, perplexed at her certainty amidst all of these strange things.

'You won't be the first person she's lost,' said Odi. 'Her mother and father, her brother and sister have all gone. She had hoped for a friend in you.'

Bea had nothing to say to that. She looked sadly at the weeping girl. There was nothing she could say to comfort her.

'The psychiatric unit is always a good place for the Hunt to watch,' went on Odi. 'When is your appointment – tomorrow, you say?'

Bea nodded. Suddenly her throat felt as dry as hot sand. So they weren't going to stop her going. She would go to the appointment. She would lose her spirit. She would lose – all this.

'What will they do to me?' she whispered.

'They will Isolate you first of all – separate you from your spirit. They have a device that will do that. It looks like a scanner. They call it the Rook. Then they will replace your stolen witch spirit with something else – a frog's spirit, perhaps, or a kitten, or a dog. Something more amenable than the spirit of a witch. Something without any gifts. Then they will give you back to your parents – cured.' He smiled grimly.

'How can you let it happen?' said Silvis through her tears. She stared at Bea. 'How can you go there, knowing what they'll do?'

Bea shook her head. She had no idea. 'I'll still know who I am, though, won't I?' She asked. 'I'll still have my memories?'

'Oh, yes. And you won't know that there's any difference. It's just that all the love will go out of your world. That's all.'

Bea nodded and bent her head, so that she didn't have to look at him.

Odi stared at Bea for a long while; then he sighed and hauled himself out of his seat, rising like an old tree pulling itself out of the ground. 'We still have our plan, though, Bea. Perhaps your parents can be shown something – your father at least. We can try. Stranger things have happened.' He took a step to the door, his head bent beneath the roof. 'Coming, girls?'

17

At the house, Bea couldn't face going in with Odi and Silvis, so she made them wait outside while she tried to creep back up to her room. But it was too late – she was busted. The police had been called, they were on their way round right then and her dad was out at the wasteland to see if she had gone to the caravan again.

Her mum grabbed her as soon she walked in. She sat her down at the kitchen table while she called off the police and her dad's search, but not before she'd locked both doors, front and back, to stop her escaping again.

'You don't have to worry,' Bea said. 'I'm not going to run away, even if I lose my spirit and live like a . . . like a frog.' She burst into tears. Her mum hovered, unable to decide whether to comfort her or scold her.

'We're your parents, we love you,' she said at last. 'We'll *always* be there for you, no matter what. But you have to trust us, Bea. We really do know what's best for you.'

Her mum made cocoa and they sat down together at the table waiting for her dad to come back. Bea refused to say a word about where she had been and what she had done. She knew Odi and Silvis were outside, waiting. Two worlds were about to collide, the outer and the inner. If only they could come together!

She didn't have to wait long. There was a tap at the back door – her dad, and he wasn't alone. Glancing at Bea as he came in, he made a little gesture to the door.

'I found them waiting outside. He wants to talk to us. It's OK, I think.'

Odi stood in the centre of the room, his hand on Silvis's shoulder.

'So this is the man you were talking about,' said her mum tightly. She stood well back from the old man, her hand clutching at the neck of her blouse. Bea could understand why. Inside her own house, Odi looked bigger and taller than ever. He stood there, bowed but still towering above them all, his one eye glittering like an icy stone in the kitchen spotlights.

'I told you they were real,' Bea said.

'Your daughter has a gift,' Odi told them. 'She can waken the spirits of things past.'

'Waken the spirits, is it?' her mum said, in a cold, hard voice. 'You mean the dead, I suppose.'

'The dead don't sleep,' said Odi. 'But I never meant that. The spirit survives death in other worlds than this one. Bea is able to invite them back and animate them again, for a short time. She did it on the moors that day, when she summoned the deer. It's a rare gift, but there are people who want to stop her growing into herself – who would capture her spirit for their own use. Her enemies are very powerful. They have branches in every part of society – in education, the police, parliament, the judiciary. The NHS.'

Bea's mum's voice dripped scorn. 'Let me guess. They go back hundreds of years, right? Descended from Jesus. Or – no. They came from outer space. They shot President Kennedy and helped fake the moon landing.'

'Kelsey,' she heard her dad murmur. He was always more patient with crazies.

'You might know them by their old name; witch-hunters.'

'You're saying that my daughter is a witch?' her mum asked. 'Well. That's *very* Hebden Bridge.'

Odi sighed, that long tired sigh Bea was getting to know.

'Tell them, Granddad. Show them,' demanded Silvis.

'Show us what?'

'The spirits. They do exist,' insisted Silvis. 'But . . . not everyone can see.' She cast an anxious glance at Bea.

'Well, fancy that,' said Kelsey.

Odi looked around the kitchen. 'There's nothing alive in here,' he rumbled. 'Not even a potted plant.'

'The garlic?' asked Bea's mum sarcastically. There was a bowl on the windowsill with three garlic bulbs in it.

Odi shook his head.

'The window,' he said. 'Look. The rockery is alive.'

He took a long stride across the kitchen, put his hand on Bea's dad's shoulder and gently guided him to the window.

'Let him go – don't you dare touch any of us! I'm calling the police,' her mum yelped, fumbling for her phone which lay on the table next to her cocoa mug. But Bea's dad lifted his hand.

'Look for the lights that aren't there,' murmured Odi.

Her father stared out of the window, dwarfed by the huge

man standing behind him. Bea and Silvis came to his side as her mum, rigid with fear, gripped her phone and glared over their shoulders into the darkness. There was a long moment of silence.

Bea stared at her dad's face, willing, willing, willing him to see. He stared ahead, hands by his side.

'What are you looking for?' her mum demanded at last, in a hoarse whisper.

'The eye interprets. Different people see different things,' said Odi quietly.

'Oh, how handy!'

'But we can talk about numbers. We can talk about where.'

Bea could feel her mum's presence as stiff as a board behind her and her father, also stiff . . . perhaps even more frightened than she was. But at least they were looking. The rockery was about three metres away, rising up before the window above a low wall. Their own reflections shone back at them, and the light from the window lit the plants only dimly behind. They were past their best and gone to seed, but they still lived and grew, and their seeds were of interest to certain little creatures that made their nests under the stones and in cracks in the old walls.

'There's a mouse,' said Odi quietly to her dad. 'There to the left, by the wall.'

Her dad looked left. Bea held her breath. *Please let him see, please let him see!* It was far too dark to see anything much, certainly not a creature as tiny and well-camouflaged as a mouse. She herself could still see nothing. She waited; the presence of Odi and Silvis might help – she hoped so.

And . . . there! She breathed a sigh of relief. The soft mossy light of a mouse spirit, trembling among the stalks.

'I see it. Do you see it, Dad?' she said.

'What do you see?' hissed her mum behind her. She sounded terrified.

'Up to the left, two more,' said Silvis. 'And babies – under that stone.'

'And there's one hiding in the corner by the bricks,' said Bea.

The mice were having a bonanza, gathering fallen seeds, hiding them in nooks and crannies in store for the coming winter. Bea saw some just as blurry lights and others as tiny greedy men and women running about – busy, busy, busy, ferrying goods to and fro, stopping every now and then to stuff their faces as fast as they could before anyone caught them. One of them was brought to such joy by so much food that its spirit spun up into the air, spiralling and spraying colours as it went.

Bea burst out laughing. 'See them?' she begged her dad, turning and grabbing his hand. 'See them? They're having so much fun!'

Her dad looked down at her, then back at the rockery. Every bit of colour had drained from his face. He looked so awful that Bea dropped her hand from his arm. She thought he might burst into tears.

'And look!' exclaimed Silvis, pointing. 'They better watch out!'

Bea followed her finger. Something was stalking the mice. Like a snake of light it was wriggling down among the stones . . .

'Weasel?' murmured Silvis.

'Look out!' shouted Bea suddenly. Her dad jumped as if he'd been shocked, and all along the rockery the little lights froze at the sound of her voice.

There was a long moment. All Bea could hear was her dad's ragged breath. She tugged on his arm and he turned to look at her.

'Nothing,' he croaked, in a voice as hoarse as a heel drawn through gravel.

'You're lying!' hissed Bea.

Kelsey sprang into action.

'I've had enough of this,' she snapped. She banged her phone on the table to get everyone to turn and look at her. She strode over, shoved her husband out of the way, pushed in front of Odi and glared up at him, like a duck looking up at a horse. 'Get out now.'

Odi stood his ground. 'Your daughter summoned the stags on the moors that day. If you want her to stay whole, you have to hide her away where they can't find her.'

'Now we get it,' said Kelsey. 'And that would be over to you, would it?'

Odi paused. 'She must be hidden. I don't know who else could.'

'And you want . . . excuse me . . .' Bea's mum's voice was quavering. Bea recognised the signs; her mum was about to blow. 'You're telling me I have to give my daughter to you in case the witch-hunters catch her?'

'We can hide you too,' said Odi. 'As her parents, you're in danger as well. And the baby. We think he might be a witch too.'

'You're the one who's been filling her head with this nonsense. Cultists, that's what you are. OK; this stops here. You hear me? Get out!' She shoved him in the chest, that big man – she was fearless for her child. 'I'm going to hand my lovely daughter over to some deranged nut job cult? Get out! Out! *Out!*'

'Dad?' Bea grabbed her father's arm and pulled hard. 'You saw! I know you did. You saw!'

Her dad, still grey, shook his head. 'Nothing there,' he groaned.

'I know you saw them!' shouted Bea.

'Just mice. I'm sorry, Bea.'

'In this light? You can't see anything in this light. They were the spirits . . .'

'Spreading lies,' Kelsey was shouting. 'Separating children from their parents. This child . . . what's her name, Silvia, is it? Where are your parents? Are they part of this, or has this gobshite lured you away from your family too?'

'He's my grandfather,' Silvis burst out. 'And you have to believe him! Bea is in danger and so are you.'

'I'll be asking the police to have a look at you two. Where is it you live? I saw that caravan. Do you really live in there – in that filth? With this young girl? Get out! Get out of my house now!'

'Come on, Silvis,' said Odi. He took hold of her and moved to the back door, where he turned for his parting shot.

'Listen to your daughter,' he commanded. For a second you got a flash of what he had been when he was young, in his heyday. Even Kelsey fell back.

Odi turned to Bea's dad. 'Bea must not go to the hospital. Run with her, hide her if you can't give her to us. If you don't, they *will* take her spirit.'

He gave Bea a nod of farewell, took Silvis by the shoulder and left.

Kelsey rushed to the door and locked it with shaking hands. 'You are never to see those people again. Do you understand me, Bea? You have no idea of the danger you've put yourself in. And you,' she turned to her husband. 'You stood there, and practically encouraged them! How dare you! How fucking dare you!' The room froze; Bea had never heard her mum swear. 'You're totally grounded now,' she told Bea. She was punching numbers into her phone. 'Police,' she said into it. 'I want the police.' She glared at Bea as she waited for the connection.

Bea turned to look at her dad.

'Bed,' he said.

Overcome, Bea rushed out of the room and up to her bedroom where she wept as if her heart was breaking.

18

Her dad woke her up with a cup of tea an hour before they were due to set out. She showered, refused breakfast, and before she knew it all three of them were in the car on their way to Calderdale Hospital.

Bea had no idea how to handle this – what to say, or think or do. So instead she nursed a sulk. She sat in the back of the car, glowering. Her parents were taking her to her own execution. They loved her. They were killing her.

'You're going to watch your only daughter get locked up in a padded cell,' she hissed.

'Oh, don't be so dramatic,' said her mum.

'I'm a prisoner in my own house, how's that for dramatic?' she asked. No one answered. 'What happens if they steal my spirit!' she demanded.

'Oh, Bea, stop this. You're not helping yourself,' her mum said irritably from the front seat. 'Just let us do what we have to. We love you . . .'

'What use is that?' Bea said.

That hurt. She could see both of them wince in the front seats.

'This spirit of yours, what does it do?' her mum asked, leaning over her seat to face her. 'It doesn't think, it doesn't laugh, it doesn't *do* anything. You know what they say about stuff that doesn't do anything? It doesn't exist.'

'Everything we do is for you, Bea,' said her dad, looking at her in the mirror. 'All we're doing is getting an expert opinion. How can that be wrong?'

'I will fight for you, Bea,' her mum said. 'I'll fight monsters and nut jobs, and dragons and wizards and witches and doctors and nurses and kings and queens for you. I'll fight anything or anyone I have to, and I will get the best there is for my girl.'

That calmed her, oddly. Her parents loved her. Even if that love killed her, it was hers. It's like a drug, she thought to herself. But it worked. Perhaps, deep in her bones, she did not believe that love could ever hurt.

Her dad pulled up into the hospital car park and tugged the handbrake tight.

'We both love you, darling,' he said.

'I love you too,' said Bea.

They got out. Her dad paid for a ticket and they led her into the hospital. The building was fronted by a tall glass atrium, and as they approached it Bea saw, reflected in the glass, images in the sky. She paused and turned – one last look. Her dad came and knelt beside her, arms around her, looking up with her, while her mum hovered anxiously behind them.

'What do you see?' he whispered.

Bea sighed. 'I see a birthday party. There's a girl who's usually there, but she's older now. She has a family. They're in a garden, having a birthday tea.'

'Balloons?' her dad asked.

'I don't think they've been invented yet. Or if they have, they can't afford them. They're quite poor. There's a pie and sandwiches and stuff. They have jelly. Three colours,' she said, glancing at her dad and smiling. The jelly was fun. 'The presents are wrapped in coloured paper. I think it's been painted by hand.' She turned to her dad. 'What do you see?'

He put his face next to hers. 'I see clouds, Bea,' he whispered.

Bea turned to look him in the eye, and this time she believed him. She nodded. He stood up and took her hand. Bea let herself be led inside.

The doctor asked the usual questions: what had she seen, what had she heard, when and where had she seen it? Had she taken any drugs that might account for her hallucinations? Were there any problems at home? At school? She asked her about Odi and Silvis, where she'd met them, what they'd said, what they did, what they asked her to do. The doctor was nice. Bea relaxed. She answered all the questions as honestly as she could. Perhaps it wasn't going to be so bad after all.

There were some tests – the doctor looked into her eyes with a light, tapped her knee with a hammer, asked about the colours she saw on a test card, looked at her tongue. A urine sample and a blood sample were taken. The usual.

When it was all done, the doctor called her parents in. In her opinion, Bea's hallucinations were almost certainly just that – hallucinations. No matter how real they seemed they had no existence outside of Bea's own mind. The real issue was what was causing them.

Bea nodded. Yes, yes. Here in the hospital, now that a doctor had told her, she recognised it as true. She was ill – how else could it be? As soon as you started to see things that other people couldn't, you were in trouble. The doctors were there to help.

'I won't lie to you Bea,' the doctor told her. 'This is a potentially serious problem, but it *is* one we can control. There are a lot of techniques, not all of them medication, that we can use to give you as normal a life as possible. Do you understand?'

Bea nodded. A normal life. That was all she wanted. Up till now she had never wanted to be normal, but now that she knew just how different she really was it seemed that normal was the thing. More than silver, more than gold, she wanted to be normal.

The doctor nodded and smiled. 'Good girl. I need to have a word just with your mum and dad now. You stay here. See if you can find a book to read.' She nodded at some shelves with magazines, books and toys. 'We won't be a moment.'

She got up and held the door open for Bea's parents. Her mum turned to look at her, unable to hide the tears glittering in her eyes. Then she followed the doctor out of the door with Bea's dad close behind.

Bea waited, flicking through a magazine. A moment later a nurse appeared. 'Beatrice Wilder?' she asked. 'We need to do a scan. This way, please.'

Bea got up and followed the woman through the corridors. She asked about her parents.

'They'll join us in a moment, they're just signing some consent forms,' the woman said, holding open a pair of double doors with a notice – Staff Only – on them. 'Have you ever had a scan before?'

'No. Is it a CAT scan?' asked Bea.

'Very similar.' They reached another door which the nurse pushed open and waved Bea in. 'There it is,' she said.

It was an ordinary hospital room, smelling of disinfectant. The scanner was a weighty-looking machine, made of solid white plastic and glass. There was a long glass tube at one end, and a long bed that slid in and out to lie on, with straps attached. At the other end was a panel of switches, LEDs, buttons and a screen.

'We're going to see what you look like inside. There might be something that doesn't belong there.' The nurse flashed Bea a winning smile, led her to the machine and got her to lie down on the sliding bed. At that moment every fibre in Bea's body was telling her that this was wrong. Her mum had promised her she wouldn't have anything done on her own – where was she now? And worse of all – hadn't Odi said that the device that would steal her spirit looked like a scanner?

Bea was panicking inside, but the sense of normal was so strong in the room that she was unable to raise any objections. Like a pet monkey she did as she was told, climbing onto the scanner bed and laying down her head. The nurse smiled and chattered as she did up the straps.

'Will it hurt?' Bea asked.

The nurse laughed and shook her head.

'You won't feel a thing, I promise.' Normal, normal, all so normal. The straps? Nothing to worry about, just to make sure she was as still as possible. Some children get fidgety. Normal, normal, normal, said the nurse. She tightened the straps over Bea's chest, across her hips, over her legs and finally across her forehead. Normal, normal. She could hardly move a muscle.

The nurse patted her arm and smiled.

'We'll just take this off,' she said, and she put her hands under Bea's neck to find the clasp to her necklace.

'No,' said Bea.

But the nurse took no notice.

'It's the sort of thing that can mess up the scan – no jewellery, didn't I say? Sorry.' She clicked the little clasp and held the stones on their silver chain up to the light. 'It's divine,' she breathed. She looked back down at Bea, and there was no mistaking the triumph in her eyes or how much she coveted the jewellery. Bea hadn't even seen her notice it. She was certain she'd never see it again.

'Don't take it away, please,' she said. 'My dad made it.' She struggled at her bonds but was unable to move an inch.

'Doctor will be with you in a moment,' said the nurse. She pocketed the necklace and turned to leave the room.

'I want my mother here,' Bea said suddenly.

The nurse nodded.

'I'll go and find her,' she said, and left the room, her hard shoes tapping on the floor. On her own, Bea tried again to move. For a full minute she struggled in silence, then gave up. She wept briefly; tears tickled her cheeks but she was unable to wipe them away. Another minute passed. Her terror was like a rock in her chest, crushing her heart. Then there were footsteps in the corridor and the door opened. Bea tried to turn her head to see who it was, but the door was out of sight.

'Little Bea! Fancy seeing you here,' said a voice she knew. A moment later, a face appeared above her.

It was Lars. Lars! What was he doing here? But she had no time to discuss that.

'Lars, Lars. Listen – I think I might be in trouble,' she whispered to him. 'I've lost my mum. Will you let me out?'

'Too late, too late, Little Bea,' said Lars. He walked round to the side of the machine and examined the controls. 'Normal, normal, normal,' he sang. 'Normal's great, isn't it? Is that what I call you from now on? Normal?'

What was going on? 'Let me out please,' begged Bea. She began to push again at the straps.

'I'm the tech. I operate this beauty.' He patted the machine she lay in.

'You work here?'

'Not really. This is just for you.' He flicked a few switches on the console. The machine murmured softly. Bea's mind was whirring into overdrive. Was Lars with the Hunt? All the time?

'Please, Lars, let me out.'

'Uh-uh. It's kill or cure for you, Little Bea.'

'I need to go to the loo.'

'Too late.'

'Lars!'

He came round, leaned over her and looked keenly down at her. 'There are times when the world is pregnant with change, did you know that? Special moments, when things are about to go careering off in some unexpected direction. Well, those are *my* moments, Bea. And I think this might be one of them. The question is: is it a beginning, or is it an end? What do you think? Will you sink or swim? Ah – here comes Doctor.'

The door was opening, and a moment later, a figure loomed into Bea's eye line. If she had any doubts that all was lost, that she was lost, that her mum and dad and everyone she loved was lost, she knew it then.

'This is the one, sir,' said Lars.

The Huntsman smiled down at her, his teeth gleaming like china. 'Got you,' he said.

'. . . tests,' croaked Bea, almost unable to speak with fear.

'The time for tests is past. You have a problem, Beatrice. We're going to cure it. Your mother asked us to. She likes the idea. She likes it so much she's having the same operation herself.'

He reached down to touch her neck, and his hand on her was cold – as cold as clay.

'There's something inside you that's making you sick,' he said. 'A little thing, a very small little thing. It used to have a purpose long ago but we're past that now.' He smiled down at her. 'No need for fire or the rope. No need for surgery. Think of it as having your tonsils out.'

The Huntsman nodded to Lars who flicked some switches. The machine – the Rook – began to hum louder and vibrated softly. Bea struggled, but the straps held her firmly in place.

'I don't want it,' she begged.

'You will,' the Huntsman said. He nodded to Lars, and the scanner bed she lay on moved smoothly into the body of the Rook.

The machine began to whir. Bea felt her head spinning, her heart spinning, her insides spinning like a whirlwind. In a space deep inside her, so deep that she never knew she had it until now, she could feel the Rook reaching in . . . deeper, deeper, deeper, towards the very seat of her being.

Then everything went black.

19

Bea opened her eyes. She had no idea where she was or what was happening. Above her she could see her reflection staring down at her. Her eyes, including the whites, had turned pure blue, but they faded back to normal even as she watched. She was in some kind of a glass box – like Snow White, she thought. There was a hullabaloo around her – people shouting, beasts roaring, little creatures squeaking and squealing. There was birdsong everywhere.

Where was she?

Tiny trembling feet were running across her body but she couldn't move her head to see what they were. Something loomed above her and she yelped in fright, but it was only the branches of a big tree, an oak perhaps, reaching across her like an arm. I was at the hospital, she thought. Then there was a violent jolt and a sudden crash that made her jump. There was a glimpse of something huge charging past to one side, roaring. She tried to sit up, and this time whatever was holding her fell away. Those trembling feet were mice, any number of them, running up and down her body and nibbling through the straps.

Bea peered out. There was a bear in the room – a huge brown bear, as strong as twenty men. It was attacking the

Huntsman, who was trying to force his way towards her through the tangle of brambles and undergrowth that had sprung out of the tiled floor. It lunged forward and swatted him, and he hurtled across the room like a rabbit and crashed into the wall behind him. Boughs of ivy thickened and spread from the wall, grappling his arms and body, trying to bind him. But the big man heaved himself free, bursting open the roots that bound him and raising his hands to grapple with the bear.

She *was* in the hospital. There were the walls, the ceiling, the floor, but a forest was growing through it. The ceiling above her had been broken up by ivy and trees. Branches reached out, dappled sunlight shone through. Little birds jumped and shook the leaves. Below her and above her and to all sides, life was appearing from nowhere.

Suddenly she was dragged backwards by her feet so fast it felt as if she'd left her breath behind. The Huntsman had her, yanking her out of the Rook with one powerful tug. The bear that had attacked him lay on the floor, its head split open. Bea could smell the blood spilling out of it.

He planted his hand in the middle of her chest and pinned her down to the protruding end of the bed she had laid on, pressing her heart in a grip as cold as the clay from deep underground. It was exactly as Odi had said. The Huntsman was not a real man. His touch made her gasp and she felt her heart actually stop for a moment before, with a wild thump, it leaped back into action.

'Do we have it?' he roared at Lars, who was still at the control panel.

'Just a moment, sir . . .' begged Lars. He looked up and paused what he was doing. 'Your hand, sir – look at your hand!'

An astonishing thing was happening; the Huntsman's hand and arm were sprouting. Roots and shoots pierced his skin and began waving and waggling towards the ceiling lights, like the speeded-up plant growth Bea had seen before on the TV.

The Huntsman gave a great shout and pulled his hand away. At the same time a huge beast – four or five times bigger than the bear – rushed towards them. Bea flinched away, but it wasn't her it was after. The Huntsman was swept away, and a second later someone else jumped into his place. It was Lars. Still in a half-trance, Bea cast her eyes back to the Huntsman. The beast that had rushed him was a huge bull, bigger than any she had ever seen before. It had knocked the giant to the ground and was trampling him underfoot. He was doing all he could to regain his feet, but the huge cloven hooves knocked him down again and again, shearing his flesh. But there was no blood. It seemed that the Huntsman really was made out of resin and clay.

Lars was pulling at her arm and she pulled back, but he held on tight. 'I'm here to rescue you, you idiot,' he hissed. 'This way, quick. We have to get out fast – this won't last.'

Bea paused, unsure whether to trust him or not; but in the distance, she heard a noise she had already learned to dread. Engines. Bikes. The baying of huge dogs. The Hunt had come to help its master.

'Hurry!' cried Lars. This time she let him pull her off the bed and across the floor, edging past the huge bull and out into the corridor. They ran between the trees across a carpet of moss and ferns, until they burst out into the glass atrium that rose from the ground floor right up to the roof two storeys above.

The forest was all around them, growing visibly. Trees waved up through it, tapping and shattering the glass with their branches and twigs. Ferns and brambles appeared swelling out of cracks in the walls. Little birds perched on the door frames and railings; a wren darted across the green shadows before her.

Mixed amongst them, nurses, doctors and patients were floundering. One little girl was dancing about in a flowing stream that had appeared from nowhere, while her mother splashed after her. Water cascaded down in a glistening water-fall from the upper floors right down to the ground. A group of men and women had gathered together, clutching at each other and screaming as a copse of oak trees shot up around them. Everywhere, people ran, hid, gasped for breath, screamed. None of them could make sense of any of it.

Bea fell to her knees in surprise. Shadows were emerging among the trees and becoming solid. Beasts. Deer – the stags were back. Wild boar, great, high-shouldered bristly beasts. Foxes. There was the great bull she had seen earlier, trying to shoulder his way out of the door; but he was too wide by far. Only his huge head got through, and he had to twist sideways to get his horns past the frame. He bellowed, so loud that the building shook and the floor shuddered beneath her feet.

A tall grey dog was coming towards them. No; not a dog. A wolf. And there – and there! Bea could see more running up the escalator, weaving between people on their way down, trying to escape. One man yelped and jumped up onto the handrail, where he balanced precariously as the wolves ran past. Suddenly she and Lars were in the middle of a wolf pack – great grey wolves, tongues out, standing around her, watching her curiously. She put out a hand to touch one on the back, and it turned round to sniff her hand.

Lars had frozen still. 'Good boy,' he hissed to one of the wolves, who had come close up to him. It stood as high as his chest. 'Gently, Bea, gently,' he said. 'I'm on your side, remember?'

Bea wasn't sure what was going on, but at least Lars was helping to get her out of here. The wolf curled its lip and growled, but didn't go for him. Gently, Lars stretched a hand out to Bea. 'Come on. Quietly, quietly . . .'

Bea didn't feel that any of this was dangerous to her – the opposite, in fact. But she took his hand anyway and allowed him to edge her away from the wolves.

'What happened?' she asked.

'You did,' said Lars. 'Oh, you beauty, you beauty! Look what you did!'

He pulled her towards the escalator, the wolves grouped around them as if they were part of the pack. But before they got there, the bikes appeared below them. Someone was riding a motocross up the escalator. Others followed. There were hunters on foot as well, fighting their way past the beasts and birds that crowded in their way. Bea recognised the nurse who had seen her earlier, her face now creased in rage.

Suddenly, as if a switch had been flipped, the light she had seen on the moors returned, illuminating everything. The trees shone green through their new spring leaves, above and below. All things were lit from all directions. Even the soil and mosses underfoot shone with light. Ahead, they could see people massing to block their way.

Lars cursed and turned to go back, but there was more danger there: the Huntsman. His body had been cleft by the bull's feet and broken up by wild roots. Behind him, a fox was pulling at his legs; he was covered in small animals, pulling, biting, clawing at his eyes. One leg dragged behind and his head was a ball of cracked resins and deformed plastic. But he was still coming.

'Traitor!' he bawled. 'Traitor!'

'Not me, sir!' yelled Lars. He looked at Bea and winced. 'Double agent. No going back now. This way,' he gasped, and darted off down a corridor, dragging Bea behind him.

They staggered across the growing floor, fleeing the bikes and the men and women after them, stumbling over roots and tufts of grass, clutching at branches and walls, dodging trees. Rocks and crags were growing up now – heaving themselves out of the floors and walkway like living things, before they hardened into place.

Bea, who had been in a half-trance still, felt the first pang of real fear as a thought struck her.

'Do I still have a spirit?' she asked Lars.

'I'll say . . . this way . . . this way . . . hurry!' he hissed. He rushed on, still pulling Bea behind him. Along corridors, up stairs, down again, towards the back of the building. They were almost out when the Hunt finally caught up with them. They turned a corner – and there they were, blocking the way forward, some on motocross bikes, some on foot. There was a pack of dogs with them – huge dogs, like the monster that had found Bea in the woods that time.

Someone was shouting at them. 'You are surrounded. Put up your hands and lie on the ground face first, or we will shoot.'

They turned to run the way they'd come, but that was blocked too. There was no way out.

Bea raised her arms to summon without even thinking about it, but the spell she had already raised inside the Rook was so powerful she did not need to.

From behind them came the clatter of hooves. The deer, the great red stags she had summoned on the moor, come to save her this time. They ran at the dogs and scattered them, harried at the bikes and people. Then came the wolves – straight for the throats of dogs and people. Shots were fired, but the men and hounds were overwhelmed. In seconds they were rolling under a wave of roiling grey fur. Then a bear. Then the cattle came – and now the Hunt was on the run.

The strange calm that had enveloped her when she first woke up had utterly gone. Bea was in full flight herself now, full of fear. Together she and Lars rushed past the raging beasts onto the back stairs and raced down. The wolves were at their sides. On the landing a bear waited and watched them run past. Down they went, flight after flight, until they reached the ground floor.

Out of the building. The forest was behind them now. Only a few shrubs and rocks broke up the tarmac. Across the forecourt and into the car park. Lars had a motorbike waiting.

He climbed on and nodded behind him. Bea jumped behind him and clung tightly to his waist – and off they shot, fast, far too fast, swerving so low around the corner onto the road Lars's knee scraped the ground; she heard him yell in pain. Fast along the roads, faster than she had ever travelled, faster than a car, faster than a train. Through Halifax, out of town, onto the dual carriageway and away, away, heading towards the motorway.

Bea wrapped her arms around Lars and held on tight. The world whizzed past. So fast! They left everything else on the road standing. She was wide awake now, full of wonder. The drone of the bike underneath her, Lars's body in her arms, the world streaming past in a blur. She was a summoner! And she had escaped the Hunt again!

But what had she left behind her?

There was a brief stop to put helmets on, and then it was hours and hours tearing along the motorways. Bea was going crazy for a pee before they stopped again, when Lars turned off onto a smaller road and let her off briefly where she could hide in some hedges. Then onwards again, too fast to talk, the wind in their ears, swerving and swooping along the country roads until they entered a forest. Bea had no idea where they were. At long last, hours after they had left the hospital, he pulled up at a tall house painted white, spotted with lichen and green algae, hidden away up an overgrown track deep in the overhang of tall forest trees. He got off his bike, took off his helmet and turned to look at her.

'We're safe here.'

Bea hobbled off the bike, stiff after such a long, tense ride, pulling off her own helmet. 'Where are we?' she begged.

'Safe,' said Lars. He shook his head and smiled. 'You are *amazing*.'

'But it can't have been me,' groaned Bea. She was tired, hungry and irritable. 'I never said a word.'

'Oh, but you did! You must have fainted. You nearly lost everything there, you know. You were just in time. You were like . . .'

He paused and threw back his head. 'I SUMMON YOU,' he cried. 'ANCIENT PLACE, YOU WOODS AND MEADOWS, BEASTS AND BIRDS. I SUMMON YOU, SPIRIT OF THE FOREST AND ALL WHO LIVED HERE. I SUMMON AND COMMAND.' He spoke in that same deep voice that Bea had used to summon – but not quite the same. There was no power behind it.

'Of course it lacks a certain something. Yes, Bea – I'm a witch too. Look!' He reached into his pockets and took out a small black object – a fetish, similar to the one Bea had been carrying.

He chucked it over his shoulder into the bushes and at once in his chest a flare of light lit up, purple, black and silver. His spirit. Looking at that, there was no doubt about it; Lars was a witch after all.

'I was sent here to keep an eye on you and help you grow your powers, Bea. My God, I thought I'd gone too far, but you proved me wrong, eh, sweetheart? Man! You proved me so wrong!'

Part Two

The Green House

20

Lars pulled a small bag out of the bike's panniers and walked to the door of the old house, rooting through it for the keys. Bea stood still, trying to get a sense of herself and where she was after that crazy ride. The air here was cool and aromatic with pine and moist earth. They had ridden half an hour through the trees to get there, and yet, although they were surrounded by living things, she could see no spirits. Unlike the wasteland outside Odi's caravan, where even the air had seemed alive, everything here was still.

'The spirits are quiet here,' said Lars. 'That way, none of them can give us away. The Hunt can use life to spy on life, did you know that?'

Bea's attention turned to the bike they had ridden in on. It was a bright red machine, with the same flames painted on it that Lars had on his skateboard. It smelt of hot metal and rubber, of petrol and oil. Even from where she was standing a couple of metres off she could feel the heat of that long ride coming off it. But there was something else there too. Bea put her hand on the tank and it seemed to throb even though the engine was off. She stepped back to look.

A shape moved – a spirit. It glowed amber and white. How

strange that the only spirit she could see here, apart from hers and Lars's, was inside a machine.

'Greyhound. How do you think we went so fast?' said Lars, watching her from the door to the house. 'Take away his legs and give him wheels and an engine – see him go!'

'Where's the dog now?'

'Him? Long dead,' Lars told her. 'Really, I've given him a second life.'

Bea turned to look at the bike, cooling from its fantastic journey. 'Does he mind?'

'The spirit doesn't *mind* things. It doesn't think or feel, it just *is*.'

'But it's the root of his being,' said Bea.

Lars looked at her thoughtfully. 'He goes as fast as the wind when I turn him on,' he said. 'In life he ran. What more could he want?' He shook his head irritably. 'Odi's been at you,' he said. 'The Salem Row crew. Witches have always used technology. Blacksmiths used fire spirits, mill owners used river spirits, farmers used the spirits of the soil. But new technology? Oh no. Far too modern. Everything was modern once. That lot live in the past, but my crew – we move with the times. Motorbikes. Computers. Skateboards.' He winked. 'How do you think you got so good so quick? I wondered if you were one of us as soon as I saw you on it. Only a witch could ride my board.' He smiled at her, the way he used to smile at her in the skateboard park.

Bea melted, and smiled back.

Lars tossed his head. 'Come in and have a look at your new home.'

He opened the door and went in, but Bea lingered by the machine that was also a dog. She had heard of beasts that had been augmented with machinery, but never before had she seen a machine augmented with life.

'Hurry up,' shouted Lars from inside the house.

She hurried after him. 'Lars – your skateboard. What is it? A swallow? Is it a swallow, Lars?'

She burst in on him in the kitchen.

'A swallow?' he scoffed. 'No, girlie. It's an eagle. A bloody great eagle!' He grabbed her wrists and spun her round in circles in a mad waltz. Music from nowhere leaped out of the walls at them.

Race across the storm
Race across the world.
Let your spirit carry me.
We're gonna fly, fly,
Into the future.

Round and round he spun her until she caught his high spirits, round and round, the two of them laughing as if the world was one huge joke. Round and round and round, until Bea collapsed with dizziness onto the floor and Lars leaned against the work surface, grinning and panting for breath.

'You're not the only one with powers, Little Bea,' he said at last. 'Every witch has their gift. I know how to fix spirits in this world. You know how to call them. Together, little one, we will make such a team!'

Bea looked up at him from the floor.

'What about my mum and dad?' she asked, suddenly serious.

Lars nodded, serious too. 'Some of us were looking out for them,' he said. 'I'll find out for you as soon as I can. Promise.'

21

There were ferns in the gutter and beds of moss on the roof. Green algae grew on the outer walls, and the forest canopy pushed against the upper windows making the house a place of green shadows. Even though it was painted white inside and out, Bea thought of it as the green house right from the start.

Her room was on the first floor at the back of the house, where the branches of the trees tapped against the panes of two tall sash windows. She could have reached out and picked the leaves, if she'd wanted. You could peer through the branches down to the garden, where the wood was encroaching. There were young birch trees in the tall grass, some of them nearly two metres high, and brambles right up to the walls.

Bea was exhausted – she'd had a day like nothing she had believed possible – but Lars was full of energy. He warmed up some beef stew from the freezer and complained bitterly about the witches of Salem Row as he gobbled his food.

'They could have used the Spook to fight, but all they did was hide. Look where it got them! There used to be twenty or more witches living up there. What's left now? Three ancient relics and a child who can hardly see.'

Lars paused, his fork halfway to his mouth, and fixed her

with his wide green eyes. 'Hiding won't help us,' he told her. 'It never has. The Hunt must be stopped. This is a war. Their aim is nothing less than complete genocide. We *have* to fight back.'

He stared at her, willing her to see his point. 'We've been weak. We haven't had the tools to fight back. But now . . .' He grinned at her. 'Those deer you summoned on the moors – the forest you summoned in the hospital! You trashed them! I can't tell you how good it was to see the Hunt on the run for once. No one has been able to do that for centuries. The power to summon . . .'

Lars peered over at her, but Bea was struggling to stay awake. Her eyelids were half down; she was almost lying on the table.

He laughed. 'But look at you – you're half-dead. You haven't eaten a thing. Go on – off you go. Tomorrow your training begins.'

Bea was happy to do as he asked. She gathered herself and headed for the door, but paused.

'When will we know about my mum and dad?' she asked again, suddenly fearful for them.

Lars waved his fork in the air and tapped himself on the chest. 'I'm not the only double agent in the Hunt. There were some pretty good people looking after your mum and dad, I can tell you that. I can't find out straightaway – this place is silent. No Wi-Fi, no data, no landline, no phones. Nothing. But don't worry! I'm on it. They'll get a message to us. This operation was planned down to the last detail. You'll know more soon, Bea, I promise.'

Bea paused. She still wasn't sure what was going on. 'How did you know?' she asked.

'Know what?'

'That I was a witch?'

'Double agent, I told you. I knew everything the Hunt knew – and you were suspected as soon as you went to the doctor.' He shrugged. 'The rest is history.'

Bea nodded. Yes. Lars had rescued her; so why not her parents too? But now she was so tired. She turned and went up to bed, where she fell at once into the deepest of sleeps.

22

Bea awoke early while the dawn was still grey. She'd had a good night's sleep, but her dreams must have been unhappy ones, because she felt sad.

Nothing was ever going to be the same again. She couldn't ever go back after what had happened and she was already missing the old ways – her friends, her town, her school, her childhood, her whole life. Most of all she was missing her family. How long would it be before she saw her mum and dad again? And baby Michael? Her mum had left him with a neighbour while they went to the hospital – she hadn't even thought to ask Lars if he was OK.

What would happen next? She looked around her as if the room could give her a clue. It was a tall, bare room. The only furniture apart from the bed was a chest of drawers. It was like camping inside – like being on holiday; but what a lonely holiday this was, away from her friends and family, one from which she had no chance of ever going back home.

Bea turned her face into her pillow and wept, and then fell back to sleep.

* * *

She woke up again much later to the smell of toast. She was hungry now and about to get up when, very quietly, music began to play. Faint as it was, she thought maybe a band was in the house somewhere.

She thought of how Lars had made music come from the air around him the night before and sat up in bed to listen. Was it more magic? This new world was strange and disturbing – but she did love the magic. Who wouldn't love magic?

From under her door, the light was changing from a thin line of grey-green to something brighter, moving and changing from side to side and colour to colour – purple, red, blue, yellow, green. The music got louder. She could make it out better now – a marching tune, quite merry, like a stepping dance, but there was something slightly sinister about it too. Soon she could make out the words.

> *Can you feel it, the Second World awaits,*
> *Calling you from Heaven's gate?*
> *Spirits stirring as the world renews,*
> *Come to take their chance with you.*

Colours began to form on the walls of her room. Bea pulled the duvet up around her chin. What was going on? Louder, nearer, merry and scary at the same time, the music advanced towards her. Bea didn't know whether to be merry or scared herself.

Yet the dead lie far beneath,
Who lost the sun when they took the wreath.
The Underworld's filled with hidden dreams
That wait for you to be fulfilled.

Your voice can bring them from the ground,
They can't help their longing for the sound.
Their lives reborn before they fade
Back down to death, their dreams unmade.

The colours around her started to form into faces that glowed and changed, some smiling, some laughing, some shouting. Louder and louder came the music. Whoever it was – it had to be Lars – was now on the landing. Birdsong broke out all around her in the air.

By how many do the dead outnumber life?
A billion lie beneath our feet.
Only you can call them back to life,
Yes – you can bring them back to life!

The door flung open wide and there he stood. Behind him the sunlight flooded in, although the day was dull and the house in shadow. He was dressed all in yellow, like the sun himself, and held a tray high above him balanced on one hand with a tall glass of orange juice on it which he swung around him as he danced. There were birds flying about his head and at his feet rabbits, squirrels and mice skipped and danced. Outside her room, Bea could see clematis, ivy, jasmine and roses tumbling over the landing, across the floor, up the walls. There were flowers everywhere. And yet they weren't real like those she had summoned the day before. Everything before her was insubstantial. Yes, it was wonderful; but it was all tricks.

The music played on as Lars paraded around her room, stepping high like something from a masquerade. The tray tipped this way and that but he always pulled it up straight before the juice spilled. Bea clutched the bedclothes to her and stared in alarm and amazement at the whole strange panoply. Through the door little birds, butterflies, moths and a few huge, iridescent beetles danced in the air. Plants began to sprout out of the walls and the shadowy shapes of young animals and little children, dressed in raggedy costumes and fancy dress, appeared and disappeared in amongst the foliage and flowers.

But all the time the Hunt was on your track.
They won't rest until they have your gift.

You better fight back,
The Hunt is upon you.
Forget about childhood
The day's getting late.
The world around you
Is dissolving in hate!
Dissolving in hate!

Lars twirled in front of her as the music played the final bars, finished with a flourish and laid the tray on Bea's lap.

'Tra-la!' he yodelled, and struck a pose, beaming down at her. Around the room, the birds and beasts and plants grew still and slowly began to fade away.

Bea gazed back up at Lars, the bedclothes still held up to her neck.

'Lordy, it's going to be hard to raise a smile this morning,' said Lars. 'Come on!' He touched her mouth at the corners. Against her will, Bea felt her lips curl into a facsimile of a smile.

'Smiling's better than frowning,' he laughed. 'There's clothes in the drawers – put them on the radiator to warm up while you shower. I'll see you downstairs. I'm going to slip into something a bit more *shamanic*.'

He danced his way out of the room. Bea waited until she heard his footsteps leave the stairway, then jumped out of bed and went to peer through the windows. Outside it was grey and overcast. The rain fell in a steady sprinkle. And yet, over her shoulder, the sunlight still streamed into her room though her half-open door.

'Magic!' breathed Bea. It was truly magic – and she was a part of it. Suddenly she was excited.

She gulped down her juice, showered, dressed and ran down to meet Lars. She was going to become a wizard – a real wizard! Her! Like Harry Potter. Imagine that!

'How did you do that, Lars?' she begged, running into the kitchen, where Lars was leaning against the sink drinking coffee. She paused. The sunlight was all gone, and the soft green light had returned to the house. Everything was ordinary again. 'Will I be able to do that one day?' she asked.

Lars waved his hand dismissively through the air and sneered. 'Those were just tricks – coloured lights and dust in the air. But you can pull real life from other worlds, Little Bea. My job is to make you so good at it you can call any spirit you like whenever you want.'

He set about making breakfast – toast and marmalade, yoghurt and honey, maple syrup and bacon and fresh berries – all Bea's favourite things. Bea drifted across to sit at the high, scrubbed wooden table and watched him at work. The fright of having her spirit almost stolen and the thrill of that mad dash north had left her. What was going to happen next? A host of questions began to crowd her brain.

As he cooked, Lars answered some of them. As he'd already said, he had been a double agent for the witches, working on the inside of the Hunt for the past few years.

'The aim was to try and steal a Rook off them – that's the machine that's given them the edge for so many years. But then we heard about the girl who'd summoned stags on the moors. At that point, everything changed. Oh, yeah. It's all about you, Bea.'

'How did they know I was in Hebden?'

'They didn't, exactly. You had a northern accent and that road you were on is fairly local, so you were likely to be around there somewhere. A lot of Hunt members were diverted up that way, including me. I was their tech, so they wanted me at hand. I stayed in Hebden for the hoarding. I bumped into you by accident.' He smiled at her over his shoulder as he shook the frying pan. 'A happy accident.'

Bea stared at him. One moment he was a friend, the next he was with the Hunt; now he was a witch.

Lars sighed. 'You're suspicious. I don't blame you. But look – I rescued you! Odi and his crew would have let them steal your spirit just because you're too young to know any better. Not one of them could rescue a pair of their own knickers from a wash pot. Damn it, Bea, you were in the Rook!'

'Yes. And you turned it on.'

'I was *never* going to let them Isolate you! Look, Bea – the thing is, you're untrained. The only times your gifts have come about is when you've been upset – right?' Bea nodded. 'That's how it always is with child witches. That hospital was heaving with Hunt followers. I had to pretend to Isolate you, to try and get you to summon. That was *the* only chance I had to get you out of there. And it worked, didn't it? Of course I'd never have actually done it! I'd already turned the machine off before you summoned the woods. OK, *maybe* you would have summoned those woods up anyway. But maybe not. And if not, that would have been too late. Once they had your spirit, we were all dead. Do you see? You have to understand how powerful the Hunt has been, and how weak we've been. You're important, Bea. I couldn't take any risks.'

Bea shook her head. How could she tell if he spoke the truth or not?'

'When did you know I was a witch?'

'I guessed you had some connection to the spirit world when you got on my board. But I didn't know you were the actual summoner until yesterday. I couldn't believe it when I walked into that room and it was you. There wasn't time to plan anything else.' He paused laying the table and looked grimly at her. 'You think I'm with the Hunt, is that it?'

Bea didn't care to nod, but she didn't care to shake her head, either.

'If I was Hunt, Bea, you would be too by now. Believe me.'

He came across with the final pieces of cutlery, bent down and kissed the crown of her head. 'Welcome to the tough old world of witches,' he said. 'It's eat or be eaten, Bea.' He spread his arms over the table, as if he was blessing the food.

'Eat!' he said.

Bea twisted round to look up at him. 'Have you found out about my family yet?' she demanded.

Lars sighed. 'Give me a break, Bea. I can't tell you any more until I've made contact with the outside world. I haven't had time. Please – let's eat, before I die of starvation.'

23

Over the course of that morning, Bea learned a great deal more about the war between the witches and the Hunt. Ever since they had invented the Rook with the aid of the traitor, Lok, the Hunt had had a huge advantage over the witches by stealing their spirits. The body, the empty husk left behind when the spirit was taken away, could be powered with other kinds of spirits – dogs, rats, frogs, other people, whatever they wanted – which gave the Hunt their servants. But the real prizes for them were the witch spirits themselves. If you captured a witch's spirit, you captured their gift as well. Those gifts could then be handed out to Hunt members, or installed in animals and machines and used against the witches.

But it was a slow business. The Rooks were heavy and cumbersome and could only process one witch at a time. That's why they were so keen to take Bea's spirit. If she was as powerful as they thought she was, her spirit could be used not just to summon up the spirits of the dead, but also those of the living. With that power on their side, the Hunt would be able to steal witch souls from the living body by the dozen. What power they would have then!

Lars's and his group's aim was to use Bea's power to fight

back. They were going to help her develop her powers properly, so that she could summon not just when she was in danger, but when and where she wanted to. Not only that – they wanted her to learn to summon the spirits of the living as well as the dead. Once she could do that, they would be able to take back the witches they had lost to the Hunt.

'Think of it,' said Lars. 'All those good people the Hunt has stolen and used their gifts against us. We can bring them back.

'There was a time when we were honoured in the world,' he told her. 'There was a witch in every town, every village. People came to us to help ease the spirits of their loved ones out of the world when they died, and into it at birth. We helped them understand the world that was hidden from them. They wanted to be on good terms with us and it. Now, they don't want to know. They mock us and try to make us look ridiculous for our beliefs, but in doing so they have cut themselves off from the spirit world. We are now on the very edge of extinction. Once there are none of us left, how will the Second World flourish then? Who will know it and love it and tend to it and see it grow? The universe will have lost its eyes and ears.

'But with your help, Bea, we can change all that. Think of it! The lives you can restore, the families you can bring back together again. Silvis's family! Yes – with your help we can give her back her family. Right now her parents and brother and sister's bodies are driven by the spirits of dogs and rats. They would attack and destroy her if they even caught sight of her. But you can put them back where they belong.

171

'What do you say, Bea? Are you with us? Will you fight? Will you be a soldier with us? Will you help heal the world?'

Her training began that same afternoon.

Lars led the way across the overgrown garden, the tall grasses and ferns wetting their feet and legs, to the edges of the woods. They wove their way past the invading trees and undergrowth until they came to what looked like a great heap of mossy branches and twigs under the trees. Only a trickle of wood smoke from the branches at the top gave it away. It was a sweat lodge.

Lars flung her a bundle – a cloak, a strange-looking thing made of skins with feathers and bones stitched into it. It stank too, although Bea wasn't sure what of. Old leather and smoke mainly, but also feathers, mud, flowers and possibly some kind of dung. Bea turned away with a grimace.

'If this was on the continent, we'd be going naked,' Lars remarked, shaking out a cloak of his own. 'But in little England . . .' He shrugged. 'You'll be better off naked under the cloak, though,' he added. 'Clothes will be uncomfortable.'

Lars turned his back and began to undress. Bea hurried round the other side of the lodge. Not much more than a week ago she'd been in the middle of a schoolgirl crush on Lars. Her relationship with him was changing, but she certainly didn't feel at all comfortable sitting half-naked in a sauna with him.

She dithered, unsure what to do. Was all this really necessary? She wished Odi or Silvis were here to reassure her, or her mum and dad. On the other hand, Lars was wonderful, wasn't he? Smart and quick and beautiful, he was much more the kind of witch she wanted to be than Odi or Tyra, for instance. In the end, she took off her outer garments but left her underwear on. Then she pulled the cloak gingerly over her head and went round to see him. Lars laughed when he saw her neat little head sticking out the top of that manky old cloak.

'Wrong hairdo!' he exclaimed. He bent, rubbed his hands in the old leaves and dirt underfoot, then grabbed her and rubbed them all over her face. Bea snarled and pushed him off – she hated the mess and she hated him treating her like a child too. But he just laughed some more. 'It bites!' he said.

He lifted a flap on the side of the lodge, ducked inside and held it up for her to follow him in. A blast of hot, wet, stinking air wafted out. Bea paused, but her curiosity and her desire for magic won out. She bent down and followed him in.

Inside, it stank of herbs, burnt flesh and urine, and the air was so thick with steam and wood smoke it was hard to breathe. The only light was the dull, red glow coming from a heap of embers in the middle of the lodge, bounded by a circle of smooth stones, each as big as her head. There was a bucket of water to the side with an old mug in it, which Lars dipped into the water before pouring it over the stones. A dense cloud of scalding steam rose into the air. He did it again, and again, until the air was so thick with steam it hurt to breathe.

'S-sauna,' said Bea.

'Sort of,' he said. He reached into a pot standing away from the fire and shook a handful of herbs and seeds around the edges of the fire. The herbs caught at once and a cloud of acrid, aromatic smoke flooded the air, mixing with the steam and making the air thicker than ever.

Lars lay down on the bench, and Bea did the same. It was cooler lower down, but her head was still swimming from the heat and the smoke. Not for a moment did she consider getting out. She was being taught magic; she would put up with almost anything to do that. She lay back, covered her mouth with her cloak to filter the air, and breathed slowly. That was all she could do – lie there and sweat and try to breathe without choking on the thick air.

She had no idea how long she remained lying there. Several times, Lars got up to replenish the steam, or the fire, or the burning herbs. At least once he burned not herbs but some kind of animal remains – the stink of burning flesh that filled the little lodge was hideous. But Bea just lay there, allowing come what will.

After an age she saw that Lars had gone and had been replaced by some other being – a creature with a huge head, eyes like pancakes, with a number of blunt horns growing through its face. The heads of various creatures hung from a belt of leather around its waist – some animal, some shrunken human heads. Bea was too drugged to care much. She stared idly at it for a while. When it saw her looking at it, it got to its feet and spoke in a slow, cumbersome voice . . .

'Welcome to the spirit world,' it said. It held out a hand, and obediently Bea rose. She put her own small, white hand into its great rough paw, and allowed it to lead her outside.

The fresh air and light was a shock after the fetid darkness of the lodge. Bea was briefly blinded, but when her eyes adjusted, the world was alive. Every tree, every leaf, every stem and flower was moving, growing, trembling. Among the dense leaves of the woods and plants around her, a thousand little faces and forms were peering out at her, forming, un-forming, moving, changing, appearing, disappearing. Some had impish faces, others like nothing on earth. So strange! – and so different from the spirits she had seen in the wasteland with Odi and Silvis not so many days before.

Bea walked around in the woods for a while. Sometimes the strange horned beast was with her, sometimes not. She saw Lars once, crashing through the undergrowth near to her. He'd changed his form now. He was on four legs like a kind of miniature cattle, except for his face, which was his own, only more devilish. He ran up to her and stared into her eyes, before running off again.

Eventually she found herself sitting in the wet grass in a hedge at the edge of the woods, staring out across a pasture. She felt at home there, as if the dense twigs growing behind her back were a part of her, and that she herself had become part of the woods. But she also felt cold, chilled deep inside, and nauseous. She leaned over suddenly and vomited into the hedge, then turned round to look out at the fields again.

As she sat there, a number of strange creatures came to inspect her. Some just sat and looked. Others crept up close and whispered secrets about this world and the next, about their own nature and her nature. Some terrified her; others fascinated her. Some made her happy, some made her feel sick to the pits of her belly. Afterwards, she had no idea what any of them had said, but at the time she was sure that these secrets were enormously important and felt deeply moved that the spirits were willing to share their knowledge with her.

After a time, a beautiful red vixen appeared, walking across the long grass towards her with quick, neat steps. She nodded familiarly to Bea and lay down next to her. The heat from her body warmed Bea, and she felt the life of it, the red, bright life of it, creep into her chilled limbs.

The fox turned her head to look up at her and smiled. 'I am your guide in this spirit world. I've come to teach you the secrets of power.' Bea nodded, and the vixen pointed with her nose along the hedgerow. 'There are field mice and voles living in this hedge,' she said. 'I beg you, Little Bea, call them forth.'

Bea understood at once that the fox wanted her to summon the spirits of living creatures, not those from the past. She was about to say that she had no idea how to, but to her surprise, she knew exactly where to find that voice which had risen into her throat from the deep earth three times before.

'I SUMMON YOU, LITTLE ONES, STILL ALIVE. I SUMMON YOUR SPIRITS FORTH FROM THE WARM FLESH. TREMBLING SEED EATERS, COME.'

She waited – and she truly expected the mice spirits to emerge. But nothing came.

The fox smiled. 'You gave them a choice. Command them, Little Bea. That is how you can bend these creatures to your will.'

Bea tried again.

'I SUMMON YOU, LITTLE ONES, STILL ALIVE. TREMBLING EATERS OF SEED, COME! I SUMMON AND COMMAND.'

And just as the fox had said, out the mouse spirits came, leaving their bodies behind them hidden in the undergrowth, creeping slowly, reluctantly through the tangle of grass and twigs towards her until they could rest their tiny paws on her legs. More and more came, climbing up onto her and then onto each other, until they covered her like a cloak of fur.

They looked so lovely, shining with a soft grey light that trembled and shook around her. She could see the thin, glowing cords that connected them with their bodies, still hidden among the hedges and grass. She touched one gently with her fingertip. It fizzed on her skin.

'Pretty little things,' she said.

The fox stood up slowly, leisurely. She reached out with her slender snout, took one of the mice by its head and tossed it up into the air and – snap! – she caught it between her teeth. In one bite it was gone. Then she moved on to the next, and another, and another after that. So the vixen devoured the mouse spirits, who had no choice but to sit there and wait for their demise. At last, when she had taken enough, she sat back and licked her lips.

'Thank you for my meal, Little Bea,' she said. Then she curled up with her nose under her tail and went to sleep. Around them, the remaining mouse spirits returned to their bodies among the brambles and grasses. Bea watched them melt away, then rested her hand on Fox's shining red coat, feeling the warmth of her, and watched her resting.

At last the shining red beast rose to her feet. She took a few steps away and looked over her shoulder, clearly wanting

Bea to follow. Bea stood, but before she followed on she had a question for her teacher.

'Where are the mice that you ate, Fox?' she asked.

The vixen looked at her and blinked slowly.

'I am a fox, Little Bea. Those mouse spirits were my rightful fee.'

'But then, where are their bodies, Fox?'

'In the bushes, among the roots, hidden and growing cold.' The fox looked into her face. 'What is it, Little Bea?' she asked. 'You are flesh, you feed on flesh. I am a spirit, I feed on spirit. The end is just the same. Isn't that so?' Nevertheless, Bea was intensely aware of all the little lives that had ended through her lesson – dozens, perhaps. It seemed very hard – but no harder, she supposed, as the fox had said, than her habit of eating meat.

Fox led the way back through the woods, across the fields, in among the trees, all the way back to the lodge where the journey had begun. Bea ducked her head and went in. The fire was almost dead, but the stones still gave off some warmth. Bea hadn't realised before how chilled she was – to the bone. She lay down close to the fire and fell into a fitful sleep.

Sometime later, she was aware of Lars entering. He stood over her and looked down at her a while, before picking her up in his arms and carrying her back to the green house, where he lay her in her bed, covered her up and left her to sleep.

24

When she awoke the following morning, Bea's recollections of the day before were flimsy and tangled. Images hung before her like unfinished tapestries; fragments of memory seemed to float around inside her mind like tangles of weed rising and falling in the murky water.

She lay in bed for a long time, drifting in and out of sleep, dreaming, waking again, dreaming some more. Three times she dreamed she got up to go to the toilet, and then woke up to find herself still lying there, wanting to go.

At last her bladder forced her up. In the en-suite, when she had done, she leaned out of the window in the bathroom and looked over the ragged meadow of the garden to the woods beyond. The visions of yesterday, those quivering little faces that had peered out at her, lingered faintly. There had been drugs involved, she was certain, but how much had been real, how much a vision? The Second World was so new to her she had no way of knowing.

Her body smelled of smoke, bitter herbs and burned flesh, along with a rank animal smell she guessed was fox. She felt reluctant to shower it all away with some sweet concoction, so she dressed and drifted downstairs to the kitchen as she was. Below, all the doors and windows of the house were wide open, and damp air drifted in among the rooms and hallways. Moths had settled on the doors and walls and there were greenfly and ladybirds on the windowsill. The barriers between inside and outside were fraying. To Bea, in her dreamy state, that seemed only right.

Lars was in the kitchen waiting for her. He quizzed her as he prepared a breakfast of scrambled eggs, standing at the cooker stirring the pan, glancing at her from time to time with a smile as she told her tale. When she told him about Fox, he crowed with delight.

'She was your spirit guide – and you met her on your first journey! I can't tell you what good news that is. It usually takes weeks. The fox is a powerful spirit – clever, cunning, very wise, able to move between many worlds. They can swallow spirits, you know. What did you do with her?'

When Bea went on to describe how the fox had taught her to summon the mouse spirits, Lars was ecstatic.

'Fantastic! Oh, this couldn't be better! She's already teaching you how to summon living spirits! And she allowed you to feed her? On your first day! Bea, you're everything I'd hoped you'd be. You'll be such a powerful witch. No wonder the Hunt is so keen to get you.'

Shaking his head, he put the eggs in front of her and commanded her to eat. But Bea had no appetite. She picked at her food, as Lars wolfed his down and talked, as usual, nineteen to the dozen.

Towards the end of the meal, he began to puff and blow, and lost his smiles. There was bad news. But he wasn't going to tell her; he was going to show her.

Bea's ears pricked up. What news? Her family? Was it about them? She was instantly terrified – she dreaded anything happening to them. When all this was done, there had to be a home to go back to. But Lars wouldn't say a word until he had finished his meal and Bea had forced down some of hers. Then she had to help tidy up. Only then did he lead her out of the kitchen to a locked door under the stairs, and down to the cellars below.

It was cool and dry down there, and very still. He led her through another locked door, then another into a small, brick-lined chamber at the back of the house. It was dark in there, but for some faint lines of bluish light sneaking out from beneath a wooden cover resting on a low circular wall. Lars slid this aside to reveal a pool of cool, clear water, and the room was at once weakly lit by the pale blue light that shone from the water itself. He perched on the low wall and gestured Bea to sit by him.

Bea sat and looked down into the well.

'Every magical object or place has a spirit inside it,' said Lars softly. He reached down into the water and pulled up what looked like a hexagonal glass bar, maybe thirty centimetres long. It was from this that the pale blue light shone.

'This is the spirit here. Little Mary Bell. She drowned in a pond in these woods over two hundred years ago. She was fifteen years old. It was a boy.' He smiled at Bea. 'A lover, I suppose. He was out in a boat and fell in and got tangled in the weeds. She jumped in to try and save him. They were both lost.'

He shrugged. 'A tragic story, but in the case of Mary Bell,

it didn't end there. Her spirit lingered on. Why?' He shrugged. 'Maybe because her lover died there, maybe some other spirit drove her out of the Underworld. We just don't know. In time, stories sprang up about the haunted pool in the woods – you know the kind of thing. A girl weeping at the water's edge. Mysterious lights seen at midnight. When a spirit, which is life itself, haunts a place like that, all sorts of strange things happen. Inanimate objects seem to come to life. People have visions and feelings they can't explain. But in Mary's case it was different. She was a witch, and a very special kind of witch. She was a sybil. Do you know what that is?'

Bea did; she had learned it when she had visited the Flint sisters, Nora and Melissa. 'They are said to see into the future, and so they can,' said Lars. But the future is not fixed, so the visions a sybil can give us of things to come are very vexatious. In fact, no one ever knows what the fuck they mean.'

Lars giggled at his own bad language. 'But a sybil can also tell us something about the past. We can more easily see things that *have* been.'

'And the present?' asked Bea.

'Most sibyls are hopeless with the here and now. Look at Odi, the greatest of them all. He doesn't know what day it is half the time. But the past, yes.'

'But if the haunted pool is in the woods, what's she doing here?' asked Bea.

'Ah,' smiled Lars. 'We brought her here. These crystal bars' – he stroked the glowing bar in his hand – 'they're a device invented by the Hunt. In the old days we had to work hard to trap a spirit in a physical thing. With these, it's so much easier.'

'So she's trapped?'

Lars shrugged. 'This water is from her pond. She'd been in it for two hundred years, she wasn't going anywhere special. This is a much nicer place to stay than that smelly old pond, which was overgrown and stagnant by then anyway. So, Bea, prepare yourself. Think about Odi and the witches of Salem Row. Think about your family. And before you find out what's happening – I'm sorry.'

He slid the crystal bar back down into the water, and the blue light shone out. His words shocked Bea. Please don't let anything have happened to her family! Or the witches of Salem Row. Not Silvis, she thought . . . not Michael!

She did as she was asked, banished thoughts about the spirit of the sybil and thought instead of her family and friends. She peered into the clear, barely moving water, and gradually the reflections within it resolved themselves into a scene. It was so real that Bea's first thought was that it was a real reflection, and she glanced behind her.

'It *is* a reflection,' said Lars. 'A reflection of the past.'

Bea turned back to the water. In it she could see the stone stairway that led them from the lobby to the kitchen in Odi and Silvis's house. Odi, Tyra and Silvis were hurrying down it – and so were her mum and dad, her dad with Michael in his arms. They were going as fast as they could . . . down the steps, through the stone vaulted kitchen, out the back . . .

And there, in the little garden, the Hunt was waiting for them. There were about ten of them, looking unhurried, untroubled. The witches turned, but behind them were their pursuers. There they stood, grim-faced men and women, some leading the great heavy-jawed dogs they used. The little garden was crowded with them.

Her mum and dad fell back against the wall. Odi for some reason sank to his knees and bowed his head. Tyra rushed forward and struck at the Hunt member closest to her with that huge right fist of hers, but the man dodged to one side and from behind half a dozen or more caught hold of her. Despite her great strength they wrestled her forward to the garden table, bent her over and stretched her right arm along its length. It took ten of them to hold her down. Then the Huntsman came out of the crowd with the wood axe in his hands. He hefted it up in the air, placed it gently on Tyra's elbow to take aim, lifted it slowly up over his hand and—

'No!' It was Silvis's voice. At once the scene vanished.

Bea looked in horror round at Lars.

'It happened yesterday,' he said softly. 'What can I say? I'm sorry. How they found out where they were I have no idea. It seems that the Salem Row witches managed to rescue your mum and dad, only to have them taken from their own house. The Spook is destroyed, and that's an end to all of them. For now. Because, Bea – this is not over. I swear to you—'

'But they've got them!' she cried. 'What will they do with them?'

'It depends. Odi, they will take his spirit and then kill him. He's too powerful, they won't dare risk him coming back. Your parents – they will Isolate them of course, but I don't think they'll kill them, not yet anyway. They'll keep their spirits safe, and you know why? As bait, Bea. A spirit can be put back in its rightful body, so long as that body is kept alive with some other spirit – any spirit. They will turn your parents into golems, animate them with the spirits of dogs, or cats or rabbits or mice. They will hide their true spirits in crystal bars of the kind I just showed you.

'And they will hope, Little Bea, that you will come to rescue them. And, Bea – don't mistake me: we will not disappoint them. We will not give up. They want you to go so that they can take you too. But no. That will not happen. We will wait, we will bide our time. You will grow your powers. Then, when we are ready and not before, *then* we shall go to them and it will not be us who are taken. I promise you, Bea. I swear it. We will not accept this. We will give your family back their rightful spirits – and Frey, and Tyra and Silvis. On my life. Together, we can do this. I believe in you, Bea. All I ask is that you believe in me too.'

Bea cried out, a desolate wail. Her mum, her dad, her baby brother – gone! Odi, Tyra, Frey, her new friend Silvis – gone. All she had left in this world was Lars. She flung herself into his arms, weeping inconsolably.

25

If only she had done as the witches had told her and gone into hiding earlier! She wouldn't have been taken to the doctor, her identity would still be a secret and her parents would not have been captured and Isolated.

The witches of Salem Row had hoped for a blessing. Instead, Bea had brought them a curse. She blamed herself, but Lars would not have it. It was their own fault! They should have stolen her away. They should have forced her, kidnapped her – anything rather than let the Hunt find her.

'I feel bad too,' he said. 'I could have stayed in the hospital longer – tried to get your parents out. But there were so many Hunt there, what could I do? And Bea – I had you. I had to rescue *you*!'

It was done – but what is done can sometimes be undone. Odi was gone for ever – Bea knew how devastated Silvis would be – but the others' bodies still lived. If she could learn how to summon their spirits from whatever the Hunt had trapped them in, she could bring them back – lovely Silvis and her entire family. Michael – still so young, and perhaps a witch like her.

The thought that she had cost them their spirits was an agony to her. But there was hope. Lars gave her hope – blessed hope that brings balm to the spirit and spurs effort towards success. She would do anything – anything! – to bring her friends and her family back to the world.

Her lessons with Lars took on new meaning for her now. Every day she went down to the lodge. Every day her spirit guide, the fox, led her to new creatures to work with. Rabbits, hares, foxes, deer – each week the beasts whose spirits she called got bigger and harder to control. Bea conquered them all. She was on a mission. She would never give up until she was strong enough to summon up the spirits of those she loved and put them back in their rightful homes.

In the hedges and among the brambles, the bodies of dead beasts lay. Fox never touched them. She only desired their spirits in their purest form. But each afternoon, Lars gathered them together – he always seemed to know where they lay. Some he burned in ditches. Some he sold to the butchers thereabouts. Others he butchered himself and kept the joints in the freezer, so that he and Bea could feast on venison, rabbit, hare and badger. Bea, who loved her meat, was grateful for that. She would have hated the thought that the animals she killed when she took their spirits rotted in the woods and went to waste. Somehow, it made the whole process seem more natural.

Months passed. By the beginning of winter, Bea was able to summon the spirit of any living beast out of its body. Now she moved on to more dangerous and powerful spirits – the elementals, spirits of woods and rocks, waterways, weather and fire.

With the summoning of elementals, the boundaries between the First and Second Worlds became blurred. Strange visitors began to call at the house; a woman with two heads sat at the breakfast table; a bear lounged in the sitting room and complained about what was on TV, although they didn't have one. Fire burned the roof without consuming it, leaves blew through the rooms even when the windows were shut, the walls turned to moss and bark and the carpet began to sprout seedlings. In the woods she heard strange voices, shouts, screams and laughter. She saw unicorns, pangolins, griffins, elves. Once there was a merman pulling himself along the ground by his forearms. She saw a manticore, a goblin, a cockatrice, a griffon. A kamarisk, with its frilled head and pretty claws, appeared in the garden. An angel flew in through her window one night and tried to remind her of her parents, of Silvis, and why she was here.

It was unnecessary. No matter how drugged she was, Bea never forgot why she was doing this; for the witches, of course, for Silvis, but most of all for her family. Her mum and dad, stolen from their own bodies and imprisoned like fossils. Baby Michael. He would have his second birthday that spring. She could give him back his whole life. Lars spoke of them often, and she almost hated him for that. But she was grateful too, because if not for this fight, what else did she have to live for?

They had a short break over Christmas. There was a party just for two, and Lars dressed up as Santa and came down the chimney into her room to lay some presents on her bed – a complete set of combats, including waterproof boots.

The months passed. Spring came and went. Bea celebrated Michael's birthday by stealing the soul of a phoenix, but it died before Lars could fix it in a crystal bar. Summer began. In all that time Bea never saw anyone except Lars. Occasionally she asked him about the other witches. He'd said he was part of a group – so where were they? Why did she never see them? Lars told her to be patient. It was best for each member of the cell to be as ignorant as they could of the others in case of capture. Even here they were not safe. But soon, soon. His leader, Cora Lynn, would not make her wait for ever.

The seasons passed; autumn arrived. By the time Bea had been in the Green House a year she was able to summon any spirit she wanted, living or dead. She could call up the spirits of beasts from other countries to attend her in the north of England; she could summon creatures from the past, spirits and gods that had been worshipped hundreds of years before. She could call up demiurges, river spirits, spirits of the road, of the seasons, of the mountains, of the snow, of rain and rocks.

There was only one type of creature she was forbidden to call. On no account, Lars told her, must she ever take a human spirit from the living flesh. That was forbidden. Only in the most dire circumstances would she be called upon to do it – and yet, before long, such a situation did arise. And it was not the spirit of any ordinary human being she was asked to steal.

It was the spirit of a witch.

26

The victim was a young man who lived in a small town on the edge of the forest – a witch gone bad. His name was Alan Thompson.

'It happens,' said Lars. They were eating supper at the kitchen table. Lars had boiled a piece of ham and put it on the table to eat with big bowl of boiled potatoes and peas. He was cutting great slabs off the ham one after the other – his appetite seemed endless, but Bea was rarely hungry any more. She liked the feeling of being empty. It made her feel light – ready to break free from the earth and fly off on the wind to who knows where. But she felt anxious too. She'd been that way more and more since she came to the Green House. Fear hummed and buzzed in her stomach more or less all the time.

Lars cut a fat slice of ham into soldiers, dipped one in hot mustard and pushed it into his mouth. 'They are *tempted*,' he said around his mouthful. 'When a witch comes into their gift, it's a race between us and the Hunt. Sometimes we get there first, but mostly they do. Then they fill their heads with lies and half-truths. They promise them anything – greatness, wealth, power, love, sex. Very quickly they come to believe the Hunt is their friend. Oh, yes – the Hunt are experts at

190

this. They drug them, talk sweet, flatter them.' He laughed. 'They blind them to reality. Once that's done, they can be led to do the Hunt's work without ever even knowing they are working for their own enemy. Then, when it's too late, when they have betrayed their friends and family – then they are taken themselves.'

'What is his gift?' asked Bea nervously. She didn't like the idea of this at all.

'His gift is shamanic; certain spirits are attracted to him. If you are befriended by such spirits they can take you to other worlds. Once there, all sorts of favours may be granted. He can spy on us. He can become invisible, by moving to a dimension or world almost but not quite parallel to this one. He can steal the spirit of a witch away into another world, so that they become helpless in this one.' Lars peered sideways at Bea as he stabbed his fork into the potatoes. 'He has done exactly this to people we are both acquainted with.'

Bea's heart skipped a beat.

'Two sisters we both know of called Flint.'

Bea turned to look at him, eyes wide. Lars leaned in. 'First he sent his attendant elementals to spy on them,' he hissed. 'The Spook was no obstacle to *them*. They stole away the sisters' spirits and hid them in the Underworld, replacing in their bodies servants of the Hunt, disguised with clever amulets. Odi and the others had no inkling of this. How were they to know that the Spook, instead of hiding them, was now broad-casting their location over half of England?'

He put a sympathetic hand on her shoulder. 'Then they came for them. It was all the work of a moment. Odi. Tyra and Frey. Little Silvis. Your parents.' He paused to watch her grieve. 'Your baby brother. All taken. All turned to feckless golems and their true spirits hidden in stones that the Huntsman jangles in his pocket. Yes, Bea – this is the witch responsible for the loss of everyone you hold dear.'

He leaned back for a moment to watch the effect his words had on her.

'I'm sorry,' he said, as Bea wiped the tears from her face with a fierce gesture. 'And now?' said Lars. 'Now he's hunting *us*.'

'Do we have to leave?' demanded Bea anxiously.

Lars shook his head. 'Geography is not an issue for the spirits he commands. No. We have only one choice. We have to get him before he gets us.' He carved off another slice of ham. 'It happens,' he said again. 'Witches are the same as any other folk – some good, some bad, some strong, some weak. From time to time, we get one who is very bad indeed. This gentleman, who lives not so far from here, is one of them.'

Stealing a human spirit from a living man was altogether different from stealing those of animals and plants. And a witch spirit too. Bea dreaded it, but as Lars reminded her, this was war; and in war, the usual rules fall away.

Did she really imagine that she was going to sit in the woods practising for ever? The enemy was still advancing. Witches up and down the country were suffering. Now they were in a position to help. Finally, it was time to act.

27

On the day of the theft, Bea got up to find a small car sitting on the mossy tarmac outside the house. It was a misty wet day in early spring with a heavy dew covering every surface. The buds in the trees were swelling and celandine were showing their little yellow flowers at the wood's edge.

'Time to see what you're made of,' said Lars, opening the door for her. 'I believe in you, Bea,' he added, as she slid in. He closed her door, got in the driver's seat, and off they went.

It was the first time Bea had been any distance from the house since they arrived over a year and a half ago. She stared out of the windows at the world whisking past. Everything was different today. The little faces she so often saw peering out of the trees and hedges always looked a little devilish, but today they seemed anxious – angry, even. Twice, a group of them flung themselves out of the hedges that lined the road towards them, only to be brushed away by the speeding car. Strange tattered shapes perched on the telephone wires and stared down at her. Past black trees and verges brown with last year's growth, past fields pearly white with dew, through villages and farmhouses crouching in the silvery air, until they arrived at the small town where their victim lived. Lars picked his way through the traffic in the town centre and pulled up to park on the high street.

'Now then,' he said. 'Tell me what you see.'

Bea had sunk down low into her seat. So many people! – they scared her. What if the Hunt was here? What if they saw her? But she did as she was told, lifted up her head and peered bravely out.

After so long, everything looked strange: the people dressed in their funny clothes like insects on a quest, popping in and out of the butcher, the greengrocer, the Spar. There was a pet shop on the corner advertising puppies for sale. The houses seemed to be watching her. All the surfaces seemed to be crawling, as if they were alive in their own peculiar way.

'Do houses have spirits too?' she asked.

'Some of 'em,' said Lars indifferently. 'Over there.' He nodded across the road. 'That shop.'

It was an off-licence. The window was one giant, bright sticker advertising wine, spirits and beer with images of giant bottles and smiling faces.

'Two people work there,' said Lars. 'One of them will come out in a minute to get coffee and pastries from the baker just there.' He nodded to Greggs, a few shops along. 'That'll be our man. He'll walk right past us. It's not far, he won't be out for long. But long enough for you, Bea, eh?'

'To take his spirit?' she asked.

'Yes, take him. Summon it out of him and into the car and I'll do the rest. He'll appear normal, no different from anyone else. But his spirit . . . When you see that, then you'll see how different that is.'

'But won't he die?' she asked.

'No! I have a replacement here for that.' He patted a neat

black case he had on the seat next to him. 'A straight swap. He'll notice nothing, I promise. He'll get on with his life, so it will seem – but his true spirit, his gifts, will be here in my case for us to use as we wish.' He turned to her earnestly. 'Think about what he's done to the people you love. Next time it could be you and me. Remember that, when you steal his spirit from his body.'

Bea nodded. 'But where's Fox?' she asked suddenly. Fox was always with her whenever she summoned.

Lars shook his head. 'She won't come here. But look!' He nodded ahead. 'Here he comes now.'

The door to the off-licence opened and a young man came out. In the flesh, Alan Thompson looked very ordinary – so ordinary that Bea was surprised he had any witch blood in him at all. He had fluffy blond hair, a mild air, wore jeans and trainers and a bit of a beard. His wide blue eyes looked permanently surprised, as if he had just seen something wonderful. She never saw so unlikely a monster. Sitting there, her only feeling about him was one of warmth.

She tried to peer inside him, at his spirit. And yes – there it was. As Lars had said, it was different from the simple lights of the people around her. Darker, richer, riper – a deep pink and blue concoction that glowed like sunlight through coloured glass.

The young man walked down the street, ten, twenty steps, until he drew up close to them. She watched him without moving. Lars reached across and shook her by the shoulder.

'Hurry! Take him now. Do it for Silvis. Do it for Michael. Do it, Bea – now!'

'I don't want to,' said Bea. But even as she spoke, she was reaching inside herself.

'I SUMMON YOU, YOU LIFE OF THIS WITCH, I SUMMON YOU TO ME. I SUMMON AND COMMAND . . .'

Alan took a few steps, then paused. He put his hand to his head and a strange light appeared around his clothing. That bright force was leaving him. Next to her in the car, Lars opened his case and she saw something green stirring inside a crystal rod.

The next thing Bea knew, she had stepped out of the car. She had no idea why she was doing it – there was no intention in her at all. She took a few steps across the pavement to where the young man stood, his mouth open, swaying on his feet, gasping as the spirit left him. She put up her hands.

'Stay,' she said.

The light paused, then to her surprise – she hadn't summoned or commanded it – it slipped back into the young man.

'Are you all right?' a voice said. It was a young mother with a pushchair who had paused next to her. Bea turned to go, but then caught sight of herself in the window of the clothing shop next to her. Someone with filthy uncombed hair looked back at her. Her clothes were disgusting – far worse than anything Silvis used to wear, since her clothes had at least always been clean. And she was so skinny! Her legs and arms, which were bare, were like sticks. Her head looked huge and her eyes were great dark globes set deeply in it. She lifted her hands to touch her cheeks and could feel the bones sticking out like stones. There was nothing to her.

'Hang on! – you're . . .' The young man had gathered himself together and was peering at her with a worried expression. 'You're one of us,' he whispered, bending down low to her so that no one in the small crowd gathering around them could hear. 'You're one of us!' he repeated. 'But – my God – you nearly killed me!'

A crowd was gathering, but that wasn't what worried Bea. Alan was reaching out to touch her, and she could not have that. She could not. So, simply, she lifted a hand and spoke again.

'Come,' she said. And his spirit, still under her command, moved again towards her. She could see it stirring behind his skin, then beyond it, glistening among the fibres of his jumper, then out into the air as it passed beyond his body. Alan Thompson sank to his knees. His teeth began to clash together, he trembled violently. Lars appeared, pushing through the small crowd that had gathered, talking rapidly. 'I'm a doctor,' he said. 'Don't worry; you're having a bit of turn. I'm a doctor. It's OK. I'm here to help.'

As he spoke, he handed one of those hexagonal crystals to Bea. Alan's spirit, like a bright shadow, moved towards it. At the same time, Lars was pressing the other crystal rod containing the pale green light to his chest.

'Come on, Al, you're all right. You been at the sauce again? *Get back in the car,*' he hissed at Bea, nudging her as the young man began to struggle to his feet. The green light had sunk into him. She could see it flickering brightly inside him – flaring up as it took root in its new home. Inside him, the spirit glanced at Bea, and it croaked.

Lars had swapped his witch spirit for that of a frog.

Clutching the crystal rod that now held his true witch spirit, Bea made for the car; but as she did so, the young mother who had already spoken to her touched her shoulder. 'Excuse me – are you OK? Are your parents here? Where's your coat? You must be frozen.'

Bea turned to the woman, who was looking into her face with a frown. Next to her, Lars was patting the young man on the shoulder. 'Good man, that's it. Carry on. You were getting pasties, remember? You stupid frog!' he crowed suddenly in delight.

. . . and at that moment Bea was overcome with a sense that she had done something terrible. Without thinking, she dropped the crystal rod, which clattered at her feet. Lars howled and snatched at it as it bounced up into the air. Bea took her chance. She pushed her way in between the people who had crowded around and fled. Behind her she heard Lars . . .

'Bea!'

. . . but she'd had enough. She was off – off down the road, as fast as she could in a wobbly run on those skinny legs of hers. She only knew that she needed to get out of town, back to the woods and fields where she was safe – where her spirit friends were, where she belonged.

Behind her the crowd seethed, but no one gave chase. Bea ran, she ran, she ran. She was out of breath in a moment but on the other side of the road farmland had already begun. She swerved across the traffic. Cars braked, horns blared – she had forgotten how to do this. Now she was climbing over a barbed wire fence, the cold wire in her hands, barbs tearing the skin on her forearm, but not stopping. She jumped down into the rough pasture, running and stumbling towards the trees beyond, her feet and shins already soaked. A voice shouted behind her – she turned to look. Lars had pulled up on the roadside. He'd opened the door, was leaning across the passenger seat, yelling her name . . .

'Bea! Bea! Quick! Quick!'

Bea gasped, the wet air filling her chest. Suddenly she was scared of Lars. She felt that she hardly knew him. Worse, she felt that she hardly knew herself any more. What had she become?

She turned and ran to the other side of the field. She was halfway up the next wire fence before she looked back again. Lars had gone. She jumped down, fell briefly among the thistle stalks, soaking her hands and her front in the wet grass, then got up and carried on, still running at a staggering trot till she reached the trees. It was only a small patch of woodland, though, and she was out the other side and into another field in a moment – then another, then another, gasping for breath and sweating in the cold wet air. At last she found a hedge, a proper thick hedge, which seemed to her to be the nearest place she had to a home now. She crept into it, right inside among the thorns and scratches, among the tight buds and the drenching fall of rain water. There she wept. How had she ended up like this? What had she *done*? Surely, it was wrong. How could she ever have dreamed it could be anything but wrong?

Weeping like this, Bea fell asleep, which is how Fox found her. She heard the vixen sniffling in her sleep and woke up when she licked her face. She put her arms around her and hugged her, and loved her. She was surrounded by so much that was strange and incomprehensible, but Fox at least she felt free to love. The vixen stayed by her, curling up around her to warm her up with her thick red coat. It was just as well she had come so soon. Already the cold water on Bea had chilled her to the bone.

She slept. She woke again at first light when Fox ran off and Lars appeared to carry her back home.

28

Bea was already little but bones. She hadn't been dressed for a wet day outdoors, and those hours sitting in the hedge, even with Fox curled around her, let in a fever. She slept a day and a night right through, only waking up to take liquids, and awoke at dawn the next day in the grip of an hallucinatory fever. She roasted and froze and sweated until the sheets were drenched and her hair was plastered to her head. Her skin was so sensitive to the touch that the bedding that lay on her was a torment, and whenever she opened her eyes, the light hurt her and sent visions of quaking shapes creeping around the room.

Even though she was so ill, Lars wouldn't take her to see a doctor. As she well knew, the NHS was riddled with Hunt infiltrators. He refused her the sweat lodge too, although she begged for it. He blamed himself, he said. He had pushed her too far, asked too much of her. The sweat lodge had played its role – now she needed to recover, to learn to eat again and build up her health.

She had a new life ahead of her as a child soldier. This was her fate; she must embrace it. Her apprenticeship was over. She must wean herself off the drugs and become a tool to save the witches.

Weak as a baby, Bea lay in bed, ravaged by withdrawal and fever, begging, begging, to be allowed back into the lodge. But Lars would have none of it. He brought her soup to sip, fed her painkillers and bitter brews of herbs from the woods until finally, after four days, the fever began to recede. She was weak, so weak – but on the mend. Soon she was able to sit up in bed and read, or play games on the console he brought her.

At last the day came when she was allowed out of bed and tottered down the stairs on unsteady legs. She had been very ill – close to death, perhaps. But it was worth it, said Lars. The mission had been a success! Bea had called out the traitor's spirit perfectly, unharmed and whole. Lars had stored it safely in a crystal rod. Even better – it had been put to use.

'By you?' asked Bea suspiciously.

He shook his head. 'As I said, I have comrades and a commander too,' he said. He tapped his lip and smiled. 'So, Bea – your training is over. Congratulations! And now I think it's time you met them.'

Over the past year Bea had heard a great deal about Lars's colleagues – about his commander, Cora Lynn, and the others in his cell. So far, she had not been allowed to see them but now, with Alan Thompson taken out and Bea active at last, they felt ready to show her their faces.

Lars led her down into the cellar again, to the small chamber at the back of the house where the spirit of the sybil Mary Bell was kept. Bea followed, excited and anxious. Apart from her recent mission, this would be the first contact she'd have with anyone other than Lars since he'd rescued her from hospital.

He moved the cover of the well to one side. There was a short pause before the water clouded over briefly and an image appeared by her side, reflected, as Lars had once told her, from the past.

A room was revealed, with a group of people sitting around an oval table, some with mugs, some with glasses in front of them. It was dully lit by lamps, and the patches of yellowish light they cast in the darkness made the scene look like a painting she had once seen. Some of them were talking among themselves, but when the figure at the centre of the group began to speak they all fell silent and turned to look out at Bea. The speaker was a woman, dark-skinned, with short black and grey hair. She was very sombre and very beautiful.

'Beatrice,' she said, and smiled. 'It's strange to talk to you when you can see me but I can't see you. But I hope our good friend Lars will make sure you get this message.

'Bea! Thank you. Thank you *so* much. For the first time in many lifetimes, we can hope that the tide is turning. I know how much you're suffering and how confusing and difficult all this has been for you. I wish I could come in person to thank you. That's not possible just now – but I want you to know that your efforts have not been in vain.

'We have the spirit of Alan Thompson. And we have used it.' She smiled. 'What a day this is! I want you to meet Davey.' She turned to one of the figures sitting by her, who leaned forward and smiled. 'Davey here now has two spirits inside him. Like you, he's a soldier. With that extra spirit he can do to them what Alan Thompson did to us – spy on our enemies, hide their spirits in other worlds and render them weak.'

The man called Davey smiled. 'Thank you, Bea,' he said. 'Because of you, I can fight. I can get revenge for what happened to my mother and father and my brothers and sisters, and I can build hope in the future for my children. Thank you so much.'

The older woman smiled fondly at Davey and then back at Bea. 'I hope you two can meet one day and be friends, perhaps,' she said. 'Bea – you've done so much, but we have to ask for more. Do you think you can? I hope so. We have a list of targets. Please understand – I know what a thing it is to steal the spirit of a living human, let alone a witch. It's something no one should ever be asked to do. The tragedy is that we must ask it of you. But understand this – we will never ask you to do anything against your will.'

She paused. Bea looked around the faces of the others sitting there – so grim, yet so hopeful.

'Take your time,' the woman said. 'You've been ill. You need to regain your strength. But remember that time is short for so many other witches all over the country. This list' – she had it there on the table before her, and tapped it with her finger – 'this list contains the details of those members of the Hunt who are the greatest danger to us and who will be of the greatest use to us. Some are traitors; most are members of the Hunt who have been given the spirits and gifts of Isolated witches. It's not a short list – some two dozen spirits. Once you've worked through them, we hope to be ready to move against the Hunt directly. And then maybe – *maybe* – we will be able to win back your family and friends. I'm so sorry that so much rests on your shoulders, but the fact is, you are our best hope. Perhaps our *only* hope. And your reward?' She shook her head. 'I have nothing, my hands are empty. *Maybe* your friends, *maybe* your family. Maybe not. We can offer you so little and you can offer us so much.'

She looked around the table and raised the glass of beer in front of her. 'We thank you,' she said.

The others there did the same. 'Thank you, Bea,' said Davey.

'Thank you,' said the others.

'We can never repay you.'

The woman smiled out at her, and slowly the view faded. Soon all Bea could see in the pool was herself and Lars and the brick-lined ceiling of the little cellar room.

Lars shook his head.

'Cora Lynn,' he said. 'Our captain. Isn't she wonderful?' He stood, wrapped his arms around himself and grinned at the ceiling.

'And this is just the beginning,' he said.

So began Bea's life as a child soldier.

29

Bea learned a great deal in her time at the Green House. She learned the names and parts of the herbs and animals, their uses culinary, magical, medicinal and poisonous. She learned which were treacherous to the spirit and those that lifted it. She learned the secrets of incantation and chant, and how poetry and song work on the spirit and mind. She learned which aspects of the landscape contain a spirit of their own, and which are simply collections of rock, soil and water.

She learned astral projection, where the spirit leaves the body, and, tethered only by a thread of belief, may travel far and wide – as far as belief may stretch. She learned how to sever that tether in others so that the spirit may become lost.

She learned how to enter the body of another living being – man, woman, child or beast – a hare, perhaps; or a plant or even a part of the landscape. She learned how to trap a spirit in a soulless thing for ever – a rock, a bottle of water, a crystal rod. She learned how to apportion blame magically; how to create love, or the illusion of it; how to change the names of things. She learned how to immobilise or otherwise injure the spirit, whilst leaving it still apparently intact, and also how to elevate it in ways as yet unknown.

Lars meanwhile was learning to swallow spirits, in the way

that Fox did. He often took a box of crystal rods up from the cellar into his room, where he would lock the door – he always locked the door – and did the deed in private. So far he was able to devour the spirits of animals and plants, but he was struggling to swallow those of the witch spirits they had Isolated, in the way Davey had. The throat rebelled against such an act. Bea could often hear him retching in his room as he tried to force them down.

More months passed, with work and practice, and more work and more practice. It was a lonely life for Bea. Lars was only interested in work. There was no friendship, no companionship. The idea that somehow her family's fate was her fault was a torment to her. It was only the thought that one day she might be able to bring them back that kept her going.

She missed Lars. Not the Lars of today, who was always working, planning and plotting from dawn to dusk. The old Lars – the beautiful, exciting, carefree boy she'd met on the slopes of the skateboard park, who could pull off such marvellous tricks, and who smiled so wickedly. Where was he gone? The Lars she knew wasn't her friend any more. He was her teacher, her officer – her boss. He dressed in military fatigues, wore his hair short and dictated her life in every detail – what she ate, what time she went to bed, what time she got up. But when she dreamed about him, his red hair was still long and he soared on the slopes like a bird, hurrying to her side when she fell, winking and clapping his hands every time she pulled off a special trick.

Every day there were more lessons; but the most important and hardest task was to perfect the dark art of stealing the magical spirits of her witch kin. That was not an easy thing, or a nice thing, or a kind thing. Only the dreadful circumstances they were in and the savagery of their enemy made it necessary. As Lars kept reminding her, this was war. War, which justifies every crime and destroys accountability. Every time Bea stole another human spirit, and she was doing it often now, it injured her inside – deep down in her own spirit, deeper than she knew how to look. She rebelled against it, mind, body and spirit, but she would not, could not stop. Everything she did was for her family and friends.

They headed out every other week on their guerrilla missions. ILD, Lars called it: Identify, Locate and Destroy. He bought a camper van and in this they travelled far and wide across England and into Scotland and Wales. Once they travelled on the ferry to Ireland to take out a Hunt cell in County Kildare that had been operating for decades. That was a successful trip. They only came back with two spirits, but both were powerful and dangerous. Lars was delighted.

Their targets, Old Tor and his wife Maisie, liked to take a pint of two down at their local pub each Sunday, and then walk back with a torch down the dark country roads to their cottage. Lars and Bea went to the pub early and listened to the old man play a drum while his wife sang in a voice so ancient it had cracked, but which was still beautiful – unearthly, wavering. They left early and waited behind a bush, wearing night-vision goggles so they could take out the old man and his wife before they even knew anyone was there.

Tor, who had been a disaster for the witches for decades, went without a murmur. His wife was trickier. She fought like a tiger and tried to drag both of them into another world to this one, haunted by rage. They had to fight hard to subdue her, and when her spirit was finally peeled out from inside her, she let out a shriek so loud Bea thought it would split her skull in half and there was a flash of pure white light that left her brains scrambled for days after.

That was her memories leaving her in a single moment. Lars had been unable to – or had chosen not to – re-animate her body with another spirit. Together, he and Bea had dragged the bodies into the undergrowth before they fled the scene.

'But it's worth it,' said Lars, on the way back. They were taking a break in a service station car park on the M62 on their way back to the Green House, drinking tea brewed on the calor gas stove he had on board and eating pasties he'd bought. The blinds were drawn so no one could see in. Pictures of Bea had been circulated amongst the Hunt nationwide, and while Lars was willing to risk a couple of hours in a remote Irish bar, he was careful that no one ever even glimpsed Bea's face in a busy place like this.

He had taken out one of the crystal bars. Inside, a strange mauve and green light flickered after his hand – seeking a home of flesh, Bea knew. No spirit ever liked to be deprived of a seat.

'Old Tor,' gloated Lars. 'Such a catch! His spirit speaks to the weather. Did you know that the weather can have a spirit? I actually think that Tor managed somehow to give weather fronts a spirit – there were always more about near him. With this, I can summon the fog, the winds, the rains, maybe even a hurricane. It's power, you see? No technology can ever get anywhere near what he can do. And now we can do it too.'

Bea was only half listening. As he triumphed over their latest catch, she was peering shyly out from behind the curtains. Just a metre or so away, people walked about and talked to their families and friends. A couple of teenage girls were chatting with a boy by a nearby car. How long had it been now since she had hung out with anyone other than Lars? Months, she supposed. Actually, it was over a year and a half. Bea had lost all track of time.

'Can't we go out? Get a coffee?'

'No way. The Hunt is everywhere,' Lars said sharply. He glanced across and softened. Reaching over, he patted her arm. 'I know it's hard,' he said. 'I know you get lonely. But you know how it is, Bea. We *have* to keep you hidden. *They* could be anywhere. Always watching, always waiting. You know what they're like. If they catch you, we've lost everything. You know this!' he said irritably, when he saw her about to complain.

Bea held her tongue. Disagreeing with Lars was unaccountably hard.

'I wish you could be a bit more triumphant,' he complained. 'This is a marvellous catch. You're so bloody miserable all the time.'

He put the crystals away in the velvet-lined box he kept them in, and started up the van. In the back, Bea lay down and closed her eyes. She felt tired – tired beyond belief at the life she lived, and the tasks she had to perform. As he pulled out of the car park, Lars launched into yet another of his pep talks.

'You're doing so well . . . your powers are growing day by

day . . . I know it's hard . . . others so much worse off than you . . .' he said. Then he got on to his favourite topic.

'This is a war, Bea. No one likes it and no one expects you to like it, but we all have our duty to do. You're too soft. You have to toughen up. It's the only way. You have to cut yourself off from your feelings – turn yourself into a fighting machine. That's difficult, especially when you're so young, but . . . blah blah blah . . . blah blah blah . . .'

The words hammered at Bea's head. She understood war well enough, but why was she kept so alone all the time? No other witches, only Lars. No play, no girlfriends, let alone boyfriends. No skateboarding, no parties, no family, no friends.

'I just want to see someone!' she cried suddenly, interrupting Lars's practised flow of words. 'I want to have some bloody fun.' The mobile home juddered, as if it was shocked by the outburst.

Lars was furious. 'You need to stop being so fucking spoiled!' he yelled back.

Bea buried her head and fought her tears in the silence that followed.

Lars grabbed at the steering wheel and brought himself under control.

'I know, I *know*,' he said at last. 'Look, leave it with me, OK? Let me think. Let's see . . . there must be some way of having fun. Even in the middle of a bloody war.'

Lars kept the spirits they had recaptured in velvet-lined boxes in the cellar of the Green House. He already had seven or eight prisoners, some of them the spirits of very powerful witches.

Sometimes it seemed to Bea that there were more witches against the witches than there were witches on the side of the witches – but either way, they had been having great success. Towards the end of May, Lars managed to swallow whole the spirit of his first witch – a girl, eighteen years old. She was able to hear things up to ten miles away. Lars had devoured her life and now he had her skills as well as his own. He was over the moon – and ready to celebrate.

'It's your birthday in a few weeks,' he said. 'Remember that fun I promised you? You'll be fifteen. You're growing up. I have some fun up my sleeve, Bea. Trust me – you're going to love it!'

A birthday treat! Bea was delighted already. What was it? Her family? Had they found a way of getting them back? Silvis! She would so love to spend a little time with Silvis . . .

'I said fun, not suicide,' said Lars. 'Oh, don't start that again,' he complained as the tears leaked through. 'Go to bed. It'll seem easier in the morning. Go! Now.'

Bea stumbled up to her room.

The fact was, she was too tender for this life, too soft to be a weapon of war. Lars understood that if she was to become what he wanted, she must somehow be changed. Somehow he had to make Bea bury that soft heart of hers. He had to make her his tool. And he knew exactly how to do it.

30

On the morning of her birthday, Lars served Bea her favourite breakfast in bed – fruit and creamy yoghurt, crispy bacon and berries. For the first time since that first day, he made the air sing for her – 'Happy Birthday'. There was a cake. When they were done he set her to do the washing-up while he went to the barn to prepare for the evening's event.

First he drove the vehicles he kept there out onto the greening tarmac forecourt – his motorbike, the car, the mobile home. He took a power hose to the floor and blasted the flags until they were spotless. Then he was up and down the walls on a ladder with an industrial hoover, sucking away the cobwebs and the dust of decades. He carried in bales of straw which he set around the walls as seats, put up trestle tables along both sides of the long barn walls and a platform made of square wooden boxes at one end where he claimed the band would play. He spread a white cloth along the trestles and made Bea go out into the summer garden and pick huge bunches of flowers and leaves to put in vases – as many as she could, great floral tributes to herself set up in nooks in the walls and at intervals on the floor.

'But who's coming, Lars? Who's it for?' Bea demanded.

'Surprise!' said Lars. She roared at him in frustration, but he wouldn't say.

He produced a huge silver bowl, as long as a small child, which he filled up with vodka, fruit juice, dark rum, sliced apples and oranges stuck with cloves, sticks of cinnamon, slices of ginger. He lined up bottles of beer and cider and row upon row of dully shining stoneware mugs and glasses.

'But who's *coming*?' cried Bea.

'You'll see!' cried Lars.

'Will I know them? I won't know them, will I?' bawled Bea.

'They'll know you,' said Lars cheerfully. He climbed high up into the barn among the great wooden roof beams to set up the lights. He put up a projector to cast light shows and cartoons on the walls, hung a great silver disco ball in the middle of the roof space and fired narrow beams of lights at it, which shattered and cast mini beams all over, an explosion of light.

'Is it my mum?' she begged.

'No mums allowed at this dance!' said Lars.

He climbed down and began to tidy up – carried the ladders out, tidied up the electric cables, put away the hoover, the power hose, all the equipment for cleaning. Then at last, he turned on the lights.

'What do you think?' he said. The space, which had been dark and dusty that morning, was filled with light. Daffy Duck was dancing on the walls and shards of colour shot everywhere.

But Bea had no eyes for decoration.

'There's no one here!' she said.

'Bea, I've worked all day for you. What do you think?'

'But what for?' she howled. 'Just me? On my own. I don't

want a party on my own. I want my friends. I want my family.'
Bea wept. She looked wildly around from side to side, in the
half-hope that her family was still there, still alive, still surviving
somehow, even though Lars had told her a hundred times that
only she could rescue them. She'd had enough. She had lost
everything, and now this idiot wanted her to dance.

Lars stood still a moment, regarding her gravely.

'Call them,' he commanded.

'Call who? There's no one left I ever knew, except you . . .'

Lars turned and flung out his arm at his handiwork. The
barn did look amazing. Dusk was falling and the lights were
brightening moment by moment. The small spirits of flowers
and shrubs were beginning to emerge around them, mingling
in with the coloured lights and projections on the walls, a
strange mix of medieval feast and modern nightclub. It was a
magical sight; but not to Bea. People, people were what she
craved. Where were the people?

'This place was used as a dance hall for hundreds of years,'
said Lars. 'Villagers for miles around used to come. Everyone
piled in and they'd dance and drink and sing and kiss, and
sneak out for a fumble and make love in the hay loft. Call
them, Bea! They're all dead now. Call them up! Fill the place
up with laughing spirits. Go on – do it!'

'But they're dead,' wailed Bea. 'What's the point of them?
They don't last.' Was that it – his idea of fun? Dancing with
the dead? She didn't want illusion and spirits – she wanted
real flesh and real blood – real laughter, real boys and girls,
real kisses.

'Bea, please? – do it for me, if not for you. Don't you know that this life drives me crazy too? I'm not that much older than you. I should be out with my friends too – but there's none of them left either. They're all gone. We only have each other. Bea, don't turn away from me. Look, Bea – look. Look at me!'

Bea had been on the edge of running out, but she turned towards him. He was lifting his hands over his head like a ballet dancer. Lights began to sparkle above his head – Lars seemed to have a weakness for Disney when it came to magic. The sparkles began to revolve one way and Lars the other.

He began to change – his clothes, his hair, his look. At the Green House he always dressed in camouflage, but now the green and grey began to fade away. The short hair he wore stretched and reshaped, his clothes grew loose and colourful. He did a couple of twirls for her – and there he was, long-haired and beautiful, just like when she had first met him.

Bea gawped. She'd forgotten how gorgeous he was. He stood in his pose for a while, waiting for her to react. When she didn't, he shoved his hands into his trouser pockets and scowled.

'I'd say let's have a dance if there was any music,' he mumbled, embarrassed himself.

Bea relented – or perhaps she had no choice. Either way, the words came into her throat . . .

'COME, YOU FALLEN DANCERS, PLAYERS, LOVERS, FRIENDS. I SUMMON AND COMMAND. PLAY AS YOU USED TO DO. FILL THIS HALL . . .'

There was a brief pause – then a creak of wood. The door opened and in they came – the girls and the boys, families, grandfathers, grandmothers, mums and dads, a chattering, excited throng. The farmers who had once ruled here, the children laughing and jumping, some sulking, some sighing, some love-struck; the fun-loving, the sad, the young, the old, all come to dance, to forget their troubles, to dance and drink and fall over and dance some more and joke and sing and make love.

Laughter and voices filled the air. Bea knew they were just guests in this world – no one knew that better than she did. But while they were here, weren't they as real as she was herself?

At the end of the barn where Lars had built his make-do stage, a collection of musicians began to tune up. Still the throng was growing. The band started up – one on a fiddle, one on the pipes, someone on a tambourine, an accordion, a bass fiddle. The band leader counted time and the dance began.

The first brave ones ran out to make their shapes on the floor. Lars lifted up his arm and smiled his sly smile. Bea took his hand and together they walked out to dance. Neither of them knew the moves of the old time, so they jiggled awkwardly about in front of one another, until the caller began shouting out instructions and couples started to whirl about the barn floor. They joined in, clumsily at first but soon getting the hang of it.

Great plates of food appeared up and down the tables, sandwiches and hams, loaves of freshly baked bread, vast hunks of cheese, roasted birds and potatoes and salads and boiled cabbage with bacon, salad, beans and baked potatoes by the hundredweight. Bea and Lars took their fill and dipped their cups in that huge bowl of punch that never seemed to empty, even though everyone there was pulling draughts out of it like elephants at the water hole.

. . . and they danced. They danced with the spirits, they danced with each other – danced and danced and danced. They stole outside to steal a puff of weed, secretly, as if anyone might actually catch them. Lars stole a kiss; they danced some more. They drank some more. As the night turned and the punch flowed, Lars swirled her out of the barn and pushed her up against the wall and kissed her again, harder this time. Bea kissed him back. They kissed until they were drunk with it. Then they drank some more and danced some more and kissed some more . . . And then at last, when the crowds began to thin, they crept up in secret to the hay loft where other lovers hid among the bales.

And oh, how tenderly did he kiss her lips, her neck, her breasts, bared to the flickering candlelight. And how sweetly did he run his hands over her as if she was his one true treasure, all his, only his, always to be only his.

Bea pushed his hand away, but he whispered with his sweet low voice in her ear, how they were two who had lost everything in this war. How they must seize their chances in times like these, take their pleasures as they could. Who would deny them this, at such a time, in such a place?

In Bea's ear other voices were whispering . . . her mum crying – Oh no, Bea! Oh no – not here, not now – not with *him*! And Odi and Silvis and her father and Tyra and Frey, and her own voice too, in among the din, warning her, begging her. Again Bea pushed his hand away as it crept lower. So soon? – too soon! But Lars whispered some more, and more and more. And at last she relented.

How tenderly did he pluck the clothes off her, that sweet little chick; and how tenderly did he touch her and make her squirm, and how sweetly he made love to her, whispering in her ear all the words she longed to hear, words of passion, of friendship, of togetherness . . . of love. Him and her against the world. It was true, wasn't it?

And oh, how lovingly he held her in his arms while she wept for all the things she had lost. How patiently did he wait for her emotion to cool, while he soothed her and hugged her. That made her weep some more. When he asked why, she said, 'Because in all these months you never touched me once till now.'

He held her still then, understanding, giving room for her grief. Downstairs, the dance had wound down. Someone played alone on a violin – so, so softly – while Bea drifted off to sleep in his arms.

In the morning when she woke up she was alone in the hay loft. Lars's door, she knew, would be locked – he always slept unseen. Later again when they were at breakfast together, he was back in his fatigues. Neither of them mentioned what had happened the night before. He ate, complained about his hangover, chatted about their next sally to war, nodded when Bea had to go back to bed.

During that day she shed some tears, but they were the last tears she was to shed in a long while. She put that night aside in a box in her mind, only to be taken out when permission was given.

Finally, Lars had made himself all things to her. She loved him, she hated him, she lived for him, she risked her life for him, she adored and feared and despised him. She was powerful; all her power was his. She no longer cared to feel – it was too complicated, too difficult, too hurtful. Her heart was ready to turn into cold stone.

What a good little solider Bea was now. She stole the spirits of young and old; man, woman and child without compulsion or compassion. She no longer considered; she obeyed. She was a soldier at last.

Once a month or so after that, Lars would casually ask if she fancied going to a dance, and Bea would look down and nod. Then there would be another beautiful, tearful, damaging night, from which Bea would emerge a little more hurt, a little more in love, a little more desperate – a little more his. She grew strong and cold. She took her pleasures when she could, as a soldier does. She did not think of others much, because to think is to pity, to understand is to forgive and no solider can afford such luxuries.

But despite all that, it could not end there. Inside Bea there beat a loving heart, and although Lars could blind her and fool her and use her, he would never be able to fully corrupt her.

31

It was autumn, two years more or less from when the Hunt had tried to steal her spirit in Calderdale Hospital. There had been another dance. Those dances were all Bea lived for, but in the aftermath of this one she had provoked a furious row. Lars tried to calm her with kisses, but for once his kisses failed. She had gone from angry to utterly enraged in a moment.

Finally, somehow, she had got in touch with the fury that had been growing inside her for months.

She was angry – but so was Lars. There was a war on! She was behaving like a fool. Did she imagine that everything would change overnight? Grow up, Bea! What had she lost? Nothing. Even her family were reclaimable. Almost everyone else had lost so much more than her and still she whined, still she demanded.

The argument had escalated; a blow had been struck. It was not the first time Lars had hit her, but never so hard, never in such a rage. As he drew back his fist she had seen something in his face she had never seen before. It looked very much like hatred.

The anger did not last. Lars was stricken with remorse. 'Forgive me, forgive me,' he wept, burying his face in her breast. And of course, she did. He was right, after all – this was war. Terrible passions could not be avoided – it was hard for him as well as for her. She had been unfair. He loved her after all – he swore it was so! The hatred she thought she had seen in him had been rage. He was under stress as well.

At last, exhausted by emotion, Bea fell asleep in his arms.

These days, Bea slept lightly, and this was no exception. She awoke just before dawn to the sight of Lars moving quietly across the wooden platform of the hay loft towards the ladder. As he turned to descend, she closed her eyes like a good girl, but Lars, who had drunk fiercely that night, slipped as his feet missed a rung on the way down and her eyes opened again. His face was on a level with hers and they looked straight into one another's eyes.

There was a long, still moment.

'Stay with me tonight?' she begged.

Lars smiled wryly. 'You wouldn't like me when I'm asleep.'

'Please?'

'I have nightmares,' he whispered back. He came back up to kiss her chastely on the cheek, although she tried to turn her head and find his lips.

'We all dream,' she whispered.

'My dreams are contagious, love,' he whispered back. 'I can't do it to you, princess. Sleep well.'

He slid away from her and down the ladder. Bea heard him make his way across the barn floor; the odd voice wished him goodnight. Then he was gone, as he was gone every single night they had ever shared.

Bea lay back and looked up into the barn roof. The electric

lights were off; it was just oil lamps now. The rafters flickered softly in the breeze as Lars let himself out.

Nothing was ever going to change.

She closed her eyes and tried to do as she was told, to sleep, but sleep wouldn't come. After an hour or so she got up, pulled on her dress and made her way down the ladder to the dance floor. The spirits below had begun to return to the world they had come from, hidden between the cracks and gaps in this one. A few still lingered for one last drink, a kiss in the shadows, a pipe or a cigarette in the corner before they too faded away. She pulled on an old coat of Lars's he'd left hanging on a nail in the barn wall before slipping out through the narrow crack of the door into the deepening night.

Early autumn. The barn had been warm, and the cool air outside was welcome as she made her way into the garden to stand by the edges of the woods. She could smell the leaf mould, the leaves changing colour as the trees prepared to sleep.

There she stood a while, looking into the darkness among the trees and imagining the world beyond. One side of her face was bright red where Lars had struck her earlier, her jaw was sore and swollen, but it was not anger she sought tonight. Her heart was demanding its time. She wanted to be loved, to be held, to be softened.

She breathed in the night air, blown in from the coast, from distant towns and villages, from moors and fields and mountains, from who knew where. That fragrant breeze tasted of freedom. Bea breathed in great lungfuls of it before turning to look back over her shoulder towards the house where Lars slept so peacefully, so alone, behind his locked door.

It seemed a cruel thing for him to lock his door on her, tonight of all nights, just when she needed him most of all.

The night air began to chill her. Bea turned back to the house, but tonight she did not go directly to her own room. Several times before she had crept up to Lars's door to stand at the threshold and listen. Once or twice she had even softly tried the handle, but his door was locked from the inside – always.

Why so secret, Lars?

Like the girl in the fairy tale, Bea wanted to see her lover as he slept. She had that right. Lars never seemed concerned with her rights, but what if she took them herself? If she slipped in unseen and lay down next to him . . . perhaps when he awoke in the morning and found her there, he'd like it too.

As she headed towards the house, she had to cross the mossy tarmac that served as a car park for the house, and there her foot found something. The car park was rarely cleared, so of course there were twigs and sticks and other woodland litter all over it. But this felt different. She bent to see what it was and her fingers found a line of small smooth stones.

A necklace. She ran it between her fingers. Seven stones.

Her heart beating, Bea hurried into the house where she flicked on the light and saw . . . yes! Seven stones – greens, browns, yellows and whites. Stones from the river.

It was the necklace her father had given her.

Used though she was to fantastic things, Bea was astonished. It had been stolen from her at the hospital two years before.

So how had it made its way here, to this remote house buried so deep in the woods – a house guarded by spirits and spells of fear and loss?

With trembling fingers she carried the precious thing to the sink and rinsed it under the tap before holding it up to the light to examine it. The high polish her father had given it was gone. The stones were chipped and roughened in places – but it was the same necklace, no doubt about it. Its beauty was undiminished. Even ground to dust these stones would shine from the spirits within them.

She lifted it up, put the slender silver chain around her neck and flicked the catch. The stones nestled in the hollow of her throat as if they had lived there for ever. For the first time in nearly two years, Bea felt happy. She pressed her palm against the stones and bowed her head.

'Thank you,' she said. Something familiar. Something from her past! 'Thank you, thank you, thank you!' As if in reply the stones warmed on her skin.

Emboldened by her crazy luck, Bea left the kitchen and quietly, quickly, made her way up the stairs and along the landing towards Lars's room. Perhaps he had left the stones for her to find – a gift? What other explanation could there be? Tonight, just perhaps, his door would be open.

You never knew.

Quietly . . . so quietly, *ever* so quietly, Bea tried the door handle one more time. Just to see.

The door was unlocked.

Bea froze for a moment in surprise and fear. Now, now, now, her heart whispered to her. But what would she find inside – good luck, or bad? A monster who took on his true shape when asleep? A prince under a spell, that took love's true kiss to end his fate . . . ?

Gently, quietly, softly, she pushed the door open.

The warm smell of man and wine-breath wafted out. Along with it were other stranger scents – was that monkey? The smell of the zoo? A horse, a cow? – as if beasts had been sleeping here. The light was shining through from the bath-room behind her, and her shadow fell on the sleeping form of Lars, obscuring her view. She stepped forward; a board creaked under her foot. Lars stirred and turned. Bea froze. He groaned in his sleep, thrashed at the sheets a moment; then his breathing stilled back to a slow beat.

She stood still, stock-still, trying to see beyond her own shadow. Something here was very wrong. What she saw in the half-light did not look at all like Lars. It didn't even look very human.

The sheet was half off him. Was it the darkness and her shadow on him that made him look so strange? He moved in his sleep and turned towards her. Bea stepped back and pulled the door to, waiting with a violent heart for his foot on the floor. But the footfall never came. She waited a moment more, then carefully opened the door and peered in again, this time standing to one side to let the light fall more fully on him.

Lars was dreaming, and as he dreamed, his shape changed. Here was a man, here was a woman, here was both; here was a horse, a bull, a hog, a bird. This was a man with no appear-ance; his flesh was unfixed. Silvis surfaced on the sea of his skin, then vanished. Her own face appeared, then was gone. As a dream gripped him he began to call in several different voices. He became a fox.

Fox. Her fox. Her beautiful red vixen.

Fascinated and terrified beyond measure, Bea held her place as the terrible show unfolded before her, dream drawn in flesh. The dream reached a climax. Lars's flesh rippled, twisted and was gripped suddenly by the form of a rocky landscape. He tensed, his flesh flexed in a rictus of rocks and scattered stones. The climax passed – he relaxed.

Bea waited, not daring to breathe, terrified that she might scream. Because a scream was in there, deep inside her, a dreadful, ugly scream, forcing its way out of her. She held it tight.

The sleeper calmed. His form relaxed, became almost human and grew still. But now a new thing occurred. Across his back, a second face appeared. It floated like a leaf on the water, as if blown by the wind. It was the face of an old man – older than any she had ever seen. Older than Odi. So old! So ugly!

The face drifted down his back and across his buttocks. Then it caught sight of her. The toothless mouth opened in shock, and at once it stopped drifting. It fled down, out of sight, behind Lars's body.

'We awaken!' it cried, and in a moment Lars awoke and turned to face her.

Bea fled. She crossed the landing in a few strides and reached the head of the stairs, where the noise behind her made her look back. Lars, partly in the form she knew, partly in several others, had risen and was heading for her, but he jammed at the door. He turned to see what was stopping him; his own leg. It had become that of a horse and was stuck against the door frame. He spat in rage, changed again wholly into Lars and hurtled towards her as if he had been thrown.

'Bea!' he screamed, in the voice of a dog. But in his rage at being discovered, he was unable to control his shape and he fell onto the floor, writhing in a mix of goat, dog and a terrible old woman.

Bea lost all control. Raw fear opened her jaws and she screamed at him. Lars screamed back at her with both faces. Bea snapped her jaws shut and ran.

Down the stairs, her feet slipping. Hands on the front door. Behind her, strange feet scrabbled on the boards, something with claws. She glanced behind and already it was on the steps. A goat, a leopard, a man, a snake. Bea howled in terror but she needed her breath to run.

Out of the house, across the garden and into the woods. In the darkness beneath the trees she could see nothing, but it was coming. She could hear hooves pounding, flesh dragging, branches cracking and splintering. Wings beat, the soft paws of wolves and lions trod, chitin clicked. Shapeless voices called and howled, several at once, like demons in possession. Where was he? She had to run, but where to? Over here? Which way, which way! What ears was he hearing her with, with what eyes was he seeing? And his voice, calling her name, bellowing, snarling, roaring.

She had lost all track of ways when he came upon her in a moonlit clearing among the trees. There he stood, demonic, enormous, high as the trees, glaring down at her, nostrils extended, eyes rolling, his neck pulsing with rage. Bea had no idea if he was trying to speak or preparing to devour her. She tried to reach inside herself, to find her voice – although what she could summon up to defeat such a creature she had no idea.

The monster advanced on her and Bea screamed for help like the child she still was –

'MUM!' she cried. 'MUM! HELP ME, HELP ME!'

The monster uttered some inarticulate curse as it swooped down for her, bending its knees to reach out with taloned hands and arms. But out of nowhere, a whirlwind came from behind. He heard it before it reached him and turned what passed for a head; but the thing was on him already. It had no form that Bea could see but it seized him anyway and sucked him up into the vortex at its heart. Bea could clearly see his flesh stretching out like spun sugar inside.

'Bea!' the monster cried, in pain. 'Bea!' – in Lars's voice. But Bea was on the move once again – let them fight it out! – getting as much distance as she could between her and these terrors. Behind her the trees crashed and thundered, the wind howled with rage, Lars bellowed in a hundred voices.

What had she done? The two-face – Odi had spoken of it, hadn't he? His brother Lok, who had no form. Lars was not her friend; she understood that now. He had lied to her. He had lied and lied and lied. Who knew how many lies? She had lived in the house of the very father of lies.

Bea ran on and on, but before she got more than a few hundred metres, that thing, that whirlwind, whatever it was, came to find her too. There was no escaping it. It sucked her up, closed around her. It threw her into the air and beat her down. It thrashed her among the trees, up in their branches, down to their roots. It whisked her up to heaven and dashed her against the trees. It carried her away in its stormy teeth, whipped her across counties, far, far away – she had no idea how far or for how long – a terrible long blizzard of a ride, until at last it dumped her bodily in a wet ditch. There she lay flat as she could, while the demon storm raged around her, flinging branches and sticks and mud at her, for hour after hour after hour, until at last she lost consciousness from sheer exhaustion, even as the wind howled and the rain whipped her already soaked body.

Close to dawn, it relented. Bea awoke and tried to stand up, but as soon as she did the thing came for her again, tore the clothes off her back, beat her with twigs and branches, until she crawled back obediently into her ditch.

So there she lay, as the day progressed, bruised and bleeding and very, very cold – so cold she was sure she was going to die. And death, she thought, was welcome. It was something she surely deserved.

Part Three

Killer in the House

32

Someone was calling her name in a voice that sounded familiar. Bea twisted over and tried to peer cautiously out of her ditch.

'There!' shouted a voice – a girl's. She'd been spotted. Bea ducked back down, hid her face in the mud and tried to pull bracken and grasses over her. But feet pounded up and paused nearby.

'She's too old,' someone said.

'She's grown up.'

Bea twisted to look, keeping her belly to the mud to hide her nakedness. A number of figures stood against the sinking sun. As she lifted a hand to her eyes, one of them stepped into the ditch. A man. He reached down, draped his coat over her and hefted her up into the air.

'Bea,' he said. 'My darling Bea. It's OK, it's OK. Oh, my darling!'

Bea was so astonished she would have fallen down if she'd been on her own legs. She pulled back her head to see. A face with a fluffy greying beard gazed down at her with tearful eyes.

'*Dad?*' she said.

'It's really you!' He cradled her in his arms and buried his beardy face into hers. 'You're frozen. Let's get you warm. We can talk later. I can't believe you're back!' He brushed his beard against her again, then set off with her through the dripping woods.

'Welcome back, Bea,' said another voice. She looked up. It was Frey. Tyra stood behind, scowling at her.

So, she thought; the Hunt had found her at last. It was almost a relief.

She awoke tucked up as warm as toast and hurting from head to foot from her bruises and scrapes. It was dark night, but a faint line of electric light shone from under the door. There was a weight next to her on the bed. Still half-asleep, she groped about to see what it was.

'Bea? Are you awake?'

'Silvis,' groaned Bea. She turned over. All she wanted to do was sleep. Then . . .

'Silvis?' she asked cautiously.

At once the figure bundled into her. She could feel breath on her cheek, an arm around her. 'Bea, Bea!'

With a fearful shout Bea leaped up and pushed her away. She flailed desperately for the light. The figure on the bed leaned across and clicked the lamp at her bedside.

It *was* her, but older. Bea scurried back up into the wall, trying to get away. 'You're . . . you're . . .' Her voice caught in her throat, trying to make it out. 'You're Hunt!' she said.

'I'm not Hunt!' insisted Silvis.

'You're a golem,' said Bea. 'Lars said you were.'

'Who's Lars?' Silvis shook her head. 'See me, Bea,' she said spreading her arms. 'Use your witch eyes. See my spirit.'

Bea did as she was asked. It took a moment, she was that scared and confused, but it came – and there she was. Silvis, silver-bright Silvis, completely herself.

'Is it really you?'

'Yes!' Silvis flung herself at Bea again and wrapped her arms around her. 'But who's Lars?' she asked once more, pulling back to look at her.

Bea pushed her away and stared at her. 'The red-haired boy at the skate park.'

'You had a crush on him.'

'He rescued me. He told me . . .'

'What did he tell you?'

'He told me . . .'

'What? Oh, Bea. What's been going on?'

Bea began to panic. *What had she done?*

'You're here now. It's all right now,' said Silvis.

'He had two faces,' said Bea. She had begun to pant.

She heard Silvis's sharp intake of breath – a genuine gasp of horror. She put her hands to her face. 'Oh, Bea,' she said. 'Oh, Bea. What have you been doing all this time?'

Silvis didn't wait for an answer. She grabbed her again and hugged her hard. Bea held her tightly and raised her eyes to the ceiling. Of two things she was certain already; that she had been with the enemy. And this; that in her heart, she had known it all along.

'I think I've done some very bad things,' she said, trying to keep her voice calm, although it was already shaking. 'I think I've done some very, very bad things, Silvis, and I don't know if anyone is ever going to be able to forgive me.'

'I forgive you, darling. Right now!'

'You don't know what I've done.'

Silvis paused. 'If it's Lok . . . if Lok is still alive, then I think I do.'

Bea waited a moment for that to sink in. She began to tremble.

'Will Odi forgive me?' she wept.

'Odi never blames anyone for anything.'

'And Tyra? And Frey?'

'I can't speak for the others,' Silvis said. 'I suppose,' she paused, 'the main thing is forgiving yourself.'

It was so unlike the Silvis she knew to say such a thing that Bea pulled back to look at her. She was older, of course. Two years had passed since they had last met. Older, wiser.

'I need to sleep,' she said. 'I think I need to sleep.'

'Frey said you should. He left this for you.' Silvis reached across to the bedside table and handed her a mug with a dark-greenish liquid inside. Bea practically snatched it off her and gulped it down. She had to sleep! She couldn't bear to be awake.

'My dad's here,' she said.

'Tyra rescued him. She went down to the hospital to try and get you. The others told her not to, but you know what she's like. She couldn't find you, but she managed to drag your dad away. He's here. And – guess what? He's a witch!'

Silvis chattered on. Only her eyes gave away how shocked she was.

Bea was already feeling woozy. She put the mug on her bedside table and thought – That's quick. She lay back on the bed.

'What about my mum?' she slurred. 'What about Michael?' The words mumbled out of her.

'Odi thinks—' Silvis began.

But Bea didn't hear what Odi thought. She was already unconscious.

33

When she awoke again, daylight was coming in between the curtains and her dad was sitting next to her in a chair.

'Bea, darling,' he said. He leaned over and gathered her into his arms. 'My darling Bea,' he kept saying, squeezing her carefully as if he might break her. But Bea grabbed hold and pulled him hard to her, and he hugged her hard back, rocking her from side to side. 'I thought I'd lost you,' he murmured. 'I thought I was the only one left . . .'

'Dad, I've been bad. I'm scared . . .'

'Shush, sshhhh, darling. Sssssh. It's OK. It's OK . . .'

'I'm so scared!'

For a long while they stayed like that, until at last Bea let him go. He sat back down in his chair, weeping openly in a way she'd never seen in him before. He'd always been so much in control.

'I thought I'd never see you again . . .' he murmured, wiping his eyes on his sleeve.

Bea got a good look at him for the first time. He'd never been entirely neat – her mum liked to describe him as a dapper man who hadn't quite got round to sorting himself out properly. So who was this scruff? There were food stains on his jumper and the lapels of his suit, the same three-piece he'd worn to hospital with her all that time ago. It had been close-fitting then; now it hung off him in folds. His grubby bald head poked out of a bush of greying hair, his beard had sprouted into a scratty clump. Bea found herself feeling suspicious of this new dad.

'Where's Mum?' she asked.

'Still at home, but it's not her, Bea, it's not her. They got her. The Hunt. Isolated her. It's her golem. She has some other spirit in her now. A rat, they think. A rat, Bea! She hated rats. Michael's there too, we think he's OK, but he's so young, Bea, so young no one can tell.'

Michael was still himself! So it was just her mum . . .

'We can get her back then, Dad. I can call her spirit. We can put her back together. Lars said . . .'

She paused. Lars had said a lot of things. How many were true?

Her dad nodded eagerly. 'We need to find out where her spirit is. If they've trapped it here and we can find it – yes, yes! But if she's gone down to the Underworld, that's different. The witches won't let you put the spirit of a dead person back in the body.'

'Why not?'

'It's dangerous. The spirit changes. It might not be her any more. And it attaches to other things. There's demons down there too. They won't let you, Bea. It's forbidden.'

'I suppose,' said Bea. She shook her head. So much going on! Lars's lies. The witches still free. Her dad alive, Michael captive, her mum Isolated. In a rush, all the things she had done with Lars came flooding into her mind. The scale of her wickedness left her breathless.

Her dad was still talking away but she was hardly listening. He was leaking tears again, which irritated her beyond reason. What about her? What about *her* tears? When was it her turn to be pitied?

He was being very odd. His gaze had changed. He always used to look her in the eye when he spoke to her, but now he was looking to one side, or up or down, anywhere but straight at her. He seemed to be talking more to himself than to her.

'What's wrong with you?' she demanded.

He stopped abruptly and glanced at her with a nervous look. 'You might as well know, I can't hide it,' he said. He paused. 'It's all been a bit much, to be honest,' he said.

'What?'

'This. The Second World. Being a witch. Spirits, Bea. I, I got a bit lost.' He closed his eyes briefly. When he opened them, he looked straight at her for the first time. He winced. 'Bit of a breakdown,' he said, nodding. His eyes welled up again; he was trying very hard not to cry. 'Sorry,' he managed to say. 'I guess you could have done with a dad just now . . .'

So that was it. And he was right. She really could have done with a dad just now.

'It's all right,' she said automatically.

'Sorry, Bea.' His eyes went to her throat, where the necklace he gave her nestled. He smiled. 'You still have it,' he said.

'Someone stole it from me in the hospital. I found it again at the house a few days ago. How did it get there, Dad?'

She'd assumed he had something to do with it, but he shook his head. 'I don't know. You can't lose them; they won't let you lose them. They must have found you, somehow. You see?'

Bea nodded, although she didn't. It occurred to her that Lars had left his bedroom door open the same day she had found the necklace. Good luck? Odi had said they might bring good luck. She could do with some.

'So you're a witch after all,' she said. And suddenly, on top of all the other feelings, there was anger. Real anger. But she had no idea where it was coming from, or why.

Her dad let out an embarrassed laugh. 'Apparently.'

'And what . . . what's your relationship with the spirit world?' she asked. It came out all sarcastic.

He looked at her warily. 'Not like yours,' he said. 'It's something to do with stones. I guess I was a jeweller for a reason.' He laughed again, awkwardly. Inside her, Bea felt the rage rise. Because . . . because . . . And suddenly she knew what it was. She turned her gaze full on him. 'You can see the spirits,' she said. 'You always have, haven't you?'

Her dad quailed. 'Not always, Bea,' he said. 'I was hiding from it. People do, Odi says. I was scared, you see. I was . . .' His voice trailed away. He looked at her helplessly. 'I'm sorry,' he said.

'The mice in the garden,' she said. 'You saw them, didn't you?'

Yet again he began to weep like a child. 'I couldn't say – I couldn't *say*, Bea. Not in front of your mum. I thought it was mad. I thought *I* was mad. I was scared you were mad too. I couldn't—'

He lunged forward to seize her in his arms again. Bea sat

in her bed, not stopping him, not responding. She beat at the bedclothes weakly with her hands.

'You're my dad,' she said. She began to cry. 'You were supposed to look after me. And you didn't. You took me to that fucking hospital and all this, all this happened because of *you*. You had one fucking job . . .'

Suddenly she was shouting. He jerked back.

'I thought I was helping you—'

'None of this would have happened—'

'Bea—'

'You let me go. You lied! You liar! Liar!'

He reached out for her again, but Bea was filled with such fury she swung her hands clawing at his face. He caught them in his, and for a moment the two of them struggled on the bed.

'Please, Bea, please, please,' he cried.

And then to her horror, deep inside her she felt the voice building up . . . 'I SUMMON . . . I SUMMON AND COMMAND . . .' She clapped her mouth shut. It mustn't come out! It must never come out again! But the desire in her to hurt her dad was so strong.

'I SUMMON AND COMMAND . . .' she cried.

The door burst open and Frey and Tyra ran in. Tyra seized hold of her.

'Stop it,' she roared; and – 'Get out!' to her dad, who scurried for the door.

'Don't let me!' she begged.

'It's all right, Bea, it's OK,' said Frey. He had a hypodermic in his hand.

'Don't let me, don't let me!' she screamed. 'I'm sorry, I won't do it again. Don't let me—' But it was coming; it was coming so fast. 'I can't stop it!' she screamed.

Tyra had her in the Grip, flat on the bed. 'Control yourself,' she hissed.

But the voice was in her throat and she was doing everything she could to hold it inside her, because once the words were out, that was it. Then the needle was in her arm.

'I'm sorry,' she gasped. And in the space of one single breath, everything went black.

34

The smell of breakfast was coming up the stairs. Toast. Coffee. Bca was starving but she didn't go down. How could she?

It was all sitting there in her mind, waiting for her.

She sat up in bed and began to clasp and unclasp her hands. Lars. Had *anything* he told her been true at all? Some of it of course. That's how lies worked. Lies, half-lies, truths, half-truths . . . fantasy and fact all knitted together into a world that suited only him. But what was the truth behind it all? Bea dreaded to find out what. Because . . .

Those spirits she'd taken. All those spirits! So many spirits. And the deaths. Yes, there had been deaths too. Those he'd not turned to golems. Their spirits had gone to the Underworld. That was death. And she'd just tried to kill her dad, hadn't she?

She was a murderer.

Bea put her fist to her mouth and bit till she tasted blood. She couldn't live with it. How could she? She had tried to do everything right and instead she was a murderer.

It was unbearable. She could not live with it. She couldn't!

Her bed was right under the window, and she crawled up onto the sill and looked out. Such a long way down. One jump, the terrible fall over in a moment. Then – peace. Do it, do it! she hissed to herself. Because, this! Anything would be better than this. Gingerly she opened the window and hovered over the sill. For two or three long minutes she stood there, staring down, willing herself to jump, but life gripped her harder than despair and she was unable to do it. She crept back down into bed. How weak she was! One way to end it, and she couldn't even do that . . .

Odi came up to see her a little later with a mug of milk and some porridge and fruit on a tray. She had no appetite, but he made her eat a little before they talked.

'I've spent a long time trying to make sense of this moment,' he told her, as he sat on the edge of the bed and watched her struggle with the food.

Bea looked up at him, that grim old man. He hadn't smiled at her, but then he rarely smiled. He banged his hands gently on his knees.

'Welcome back,' he said. He waited until her breathing was calm enough for her to speak before he went on. 'Now you must tell me exactly what happened.'

Bea had decided she was going to recount the whole thing as honestly as she could. She would leave nothing out, no matter how shameful it was. She would lay her sins bare and she would go on till every word was spoken. She owed them that, for who had ever been as foolish or as wicked as Bea? Her hopes and dreams had been stolen and misused, her strengths had been turned to weakness, her conscience cast aside. She was useless. She was worse than useless. She was death itself.

All through the telling she howled and gulped for air. For minutes on end she was unable to get a word out and could only beat her hands on the bedclothes in frustration and self-loathing. Sometimes she was reduced to nodding or shaking her head as Odi asked her questions. At the end of it she wept straight for fifteen minutes while he held her hands.

'Brave girl, Bea,' he said. 'And bravely told.'

She shook her head. 'How bad is it?'

He sighed. 'These things are crimes.'

'I didn't know,' she said. 'I thought I was helping.'

Odi regarded her carefully. 'In other worlds than this, you said no to him.'

She nodded.

He tipped his head lightly to one side. 'And in others, you stayed with the Hunt. Yet here you are among us again.'

'It was Lok, wasn't it?'

Odi shifted on the bed. 'Yes, you were with my brother,' he said.

'You said he was dead.'

'We thought so. This is not a . . . not a common world.' He looked guilty himself. He, after all, had failed to see it. 'So he's alive and he's still working with the Hunt. In what capacity, we don't know. Many years ago there was a power struggle between him and the Huntsman. We thought the Huntsman had won.' He shrugged.

'So he may be in charge now?' asked Bea.

'I wouldn't put it past him. He has so many gifts.'

'He can change his shape, can't he? So he can look like

anyone?' said Bea. 'I've been trying to work out who was who. Was it all him?'

Odi stroked his chin. 'The boy Lars was him, we can be sure of that. Did you ever see the fox at the same time as him? No? That was him too, most likely. Cora Lynn and the others you saw were him, although I don't how he did the trick with the pool. The creatures you saw after the lodge were almost certainly him as well. We don't use drugs,' he added, glancing at her. Bea tossed her hands in the air. Among all this, so what?

Odi leaned forward and stroked her cheek with the back of one big finger. 'Lok was always the master of lies. There's not one of us who hasn't been fooled by him in the past, if that's any comfort. You will have guessed,' he said; he paused. 'You will have guessed that the spirits you took were our people, not the Hunt's.'

Bea could only nod.

Odi took his hand away and sighed. 'This business of swallowing spirits,' he said. 'That's very bad. If Lok has learned that skill . . .' He shook his head again. 'The spirit takes up no space in this world. He could swallow ten, or a million if he had the time. If he's learned to do that, who knows what he can do?' He looked at Bea thoughtfully. 'So many gifts, all his. Well, it's lucky he couldn't take yours. He must have wanted to very much. Yours is a very great power.'

'But why did he rescue me from the Rook?' Bea asked.

Odi smiled grimly. 'He didn't,' he said. 'You did that by yourself. All he did was kidnap you and lie to you and hold you while he planned how best to use you.'

Bea nodded. Yes, he had used her. And how well she had let him do it.

'Thank you for your honesty, Bea,' said Odi. 'You're a good person. Yes,' he added, as her eyes slid away. 'Good people can do terrible things too. You're a brave person as well, but now you have to do something even braver, and learn to live with your crimes.'

Bea shook her head. 'Can it be undone?'

'If you match the body with its true spirit, they can reunite, if the spirit wants it.'

'And I can do that with my mum, can't I? Bring her back?' she begged.

'If we can find her spirit. If we can release her from whatever prison they have put her in. If she isn't already in the Underworld. Then, yes. It's a lot of ifs. I don't want to raise your hopes, Bea, but she may be closer than you think. Wait,' he said, interrupting her as she was about to speak. 'We can talk more about this when you're rested.'

She nodded. Then she asked him the question that had been preying on her mind all along.

'What's going to happen to me?' she said.

Odi sighed. 'I wish you hadn't asked me that,' he said. 'But since you have, I'll be honest with you. There will be a trial, Bea. There has to be a trial. You must tell those who have been affected what happened. They will tell you about your victims and how their lives have changed. Then we will sentence you. Witch justice can be severe, but it can also be merciful. Everything will be taken into account. Your guilt will be put to the vote.'

'What will the sentence be?'

'That will depend on how many vote guilty.'

Bea bent her head and her tears dropped freely onto the bedcover. 'I've been trying,' she wept. 'I've been trying so very hard but I got it so wrong. I get everything so wrong.'

Odi put an arm across her shoulders and kissed her head.

'It won't always feel like that,' he said. He waited for her tears a moment before straightening up and looking down at her gravely. 'Now let's talk about your father.'

Bea turned her face away. She didn't understand herself how it was possible to love someone so much and be so angry with them at the same time.

'Don't be angry with your father, Bea. He didn't believe his eyes. Do you truly believe yours? Life is a million times stranger than any of us can hope to imagine. It takes time to accept that the world you thought you knew is just another story. You of all people should know that.'

He reached down and ran his finger across the row of little stones around her neck.

'These are such precious things. He gave them to *you*, Bea. Don't you see what that means?'

Bea reached up to touch them. 'They were stolen at the hospital but then they turned up at the Green House. Dad said he didn't do it. So how did that happen?'

'They must have found you themselves,' he said.

'Is that their power? Is that his gift?'

Odi frowned in thought a moment. 'The stones love him,' he said. He rubbed them lightly between his finger and thumb. 'There's love in them,' he murmured. 'There's beauty. Maybe they just cleave to your presence. It could be luck . . .' He shook his head. 'I can't tell. There's no other world I know of where this necklace exists. How can that be?'

For a moment he looked troubled, but then his face brightened suddenly. 'I've no idea,' he said. He beamed at her. 'I'm old in so many worlds, but things still happen that I haven't got a clue about.' He nodded happily. 'Stone spirits are very rare. I suppose it'll come clear in time.'

So her dad was right – it was not possible for her to ever lose them. And Odi was right too. Her dad loved her that much! But . . .

'I don't know how to forgive him.' She looked at Odi sideways. 'I suppose you're going to tell I have to forgive myself before I can forgive him.'

'No,' said Odi. 'You must *never* forgive yourself. You must live with your sins for ever.'

35

How many spirits? Two dozen? Three dozen? How many murdered? Ten? Twelve? Something like that. Bea didn't even know. Hearts broken, lives ended, dreams shattered. And the worst of it was this; she had known. In her deepest heart, she had known all along that she was being lied to, but she had been too weak – too greedy? Too cruel or too selfish – to act on it.

Odi was right. Should she live to be a hundred, not a day would go by without bitter regret.

Before he left, Odi picked up a drink left by the door and stood over her while she swallowed it down. The witches were well aware that Bea was in danger now by her own hand. The drink sent her straight into blessed sleep before dark thoughts lured her.

She slept for three days, waking only to eat very little and swallow down another draught. When, finally, they let her come to, the initial shock had been absorbed. Medicine had helped with that. But the guilt and the shame were hers for ever.

Bea was well enough now to get up, but she was scared to go downstairs. How could she face the witches after what she had done? She refused to see her dad – not yet. She was still so full of rage and she was scared she would turn it on him again. Frey turned up daily with her medication and spoke kindly enough to her, although she could only imagine what he really thought. Odi came up to keep her company once or twice. Tyra looked in on her once – said nothing, just looked at her as if she was reminding herself what exactly a murderer looked like. She left without a word. Bea did not expect any mercy from her.

Mid-morning on the day they let her wake, visitors began to arrive, which gave Bea even more reason to stay in her room. About midday there were more. In the afternoon, still more.

'Who are they?' she asked Silvis.

Silvis frowned. 'Didn't Odi tell you? He's such an idiot. You know why, Bea, don't you? It's . . . you know . . .' She pulled a face. 'It's the trial.'

Bea's heart froze inside her. So soon?

'Not for a few days, though,' said Silvis.

Bea bowed her head. She was so, so scared.

'What will they do to me?' she whispered. *Murder*, whispered her fears. *Murder . . .*

Would it be death?

'They'll have to come through me first,' said Silvis.

Bea shook her head. 'You know that's not true,' she said. And Silvis did not deny it.

Whatever the others thought, Silvis never judged. In her eyes, Bea was as wonderful as ever. She was there on her bed when she woke up and again when she went to sleep. While the other witches gathered downstairs, Silvis spent hours with her and helped her catch up with her news.

Jenny had died shortly after Bea had disappeared. The witches had buried her secretly in the woods – they hadn't dared do it in the usual way in the cemetery. She was so old – older than any of them knew. If the doctors came across someone so ancient, the Hunt would have known about it at once.

Silvis was so proud of Tyra for going in and rescuing Bea's dad. 'The others tried to stop her but she just did it anyway,' she said. 'I tried to sneak out with her, but Frey caught me. I think they were secretly pleased, just terrified for Tyra. It was such a shame she missed you!'

'How did she persuade him to go with her?'

Silvis smiled lazily. She'd grown up so much in the two years since Bea had last seen her. She'd been a skinny little thing then, but she was quite plump now, with a bust and a bit of a tummy, as she called it, patting it proudly. She was as tall as Bea.

'She used the Grip,' she said.

'A fist?' Bea asked.

'That fist can be quite convincing,' said Silvis, and laughed. 'But no, she just picked him up and flung him over her shoulder.' Silvis lit up. 'Oh, I wish I'd seen what you did there, Bea! It must have been *fantastic*! People were going *crazy*. The Hunt had a terrible job covering it up. They had to make out that some poisonous gas had been released, like it was all some kind of mass hallucination. There's all sorts of stuff about it online. Alien abductions. Gaia striking back. Even witches. Imagine!'

Silvis shone, and willed Bea to shine too. But Bea wasn't doing much shining at the moment.

And what about Silvis? Her voice? Her beautiful, beautiful voice?

Silvis pulled a disappointed face. Just the same.

'It still pops things open?' asked Bea.

'*Sometimes*. I'm only just thirteen, so maybe it's still developing. You came into your gift when you were thirteen, right? Otherwise I'll be good for nothing except letting the rabbit loose. But it *is* beautiful, isn't it?' Bea nodded. There was no doubt about that. 'Maybe my gift isn't about opening things. Maybe it's something to do with beauty. Not very useful, but . . . that's something. Like your dad. He makes beautiful things. It's a gift, isn't it?'

And of course Bea had a million questions about her family.

As her dad had told her, her mum's golem was living with Michael, now aged three, in their old house down in Hebden. The golem believed that her husband had left her and taken Bea with him. She missed them both, of course – but never quite enough to be bothered trying to track them down. Like all Hunt golems, she was driven with a hatred for the witches.

Michael was different. He still had his own spirit intact, but not because the Hunt were letting him go. They were waiting for him to develop his gifts before they took him. He was like a lamb, fattening for slaughter. It was just a matter of time.

'He must know it's not his mum, whatever she looks like,' said Silvis. 'Poor kid.'

Bea didn't answer. The truth was, she blamed herself even more than her dad.

'Your mum's not gone for ever,' said Silvis. 'We can rescue her. You have to call the golem spirit out of her and show her true spirit its old home. She's bound to go to it. Your mum will be as good as new.'

'But we don't know where her spirit is, do we?' said Bea. 'She could be dead for all we know. She probably is.'

Silvis came to put her arms around her. 'We think we do know, darling,' she said.

'You know? Where is she?'

Silvis fixed her with a firm look. 'The spirit that rescued you from Lok. We think that's it. Your mother's spirit.'

It took Bea a moment to realise what she was talking about. The spirit that had *rescued* her? The spirit that had beaten her, that had scraped half the skin off her, that had bruised her from head to foot, trapped her in a freezing wet ditch all night until she was half-dead from the cold? That spirit? *That* was her lovely mum, who had never raised a hand against her in her life? No way!

'It rescued you. It took you to the only place where you'd be safe,' said Silvis.

Bea shook her head. She'd been bloody and bruised from head to foot. Why would her mum do such things to her?

Odi explained it to her that evening. 'Your mother's spirit loves you and wants to look after you, which is why it rescued you. But it's angry at your crimes, which is why it beat you.

It's exactly because it did these things to you that makes me certain it must be her. Nothing else on earth can love you like that. You must understand that this is not your mother as such – it's her spirit,' he added. 'All her memories and understanding remain with her golem. The raw life of her, and the feelings of her life, are all that remain.'

Bea had been so frightened the night of her return that she had very little recall about exactly what had happened. But she did have a vague memory of calling out for help. Could she have called up her mother by accident?

'She was there so fast,' she said.

Odi nodded. 'The spirit doesn't know time and space as we do. But Lok might have been keeping her in one of those crystals you spoke of. Keeping her close, in case he needed her.' He smiled. 'Even Lok makes mistakes, you see.'

'And can we really bring her back?'

Odi nodded. 'With luck, yes. We really can.'

Bea sat up in her bed. Yes! she thought – yes. This was something to live for.

'I have to summon her again . . .'

'No. Summoning is a temporary measure. If she's to stay, she must stay of her own accord.'

'But how?'

Odi sighed. 'There are ways, but we can't wait too long. Now that her spirit is free from whatever they trapped it in, it will begin to move to the Underworld. Once that happens, it's lost to us. But before that, Bea, you have other business. Tomorrow your trial begins. Prepare yourself. You must be strong. Above all, you must be honest. Remember that. A witch trial is as much about openness as it is about judgement.'

'I'm not ready,' said Bea. She was literally quaking with fear.

'Of course not. You never will be. But the trial will go ahead nevertheless. So make peace with your father, Bea. You're going to need his support.'

Bea held back her tears and nodded. 'What will they do to me?' she asked.

Odi dipped his head to her bravery. 'We have laws and you have broken them. You will be found guilty, no doubt about that. The law must be upheld. The trial itself will be an ordeal, I won't hide that from you. You will be expected to face your victims' families. They have the right to know how their loved ones were taken. On that count, you will be shown no mercy.'

Bea nodded. She understood. Why would she be shown mercy? What mercy had she shown to her victims?

'There can be mercy in the final judgement though,' said Odi. 'Understand, Bea. We know you. We've seen your heart and we believe it to be loving and true, but there will be those at the trial who will want vengeance and punishment for its own sake. A trial is only as fair as the people who judge you. I can answer for your heart, Bea, but I cannot answer for theirs.'

36

Bea met her dad in an old-fashioned little parlour at the front of Tyra and Frey's house. Neutral ground. Tyra and Frey came with her to stand guard behind the door in case she lost control again.

She had to stand outside herself for a few minutes, calming herself. She was so angry with him! She knew she was being unfair, but she couldn't help it. Mainly, she was terrified of herself.

He was sitting on a little wooden settle in a corner, but he stood up when she came in, looking madly formal in his dishevelled way and greeting her with an anxious smile.

'I'm sorry—' she said, but he stopped her.

'No. I let you down. Like you said, I'm your dad. I'm the one who's sorry.' His lip quivered as he spoke. Bea thought – Oh God, please don't cry! Where were the dads when you needed them?

'Let's forget it,' she said, lowering herself into a chair opposite him.

'I just want you to know, Bea' – he coughed to clear his throat – 'that whatever I did or will do, and whatever mistakes I make, I always have and always will love you. I always tried to do the best for you. I just get it wrong sometimes.'

Bea smiled. It was a little speech he'd rehearsed for her. 'I know you did,' she said.

He looked sad, so sad. But this wasn't the time to be sad, thought Bea irritably.

'I missed you so much,' he said.

'Can we talk about Mum?'

'I miss her too. All of you. I thought you were dead.' His lip began to tremble again, but Bea was not in a mood for tears – not his, not her own, not anyone's.

'Stop it,' she said fiercely. 'I don't want your tears. I want you to be my dad. I want you to *help* me.'

He took a breath. 'I'm here for you,' he said – which made her laugh a little. He looked indignant. He fixed his eye at a point over her head. 'I know what I did, Bea, and I'm sorry. But I'm here now and I know the truth, and I swear to you I will do everything I can to get you through this. To get *us* through it.'

Bea thought – What can you do? But she didn't say it. Why be cruel?

'I know I'm not myself at the moment,' he said. 'I'm just trying to hang on. I'm just trying to hang onto you and Mum and Michael. *For* you and Mum and Michael, I mean.'

Bea shrugged, before she could stop herself.

'I'm getting better, you know,' he added. 'You think this is bad? You should have seen me when I first came here!' He stared at her for a second, then stuffed his fist into his mouth and started to laugh silently. It was a crazy kind of laughter, but it made Bea laugh too – and she knew then she had forgiven him. She went across to him on the settle and put her arms around him. They stayed a moment in an embrace, each facing behind the other with their chins on one another's shoulder.

'I want my dad back,' whispered Bea.

'I'm on my way,' he whispered. 'I'm climbing back out. I'm trying to be strong for you. It's such a long way up but I'm climbing towards *you*.'

'Mad Dad,' said Bea.

'Yes.'

'Why did you lie to me about the mice?'

He shook his head over her shoulder. 'I spent so much of my life keeping all the impossible things out, that when they all came rushing in I sort of broke. It was like nothing was real any more. But I always loved you, Bea, through it all. And Michael and your mum. That's my starting point. That's the beginning and end of me. I just . . . I just need some time to get myself better.'

'I love you, Dad.'

'I love you, Bea.'

They stayed there for a while. This is the start of it, thought Bea to herself. She was going to get her family back. All of them. She was a summoner. She could do this. And not just her family. *All* of them.

'All of them,' she whispered fiercely over her dad's shoulder, and although he had no idea what she was talking about, 'Yes,' he said. 'Yes. Yes.'

37

Over the next day, more witches arrived. From her room, Bea peeped out from behind the curtains and secretly watched them coming and going. They were all friends or relatives of people whose spirits she had stolen, or who she had helped to kill. But who was who? She tried to work it out in her head, and the memories of what she'd done came flooding out at her in a torrent. She gave it up. There would be enough of that tomorrow.

The witches' meeting room had once been an elegant place, beautifully furnished, hung with brocade, full of life. Now it was mainly used as a storeroom. Four great brass lanterns hung from the ceiling on rusty chains far overhead; none of them worked. Huge pieces of dark, dusty furniture lined up around the walls, all heaped up with books, chairs, jars, old cookery utensils and other rarely used things. Wherever you looked, junk, antiques and bric-a-brac tumbled together.

Bea had been expecting some kind of a court – a judge, a jury, lawyers – but as she came into the room with Silvis on one side and her dad on the other, there was nothing like that. In one corner of the room the witches had set up a leather settee with an old wooden carver flanked by two upright chairs at angles to it. Scattered before them was a mixture of armchairs, uprights, benches and pews for the visiting witches. There were thirty-odd of them, men and women plus seven or eight children.

Bea was terrified, trembling so much she almost had to be held up. Her sins were monumental; what difference did it make that she had committed them in good faith? Another, better person would not have done it. She believed that. As she crossed the room to take her seat in the woodwormed carver all eyes were on her.

So this was what a murderer looks like, their eyes seemed to say. She seems so normal. Who would have guessed that this young girl was capable of such terrible deeds?

She sat down on the carver, Silvis and her dad on either side. Odi sat on the settee with Frey and a tall, pale, grey-haired woman, who watched her closely as she came in.

Odi leaned forward to speak directly to her.

'All the people here had connections with the victims of your crimes,' he said. 'They all know something of your story, about Lok, how he seduced you and tricked you, but now they need to hear it from your own lips. That's how we'll spend today. Tomorrow they will be asking you questions about the individuals whose spirits you stole and those you helped to destroy.

'We have appointed someone to argue your case and one to argue against you. Frey will speak for you. This lady is Gila. She will speak against.'

Bea nodded.

'Much depends on your honesty,' said Odi. 'I can't emphasise that enough. You must tell us everything and you must tell it as honestly as you can. You won't be warned of this again. Do you understand?'

'Yes.'

'Scrupulously honest,' he added; and Bea saw Tyra, sitting a little further back, roll her eyes and tut. As far as she was concerned, Bea had had enough already.

'Tell us your story, Bea,' said Odi. 'Begin at the hospital.'

Bea dug her fingers into the wooden arms of her chair, cleared her throat and started to go through the events of the past two years as she remembered them. As she talked, the silence seemed to darken around her. It took some telling. Acts that had once seemed brave now felt cowardly. She had to keep her eyes down, especially when she was talking about the thefts of people's spirits and the deaths – it was just too hard to look around, wondering whose son or daughter, whose lover, whose father or mother she had destroyed.

On it went, crime after crime. Silvis held her hand tight and her dad shuffled anxiously on the other side. She faltered often, but did not stop. There were two breaks of fifteen minutes, and an hour for lunch, which Bea ate away from the others with her dad and Silvis. It was well into the afternoon by the time she was done.

She hung her head, and waited. Opposite, she heard Odi let out one of his long, tired sighs. Next to him on the settee, Frey got to his feet and addressed the witches.

'We all know Lok,' he said. 'Even knowing him, there is hardly anyone here of the right age who hasn't been tricked by him in one way or another. This child is not a perpetrator; she is a victim. She has been abused in every way. He isolated her, he frightened her, he spun her a web of lies, he slept with her. He took everything away from her – her family and friends, her witch gifts, her intimacy, and he made her love him as he did it. How can she be guilty under those circumstances?'

Bea had hardly thought about the sex, but now that it was out in the open, she had to bury her face in her hands. She was so ashamed, felt such a fool. But two things Frey had said she knew were true. She was a child and she had been let down.

Frey sat and Gila got to her feet.

'Frey is right,' she began. 'We all know Lok. None of us are surprised at his deeds any more, but we are right to be surprised at the crimes this young woman has committed. In two years she has destroyed more of us than the Hunt was able to do in ten. Yes, she was tricked into thinking she was fighting for us. But when did we ever use tactics like hers? Her actions are crimes no matter who she was fighting for. No witch steals souls and puts them into a machine. No witch kills. But how willingly she did it!

'This trial is not about Bea. It's not for her. We are here for her victims. Remember that, when it comes the time to judge.'

Gila spoke clearly and well – her voice sounded so much more convincing than Frey's quiet tones, to Bea's ear at least. She had kept her eyes down throughout, but risked a quick glance upwards when it was over. The witches' faces gave nothing away.

Odi announced the end of that day's session. Bea was led out by Silvis and her dad, who took her up to a couple of rooms that had been put aside for her on the first floor. As the door was closed behind her she could hear the others leaving and their distant chatter, but she couldn't make out a word they said.

The next day, the trial resumed.

Once everyone was gathered, Odi explained that today would be spent talking about her victims. She would be questioned about them, one by one. There was no hurry; it would take as long as it took.

'We shall go through them in order of date,' he announced. 'James Thompson. I call on you to question Beatrice Wilder about your son.'

A man sitting a few rows back rose and cleared his throat. 'My son Alan lost his soul early this year in Haltwhistle, Northumberland,' he said.

Bea knew that name. Alan Thompson. Her first victim.

'Alan was twenty-seven years old,' the man went on. 'He worked in an off-licence in Haltwhistle, where he lived with his girlfriend Angela. I think the best way to start to describe Alan would be with his kindness. There was a warmth about him. It wasn't necessarily that he did anything for people – although he did that too. People just felt good in his company. The spirits loved him. They'd cluster around him like butterflies on a bush.' He smiled at the memory. 'They just liked being near him, I suppose. Well, so did we all.

We often wondered if that was part of his gift. It's something you can't explain, isn't it, that warmth some people have?

'His main gift wasn't a remarkable one. He had an affinity with animal spirits. His ambition was to be an animal trainer, once he'd saved up enough to get a payment on premises. Their spirits would come to him. Do him favours, if he asked. Find things for people that they'd lost. Gathering cattle or sheep that had strayed. Training dogs or horses. You know? Simple stuff.

'We couldn't believe that anyone would harbour bad feelings towards Alan, but one day he came back home and his spirit was gone. I'd like you to tell us what happened that day.'

As the man spoke, Bea gripped the arms of her chair in panic. In her heart, she realised for the first time, she had never really thought of her victims as people.

'I can't do this,' she hissed.

Silvis tightened her grip on her arm. 'Yes, you can, darling,' she said calmly. On her other side her dad flung his arms in the air.

'Is this really necessary?'

'Yes,' said Gila. 'For every single one.'

Bea looked to Odi, begging for reprieve.

'Speak,' he said.

So she had to do it – word by word, blow by blow, every detail of what she'd done that day. With each word she spoke, the father's quiet stance, the deepening silence around them, the way he fought his tears, all tore a fresh hole in her heart. She tried to drop her eyes, but the witches insisted she looked the man in the face. At the end of it he stood up again to tell her how her crime had affected him.

'I had two children. The Hunt took our eldest four years ago. Alan was the last, our only son. He lived nearby – we saw him every day. We were very close but he doesn't care for us so much now – he doesn't care for anything. We're lonely, we miss him. I think Alan is lonely too. He's lost his friends, the spirits avoid him . . .' He lifted his head to look at Bea directly. 'My wife' – he made a futile gesture with his hand – 'my wife chose not to come. We try not to be bitter towards you, but we miss our son every day of our lives.'

The old man sat. Friends on either side of him comforted him. Bea was beyond horrified, but there was nowhere to hide from all those eyes. Each face seemed to say – 'You did this . . .'

And then the next. And the next. Over the course of the day, each one of her victims became a person to her.

So it went on. There were many breaks and pauses in the proceedings, when Bea or one of the other witnesses needed a break. Her dad couldn't keep quiet and was sent out the room twice for making a fuss.

At the end of the day they were some two-thirds through. Bea had never felt so exhausted in her life.

The next day, the same thing. One after the other the witches stood, named the loved one they had lost. Mothers, sisters, wives and husbands, lovers, brothers and friends. So many lives ruined with each victim. Remembering Odi's words to her, Bea did her best to tell the whole truth but it wasn't easy. With every word she spoke the temptation to soften the blow was there, sometimes for herself, sometimes for her victims. There's a gradient between lies and the truth on which we all slide. Bea played down the moments when she had felt exhilarated by her power or enjoyed the cruelty. She exaggerated the role of Lok. She emphasised her hatred of what she was doing.

At the end of it, Odi heaved one of his deep sighs and Frey stood up to make her final defence.

'Bea understands what she's done. No one who has watched her over these past days can doubt that,' he said. 'And no one who has watched today can doubt that she is no murderer. It's Lok who should be answering for these acts, not her. She believed he was dead because we told her so. She was unprepared for him. If Bea is guilty, so are we all.

'Gila has said that no one here would have committed the crimes Bea has, but is that really true? Look into your hearts. Her crime, if it is a crime at all, is this; she was a soldier. We are at war. The rules change at such times. If her acts had been aimed at the people she wanted to aim them at, would she really be here now? Would you be judging her in the same way? We give soldiers at war permission to act in ways we'd never even consider in peacetime. Sometimes, they get it wrong and the consequences as we can see can be terrible. But while we can judge our soldiers for wilful crimes, it is unfair to judge them in the same way for their mistakes.

'Bea is one of us. She is on our side. You can see the guilt she carries. She will carry that guilt to the grave. Let that be her punishment.'

Frey paused, giving the witches time to think about what he had said.

'This is a case where we can reasonably and honestly show mercy,' he concluded, and sat down.

Then Gila got to her feet. 'Look around you,' she said. 'How many are here? Forty, I make it. Forty-seven, counting the children. Every single one of us here is a survivor. If this young woman – I cannot call her a child – if this young woman had not done her work so well, how many more would there be? Think of *that*. Think of them, your lost loved ones. Sons, daughters, mothers. Fathers, brothers, lovers. Gone from our lives.

'She says she's *sorry*. She didn't know, she didn't mean it. I say she *did* know – not that these people were on our side, perhaps, but she knew well enough that what she was doing was wrong. Witches do not fight like that. We do not steal souls! This young woman has broken our most basic rules.

'Frey says she was simply being a soldier. But what do we call soldiers who kill their own? Let me see . . . what's the word? Ah, yes. Traitor. Yes – traitor. Beatrice Wilder is a traitor to us, to our cause, to every one of us here.'

She turned on Bea. 'Your instincts should have told you not to do it,' she declared. 'Even a baby knows right from wrong. Trusting someone foolishly is no crime. Stealing spirits is. And so is murder. You are guilty, child. You know it, don't you?'

All Bea could do was nod. There was no arguing against it.

Gila turned away and nodded to the assembled witches. 'There you have it out of her own mouth. Guilty.'

38

Each person there was given two slips of paper: one white, one black. A small wooden box, very old and scratched, was passed round and everyone put their paper through the slot in the top. When they were done, a table was pulled to the front and the box tipped up on it for all to see. There was no need to count. Out of nearly thirty slips, only two were white.

Silvis gripped her arm tight. Bea shook her head. Guilty. It was right. Even so, she was shocked because . . . because you can always hope, can't you?

Her dad jumped to his feet. 'But you all heard what happened! It wasn't her, it was Lok. This is wrong. You should have warned her. You should have protected her—'

He was whipping himself into a rage but Frey gripped his arm and pulled him down. 'Control yourself,' he commanded. Her dad glared at Frey, but then sat down suddenly and buried his face in his hands.

From a few rows back, Tyra called out flatly. 'She's a murderer.' There was a shocked silence in the room. Bea herself felt as if the breath had been sucked out of her body. But it was right. She *was* a murderer.

'She will punish herself,' said Frey. 'Every day for the rest of her life. She has a good heart, we all know that.'

'Punishment isn't for her. It's for her victims. That's what justice is,' said Gila. 'That's why we're here.'

Odi nodded and rose to his feet. Silvis, who had plainly thought it would never come to this, yelled in outrage – 'Whatever you do to her, you have to do it to me too.'

'Don't you understand what she's done, this *child*?' demanded Gila furiously. 'These golems she's left behind are the most miserable creatures in the world. Their families and friends mean nothing to them. *We* mean nothing to them. Their own memories mean nothing to them. They have forgotten how to love, how to share, how to be happy or sad. They are worse than dead. Magic has left them for ever.'

Her dad had flushed and was stuttering to speak again, but Bea took his hand. 'I'm guilty, Dad,' she said. 'Anyone can see I'm guilty. Drop it.' Her dad fell quiet again and began to mutter and weep. Tyra gave her one hard, brief nod, then dropped her gaze.

'So be it,' said Odi, and he got to his feet. 'The sentence is exile,' he announced.

'No,' cried Silvis.

But Bea was so relieved she almost fainted in her chair.

'You will be sent away from here,' Odi went on. 'No witch will meet you or greet you or offer you help of any kind, or give you comfort. Any who do must share your fate.'

'But she'll die!' cried Silvis. 'You know that. The Hunt will get her in moments!'

'It's the law,' said Odi.

'You value her so highly, maybe she can save herself. She did it once, didn't she?' said Gila.

'This isn't just cruel, it's stupid,' said Frey. 'The Hunt will take her spirit. You're handing all her gifts and powers straight to them. You're not just signing her death sentence; you're signing ours.'

Gila nodded; she'd thought it all out. 'I'm not thinking of releasing her here,' she said.

'Where, then?'

'Somewhere the Hunt will never find her.' Gila turned her stony gaze directly onto Bea. 'In the roots of a mountain. The ocean trenches. The moon. I don't care. The further away the better.'

In the shocked silence that followed, Odi cleared his throat.

'You want us to exile her spirit.'

'It's been done before.'

'And her body?'

Gila broke her gaze and looked at Odi. 'It's been done before,' she repeated.

'But that means death!' said Frey.

Gila tipped her head as if to say – 'So who cares?'

Bea began to tremble again. Every eye in the room turned curiously upon her.

'No,' begged Silvis. 'You can't do that to her.'

'We can and we will.'

'Can we vote?' begged her father.

'There is no vote on the law,' said Odi. 'And this is not just within the law; it *is* the law.' He looked down gravely at Bea. 'Do you accept the sentence, Bea?' he asked.

Surprised at the suddenness of it, Bea struggled to stand.

'Mercy,' she said. 'Can't you show me mercy?'

'The law has no mercy,' said Odi.

'Then can I speak?' she begged.

'It's her right. That's the law too,' Odi said to Gila, who was about to protest. Gila shrugged as if to say – it makes no difference.

Bea was still shaking, but she did her best to stand upright and look her accusers in the face.

'I made myself a promise the other day,' she said. 'And I want to make it to you now. It's this; I will get them all back. All of them. Every spirit I lost. Every single one. Even if you lock me in the middle of the world, I will try.'

'Not possible,' someone said.

'I'm a summoner. That's all I have now, to undo all this. I won't stop until I'm stopped. I'll pull them out of the Underworld if I have to . . .'

'That's forbidden,' growled Gila.

'What have I got to lose? I'll break all your rules if I have to, but I will get them back, I swear it.'

. . . I've overdone it, she thought. But she meant it. It had taken all her strength to say it and now it was time to go. She tugged at her dad's hand for him to help her out. He looked up at her from his seat. His face was white.

'You see?' demanded Gila. 'She *still* doesn't understand what she's done. You heard; she'll break every rule. She's prepared to pull apart everything we hold dear. That's her repentance. Answer the question, girl. Do you accept the sentence? Will you send yourself into exile, or do we have to force you?'

Bea stood as tall as she could. 'I accept it,' she said. 'I don't know if I can summon my own spirit. I'll try. But give me a day to say goodbye.'

'Not to me,' said Silvis. 'I'm going to help you, so I have to go too. It's the law, isn't it?'

'You're being an idiot,' snapped Gila.

'And me. I stand by her.' Her dad stood up and grabbed her hand.

'Into the heart of a mountain? For eternity?' sneered Gila. 'Do you have any idea what that means?'

Frey got to his feet. 'I think I'll come along and help you pack,' he said. 'And therefore I suffer the same sentence. We shall go into exile together.'

Odi tipped back his head and laughed. 'And I shall make some sandwiches to eat on the way – which means I'm helping her too. So I'm in exile. Tyra? What do you say?'

Tyra rose from her seat and made her way to the front. 'Come here, child,' she said. Uncertainly, Bea did as she was told. To her shock and embarrassment, Tyra got on her knees before her and put her arms around her.

'And I offer you comfort,' she said, 'and so I join you in exile too. The law is without mercy, but we don't have to be merciless ourselves. I forgive you, Bea. I do it because I know you will never forgive yourself. Every day you will think of the things you've done, of the spirits that have been lost, and the lives that have been ruined because of you. That is a terrible burden, but you must bear it because the day you forgive yourself is the day you lose your humanity. On that day, I swear I will hunt you down and kill you like a dog. You have made an oath today to recover the lost souls. I hold you to that oath. You are a soldier, although I'm amazed to say it. So am I. I will be your comrade from this day on. I will fight by your side, I will never leave you. I swear this oath on your oath. So I go into exile with you.'

Bea flung her arms around Tyra's fat neck and hugged. Tyra stank more than a bit. She wasn't too regular with her showers or baths, and there was a distinct waft of booze about her. But Bea had never been so glad to have someone on her side.

Gila, who had been watching this in disbelief, exploded suddenly with anger.

'This is a trick,' she shrieked. 'You planned this from the beginning. There was never any chance of any kind of sentence. You've turned this trial into a joke.'

Odi turned to face the witches around him. 'Justice has been served,' he announced. 'Repentance has been shown, penance has been performed. Mercy has been given and solidarity has been joined. A good trial! And now, we don't ask you to join us, but it will be a lot easier for us if you were to decide to leave us in exile here in our own home, rather than lock our spirits up for ever.'

Uproar broke out as the witches rose to their feet, some arguing against, some for; some shouting in anger, some cheering. With a great roar, Tyra tugged Bea's hand up above her head. 'Victory or death!' She swung round, seized Bea by the waist and held her up in the air. 'You beauty!' she cried, and planted a great hairy kiss on Bea's face.

39

The arguments raged for hours. Some of the witches were so angry with the outcome they left the house refusing to speak to anyone from Salem Row. Some stayed – joining them in exile in their own home, in effect. Others, including Gila, violently disagreed, but refused to go.

'I can't make you leave, but to ask me to leave? I'm not going along with that,' she said. There was to be a meal that night – not a celebration of any kind, but a more sombre affair in memory of Bea's victims. Gila and two others insisted on their places at the table with the others, despite disagreeing with the result.

Bea went up to her room straight after the trial to sleep – she was utterly exhausted. But she was woken by Frey an hour or so before the meal. He had over his arm a gown for her to wear.

'It's traditional when you've been shown mercy,' he said, shaking it out. It was plain white, with a high collar and a tie under the bust. 'We want you to serve the wine.'

Bea groaned but pulled herself out of bed. She ached from head to foot – tension, Frey suggested, since she had done no exercise for days.

'It's the last thing,' promised Frey. 'But there is this.' He had a bag with him which he opened to show her. Ashes.

He shrugged. 'It may seem silly, but ritual still counts among us. Cover yourself with these from head to foot,' he added, and left her to get ready.

Bea stripped and did as he asked – rubbed the ashes all over herself and into her hair. Then she pulled on the gown and went down, barefoot, to serve the wine.

There were sixteen people left out of forty, and three of those were Gila and her friends who had refused to go along with the mutual exile. When Bea went to pour wine into their glasses, they held their hands over them, refusing the service. But the others accepted graciously. No one spoke much to her – even Silvis had been forbidden to chum up – so Bea spent the meal in silence as the witches drank toast after toast and talked about the lives of those who had gone.

At the end of it, though, when everyone was actually leaving the room, Gila beckoned her over. Bea came to stand by her side, and the old witch held out her glass. Dutifully, Bea poured.

'Don't think I forgive you. I don't. Don't think I approve either,' said Gila. 'I accept the wine only because I'm here to hold you to your oath. You *will* get them back – every last one, just as you said. But you are *not* to continue to break our laws. They're there for a reason. Once a spirit has gone to the Underworld, it undergoes a transformation. They are no longer who they were in this world, and calling them back to life is dangerous. Not only that, but they can bring other spirits with them – inhuman spirits. People call them demons.

They've nothing to do with the Devil, of course, but you would be forgiven for thinking that they do if you could see the destruction they bring about.

'Those who have gone to the Underworld must be left there. Do you understand me? You must renounce that part of your oath. Devote your life to bringing back those whose spirits are still here and leave the dead to death. No one ever came back from there unchanged to recover the lives they lost. You will only bring more destruction on our heads if you follow that path.'

Bea turned to look at Odi, who sat nearby eavesdropping. He didn't turn to look at her, but slowly nodded.

'I promise,' said Bea.

Gila nodded, put down her glass without drinking and left the room. Bea went back to her place and waited quietly until everyone was gone. Then Silvis and her dad came to her. Together they got her upstairs, where Silvis helped her undress and put her to bed.

Two days later Odi called a meeting to discuss how to proceed with fulfilling Bea's oath.

Bea assumed they were going to talk straightaway about tackling Lok and the Hunt, since they were the ones who held the spirits of the witches she had Isolated. She dreaded that, but to her relief, they didn't expect her to go there yet. In fact, there was only one person they could deal with just then – her own mother. Bea hadn't taken her spirit, of course, but at least it was accessible.

Bea and her dad were delighted. Once more, the witches' generosity had surprised her.

Kelsey's spirit had taken refuge in a dead elder tree close to where she had dumped Bea, in the form of a colony of honey bees. The year was getting older and colder and the bees were getting ready to hibernate. Soon her spirit would begin its strange journey down to the Underworld. They had to move swiftly.

Bea had been thinking of her old household down in Hebden Bridge. What must it be like for her mum, to have all her memories and intelligence intact, without any of them meaning anything to her any more? Was she aware of how pointless her own life had become to her? And Michael, alone with her. Did he understand that his mother had gone? All he had left now was an automaton of flesh, going through the motions, seeing, thinking, but never able to feel or relate?

He must sense it. Without understanding why, he must know that something was terribly wrong.

So the witches knew where her mother's spirit was, and they knew where her body was. In order to reunite them they had to bring the two together and chase the golem spirit out of her. Then, if it so wished, her spirit could re-enter and Kelsey would be herself again.

The whole enterprise was riddled with danger. The Hunt knew Bea would want to contact her mother, and her old house would be watched, and not just by the neighbours. The Hunt could use life to spy on life, just as Lars had said. Even the birds could be spies. Nevertheless, the witches were going to have to go down there one way or another. They decided that the best way was to take the mother-spirit down to Kelsey, rather than the other way round.

'First we need to find a temporary home for her spirit,' said Odi. 'A fetish. A place where she'll feel comfortable. Any ideas?' he asked.

They didn't have any obvious options. Nearly all Kelsey's things were back at the house in Hebden, owned now by her golem. Going down and trying to take something would only alert the Hunt. Two trips? Not worth it. Even Tyra, who loved a fight, was wary of doing that.

Bea's dad suggested going into Manchester to buy something lovely and costly, like a present for her, but Frey shook his head.

'Costly or cheap, the spirit doesn't care,' he said. 'It needs to be something she knows.'

'A shoe box?' suggested Bea. Her mum used to keep some of her favourite old photos from when she was a child in a shoe box. It didn't seem much to keep someone's spirit in – her dad hated the idea, but he had no other suggestions to make.

So a shoe box it was.

They needed to fill the box with a sense of themselves and the family they had once shared with Kelsey. Again, they were short on Kelsey's own things. Bea had lost her phone – it had disappeared at the Green House – but her dad had his, full of texts and photos of the family: exactly the kind of things they could put inside the fetish to make the spirit feel at home.

Bea and her dad did the job together, trying to make it look as much like something Kelsey would love as they could. Her dad put in his wedding ring and printed off photos from his phone. He downloaded as many of the texts and messages he could find between her, Bea and himself and put them on a USB stick.

He'd abandoned the shop in Hebden so he had no jewellery with him, but he made a charm bracelet and some earrings out of copper wire and little bits and pieces that had taken his fancy – a couple of stones, some pieces of twig, an acorn. Bea looked long and hard at it, but she saw none of the magic he had put into her necklace. It looked like him – a bit crazy. Maybe after all, finding those stones had just been luck.

Kelsey loved reading and poetry – she was a poet herself – so there had to be some written matter too. Kelsey used to write out her own favourite work and frame it on the wall, if it meant a lot to her, so Bea's dad spent hours writing one out on a scroll for her. There was limited space, so in the end they picked just two physical books – a novel by Jane Austen and a slim volume of Sylvia Plath poems. Kelsey had adored Sylvia Plath above all others.

They decorated the box with printed-out pictures, text messages and emails between them all, designs in her favourite colours and so on. When it was done, Bea thought it really did look like something her mum would have liked. She'd have loved all the things they'd done by hand too – the little drawings and messages, the in-jokes and the rest of it.

Her dad seemed pleased too – at first. While they were

making it he was absorbed and happy, but once it was finished he started to go off it, and over the course of the day he became more and more agitated. As the others were discussing how to make a little procession and ceremony that might please the spirit, he was walking up and down, biting his knuckles and glaring at the box as if it was his enemy.

That night it began to rain – bad news for the ceremony the next day, as the bees would be unwilling to fly. Frey had told Bea not to be surprised if her dad got upset – he seemed to be affected by the weather in his current state. Sure enough, at about nine at night, he suddenly blew. The rain was hammering down. Bea was upstairs reading when she heard him shouting downstairs.

'This is nonsense. You wouldn't keep a beetle in that,' he shouted.

There was a noise – banging and thumping. She guessed that he was attacking the fetish and got to the door in time to see her dad running out of the sitting room. The box itself lay trampled on the floor. Bea, who had spent so long trying to love it, burst into tears. At the same time, in her heart, she knew that her dad was right.

He was off out of the house into the pouring rain, Tyra shouting and cursing at the open door he left behind him.

'Follow him,' Odi commanded her.

'Bugger this. Bugger him!' snarled Tyra. But she did as she was told, grabbing some waterproofs off the hooks in the porch and running out in the rain after him. Bea set off after her, but . . .

'You stay here,' said Odi. 'We don't want you falling into

the wrong hands again. It's dangerous out there. Tyra will look after him, I promise.'

An hour passed, then two. Frey tried to get her to bed, but Bea wasn't having it. She went to park herself in a deep windowsill at the front of her house to wait for them to come back. Silvis joined her – didn't say a word, just plonked herself down on the other end, kicked off her slippers, rubbed her bare feet against Bea's, and took out her book.

It was a long wait. The rain and wind came in waves. Frey joined them at midnight and an hour or two after that, Odi joined the vigil too, but it wasn't until dawn was edging the sky that the door banged open and her dad came staggering in. He was slathered in mud from head to foot and he looked dreadful – grey with exhaustion. He crashed into a chair as soon as he was inside, filthy with mud, and fell straight to sleep. Behind him Tyra stood in the doorway like a mud spirit. Over her shoulder she carried a rucksack.

'That was a night of it,' she said.

She came in, sat down on an old church pew they had up against one wall and presented her filthy boots to Silvis, who bent to pull them off her feet. Standing up she pulled her waterproofs over her head and stripped her trousers off. Then she unzipped her rucksack and rolled something onto the table, wrapped in a polythene bag. Inside was a skull, fresh from the grave, filthy with dirt – teeth bared, eye sockets full of mud, stained brown and orange from underground. Odi picked it up and examined it closely.

'You bloody idiot,' groaned Frey. 'Where did you get that?'

Tyra flopped back down in her seat. 'He went galloping up that hill like an idiot, never mind the rain, and started clawing at a grave like a dog after a bone. I managed to convince him to come away and get some shovels and then we both got at it. Should have seen us! Slipping and sliding in the grave-dirt like a pair of ghouls. No one out in that weather of course. Hard work! Haven't had so much fun in ages!'

'Who is it?' said Frey.

Tyra leaned forward and tapped the skull with one finger. 'A poet used to live in there,' she said.

Frey groaned.

Tyra looked up at Odi, who was still turning the skull over in his hands. 'Well?' she demanded. 'Was he on to something or have I been wasting my time?'

Odi nodded and smiled. 'It's perfect.'

'But why? Is the spirit still in it?' asked Bea, squinting at the skull – trying to look at it with her witch eyes.

'Her spirit is gone,' said Odi. 'But I think she's left some of her poetry behind.' He reached a finger inside the mouth of the skull, poked around and retrieved a small muddy stone stuck in there, which he held up between his fingers.

'Is that poetry?' Bea asked.

'She wrote such beautiful poems. This one was never finished,' said Odi. He polished it on his sleeve and it began to shine, purple, red and blue. 'Over time it's turned into a jewel. Your father is a wonder, Bea. If this doesn't work for your mum, nothing will.'

* * *

By midday the skull was there on the breakfast table scrubbed clean and polished, its teeth brushed and gilded, its eye sockets painted deepest blue, its cheeks red, its dome orange – Kelsey's favourite colours. Bea and her dad had spent the morning decorating and furnishing it. They rolled photographs of the family into thin cigars and pushed them into the brain cavity, glued ribbons to its dome, painted little images of the family around the forehead and rested it on a cushion, like a crown.

Odi had attached the jewel right at the back of the mouth, where the root of her tongue had once been. He looked down at it and smiled.

'Listen,' he said. They all bent their ears low to the skull – and yes, there was a voice again for the long-dead poet. Bea bent as close as she could, and she could hear singsong whisperings, a faint but lovely tune. But no words she would make out.

'It's not a language of this world,' was all Odi would say. He smiled. 'Thank you, Jamie; and Tyra. This is wonderful. There's nothing more to be done. It's ready.'

40

The following morning they set out. Bea's dad walked ahead, carrying the fetish. Odi, Tyra and Frey followed and behind them came Bea and Silvis. A thin drizzle fell, but the air was sweet and cool. The dead elder was rooted in an outcrop of rock on the lip of the valley, surrounded by stunted oaks, bilberry, heather, ferns and rushes. A few bees flew to and fro, gathering the last of the nectar from the ivy that grew nearby, but most of them were already keeping warm in their nest. Bea's dad took the fetish carefully out of the box and put it on the ground a little way back from the tree. He sat on the ground behind it on a cushion wrapped in a black bin bag – it could be a long wait. The others sat in a loose ring behind him except Odi, who went up to the elder tree and knelt on the ground in front of it.

'Here we go, then,' whispered Frey. 'Good luck, all.'

The drizzle gathered in tiny beads on their coats, and the sun shone thin beams from behind the clouds. Odi, Tyra and Frey began to chant and mutter in low, garbled voices.

Bea had been waiting for this moment for so long. All the time she had spent at the Green House . . . all the training she'd gone through, the hours of study, the terrible deeds she had committed – all of it had been with this one aim in mind: to bring her family back together. She had been fooled, twisted out of shape, lied to, abused, but after everything that had happened, here she was still, with that same aim in mind, that same willingness to do whatever she needed to achieve her goal.

For a long time, nothing happened. Hours passed. A blackbird flew into the clearing and was landing on the grass before it saw the group sitting around and rushed off again, squawking in panic. More hours. Bea lost concentration. She was almost dozing when she was woken up by a nudge from Silvis, who was pointing at the tree. There was some movement around the crook of one of the branches.

'The bees,' she whispered.

Yes, the bees. A group of them were buzzing around a small crack in the bark. Another emerged, and another. Others were crawling out from various nooks and crannies in the old hollow tree.

'Your mum's showing herself,' crowed Tyra. Frey hushed her and she clapped her hand over her mouth.

A low buzz sounded in the air. Soon the bees were popping out of the hollow trunk one after the other, as if the tree was firing them into the air . . . more and more of them, flying in circles around the glade. Still they came, rushing in droves now, hundreds of them – thousands. The air was thick with little dots swaying in the air, filling the glade with an intense loud buzz.

There was a tickle on Bea's hand. A bee had landed there. She had to resist the temptation to slap at it.

The bees had begun to move away from the tree towards

Jamie and the fetish. The swarm was now three or four metres across, a loose cloud of swiftly moving insects with Bea's dad at the centre of it, his hair stirring in the wind from thousands of tiny wings. The buzzing grew louder and louder, filling the whole glade. Her dad turned slowly to Bea and beamed. 'Can you hear it? Her voice, in among the bees. Can you hear her?'

Bea listened carefully – and yes. The bees were buzzing in her mother's voice. She smiled back – Yes! Yes! It was working! But even as she did so she felt more movement on her hand. Not one, not two, but maybe a dozen bees were settling on her. There were more around her. Was this right? Weren't they supposed to go into the fetish skull?

'Stay still, Bea,' said Frey quietly. Bea did as she was told, but it wasn't easy. The bees were gathering on her now – not just on her arms, but on her hair, on her hands, on her face. It was the bees on her face that she found hardest. More were settling on her all the time.

The buzzing around her went up a notch in pitch.

'OK, Bea,' said Frey calmly. 'I want you to get up very slowly and walk away. OK? Do it now, please.'

Bea stood up, very slowly as she had been told. The bees rose from her skin and buzzed louder, more angrily. She turned – and they went for her. The first sting was on her face. In that moment the rest of the swarm that had been gathering about her father swooped into the air and headed for her in one dark cloud.

'Run!' yelled Frey.

Bea turned and fled, but the swarm was faster. She put her hands up to protect herself but they were all over her, stinging,

stinging, stinging. Someone grabbed her from behind, scooped her up and wrapped her up in a coat – she knew by the smell it was her dad. He ran with her in his arms for home, the bees in pursuit. It wasn't just Bea they wanted now, but anyone who got in their way. By the time the witches gathered back at Salem Row, everyone had been stung, although no one else as badly as Bea. Her face had swollen right up, especially where they'd got her on her eyes and lips.

Frey treated her, gently dabbing her wounds with a herbal mix that soothed the pain. But Bea was distraught.

'She hates me, she hates me,' she wept.

'She doesn't hate you,' said Frey scornfully. 'She's angry with you. It's not the same thing.' He continued dabbing at her swollen skin for a while before he added, 'If she had wanted to re-join us, Bea, she would have. I'm afraid it's not looking good.'

The others were sitting at the kitchen table, waiting for their turn to be treated, and Odi cut in when Bea was about to protest.

'It's her choice and her right, Bea. We've offered her a home in this world and she's said no.'

'She hasn't said no,' said Bea. 'She was going into it – it was me being there put her off. You have to try again without me there.'

Odi looked at Frey, who shrugged.

'One more time, maybe,' he said.

So they did try – one more time. But this time there was no movement at all. The bees stayed inside the tree.

'She's begun her journey to the Underworld,' said Odi.

'It would be dangerous to try any more. As Gila told you, there are other spirits who share that world with the dead. It's over, Bea. We did our best. Respect her wishes. It's time to say goodbye to your mother. Let her rest in peace.'

41

The witches did their best to help Bea move on, Tyra in particular insistent that this was just a setback. So her mum had refused to return – all the more reason to move on with the fight. There were so many other lost souls to rescue.

'Remember your vow at the trial,' she said. 'You have an obligation. It's time to set your sights on the others.'

And Bea tried, she really did. She sat with the others and talked and made plans and discussed options. But it was no use. She had been through so much – fooled and abused by Lok, humiliated and shamed in the ordeal of the trial and now finally, with her failure to rescue her mum, her spirit broke. For three days she forced herself to face the world. On the fourth, she simply didn't get up.

Frey tried to fetch her down for breakfast. She said yes, in just a moment, but didn't move. Her dad came next. He sat by her bed and tried to get her to talk, but she just lay there with her back to him. He went downstairs alone.

In the afternoon Tyra came up and roared and bellowed around her room: 'What is this shit? You think Lok is going to come here to find you? You have to go and find him, you silly little cow. Bea! I'm talking to you – you better get yourself together—'

She didn't get any further. Odi came up and ordered her out. Odi waited until Tyra's feet left the stairs, then sat himself down on the edge of the bed and put his hand on Bea's back. She didn't respond, just lay there with her face to the wall.

He patted her gently a few times and left. A little later, Frey came up with another brew for her to drink.

'It's time for you to take care of yourself,' he said as she drank it down. 'Rest for now. You're safe here and so are we. You can pick up again when you're ready.'

Bea drained the cup and flopped back down. Frey paused at the door.

'I know it doesn't help just now, but you won't feel like this for ever,' he said. He closed the door quietly behind him, and left her to it.

He was right; it didn't help. What was she good for? Killing her friends and letting people down. She had failed to save her own mother. What was the point of even trying?

Silvis was out that day, but when she came back in the evening, she went straight up to see Bea, still wearing her coat.

'I just want to be left alone,' Bea told her.

'I know,' said Silvis, pulling off her outdoor clothes. 'But I'm staying here anyway.' And she did, for hour after hour. She was undemanding, didn't need to talk or do anything – just lay and read her book and cuddled up to her from time to time. Bea found what comfort she could in her friend's loyalty.

* * *

Mid-morning, four days later; a tread on the stairs. The door creaked, a pair of boots scuffed the floorboards. Tyra had been on a binge for a few days, according to Silvis – out on the town getting drunk. Bea's back was turned and there was a pause as Tyra stood next to the bed looking down at her. Then the rough sound of wood on the threadbare carpet as she pulled the bedside chair over to the wall. Tyra sat.

Bea kept still; if she thought she was asleep, the old witch might leave. She did almost doze, and when she came to, she turned her head quickly to take a peek. Tyra was still there, her arms resting on her thighs, leaning forward, staring at her.

Great.

Bea turned back. There was another long pause.

'I don't suppose they've told you the news, then,' said Tyra at last. 'They're being so careful with poor little Bea! You want to hear it? It seems that your murderous little spree goes on.'

Bea froze. That wasn't possible. She hadn't left Salem Row.

'The good news just keeps rolling in,' sneered Tyra. 'Yes – Lok is on the move. Carlisle one day, Leeds the next. Manchester, Burnley, Halifax. All around the northwest. Nice folk, I knew most of them. Gila, remember her? Her golem is run by a mouse now. A mouse! You can't ever accuse Lok of lacking a sense of humour, can you? Well, well. Dear Bea. You're the prize that just keeps on giving, aren't you?'

Bea swung round to face her. 'But it can't be, I've been here all the time!' she exclaimed.

'Oh, it speaks – to defend itself, of course. You don't need to *do* anything any more. You already did it. My God, you're

like a fucking plague, girl. You don't even have to be anywhere
to kill people. How do you do it?'

'It's not me!'

'Of course not. It's Lok. Who else?' Tyra demanded. 'All
those spirits you stole for him.' She shook her head in disgust.
'They're all beating their brains out trying to discover what
sort of powers he has now. He's certainly learned to locate
witches – he's going directly from one group to the next. He
must have a small fleet of Rooks going round with him, the
way he's going through us. You must be so pleased with yourself – you little shit.'

Tyra was leaning right forward, almost hissing at her. Bea
heard it with disbelief. It was getting worse? How could it get
worse? More deaths, more thefts, more horror.

'Why are you telling me this?' she wailed.

'Oh, I think you need to know. I think you *deserve* to know,'
said Tyra.

'I hate you . . .'

'Yes, and I hate you. And you know what I hate most of
all about you? The way you've just given up. You just lie there,
wallowing like the little shit you are. You had one setback.
Now look at you. *Oh, I'm all so depressed.* Fuck off.'

Bea was astonished that she was being spoken to like that.
'I tried, didn't I?' she yelled. 'I couldn't even get my mum
back – I'm allowed to be depressed. It didn't work!' she
screamed suddenly, finally losing her temper. Downstairs there
were calls and the sounds of people running to see what the
matter was.

'You gave up on us, you little bitch. You gave up on me,

you gave up on us, you've given up on your own mother,' sneered Tyra. 'God, how I despise you—'

Behind her, someone banged at the door. Tyra stood up and jammed her foot against it.

'What's going on?' yelled Frey.

Tyra stared at Bea and spat. A glistening gob of it landed on her chest. Suddenly Bea had had enough. She launched herself at Tyra, went for her eyes with her nails, but Tyra just seized hold of her, not even with her big hand, held her at arm's length and shook her until her teeth rattled.

'You think you can take me on?' she hissed. With her free hand, her big hand, she reached out, dug her fingers into the wall and pulled out a handful of crushed stone. 'I'm the Grip, girlie. Don't mess with me.'

Bea stared in amazement. The sheer force of it stunned her. The old witch flung her down onto the bed, where she scurried back against the wall and crouched fearfully.

'What do you want?' she begged. 'I tried. I tried! It didn't work.'

Tyra seemed to literally bulge with rage. Suddenly she reached down, seized her by the throat and pulled her right up to her face. 'You're a fucking *summoner*,' she hissed, low so that the others pounding and yelling on the door wouldn't hear. 'Your own mother is in the process of leaving this world and you lie in bed doing nothing.'

'But . . .' Bea was astonished. 'Odi said no.'

'Odi said, Odi said,' mimicked Tyra in a hoarse whisper. 'A stupid old fool who doesn't even know what world he's living in. You are a summoner. So *summon*.'

She took a slip of paper out of her pocket and jammed it down Bea's front. 'You can get your mother back, girl. You just have to tell her where to go.'

Tyra took another moment to watch Bea cringe before her, then dropped her abruptly back on the bed and opened the door. Outside, Frey, Odi and Silvis all crowded in the entrance.

'What's going on?' demanded Frey.

'Just a minor disagreement,' said Tyra. She spread out her arms and herded them away like sheep. 'Nothing to see here. Move on please, move on.'

Silvis slipped under her arm and dodged into the room. 'What happened?' she asked; but Bea shook her head and refused to say. Silvis climbed onto the bed and stared at her anxiously. Seeing she was OK, the others left, still arguing on their way downstairs.

Bea lay gazing at the ceiling, her eyes darting from side to side as she tried to work it all out.

'There've been more deaths,' she said.

Silvis let out her breath in a rush. 'She's told you.'

Bea looked at her. 'Why didn't *you* tell me?' she demanded.

'We didn't know if you—'

'What?'

'If you could take it! Be fair, Bea. You've been through so much.'

Bea nodded. 'How many?' she asked.

Silvis shook her head. 'Bea . . .'

Bea sat up to confront her. 'Tell me.'

'I suppose it's out now.' Silvis hung her head. 'About twelve, as far as we know.'

'Dead? Or turned to golems?'

'Both. The most powerful ones are killed so their spirits can't be put back.'

'In how many days?'

'Oh, Bea. About a week. But it's stopped now. There's been no news of more for a day or two.'

Bea shook her head. But it would start again, of course.

'Bea, yes, of course we all want you to fight Lok – to summon the spirit out of him. It's the only thing that can work. But look at you! You can hardly get out of bed. And now you've lost your mother. You have to get over that. We're trying to give you time.'

'While more witches die,' said Bea quietly.

'You can only do what you can do,' said Silvis. 'Your spirit is wounded. No one can do good work while their spirit is sick.'

Bea leaned back. Silvis watched her, frowning. 'Now's not the time. You'd fail,' she said bluntly. 'Give yourself a break, Bea. You're our last chance. Listen to your spirit. Are you really ready?'

'No,' said Bea. 'But witches are dying. I can't keep letting that happen.'

Silvis came to put her arms around her. 'As I said, it's stopped for now. Be sensible, Bea. Wait until you've got at least a fighting chance. Promise me, Bea. Please?'

Bea nodded. 'I promise,' she said.

Silvis kissed her, then clambered off the bed. 'I need the loo, I'll be back in a sec. Do you want anything?'

'Cheese on toast,' said Bea. Her mum always used to say

that if you were feeling down, cheese on toast was the best remedy. In the past, it had even worked.

Silvis left the room, glad to have something to do, and Bea reached down her top to find the slip of paper Tyra had shoved down there:

'Tonight. Keep quiet. I'll be waiting outside.'

42

Silvis came back in the evening and spent the night curled up on Bea's bed like a cat. Bea lay still and breathed slow, as a sleeper would. She actually fell asleep at one point, but her purpose that night woke her past midnight.

Silvis's breath was deep and slow as Bea slid quietly from under the duvet. She didn't put on any clothes in case she awoke her friend, but dressed in rainproof trousers and a coat from the hooks in the porch when she got downstairs. Then she pulled on a pair of welly boots and stepped out into the night. It was damp and blowy outside, the wind heaving at the trees in the darkness, tugging down the remaining leaves. She closed the door gently behind her and walked up the road towards the path that led to the rocky edge where her mother's spirit still hid in the old elder tree.

Tyra was waiting at the end of the row with her father.

'What's he doing here?' Bea asked.

'Maybe he can protect you.' Tyra looked critically at her. 'Well? Do you think you can do it?'

'No,' said Bea.

Tyra grunted. 'I have the fetish,' she said, patting the bag she carried over her shoulder. 'So let's go, summoner.'

'You don't have to do this . . .' began her dad.

'Jamie,' said Tyra over her shoulder. 'Shut up.'

He looked at Bea; she nodded. The three of them set off to the hollow tree.

It was a dark night, pitch black. Tyra didn't want light in case they attracted attention. 'Use your witch eyes,' she said. Of course, the spirits of the living things around them shone with life but Jamie was blind to so much of it that he was stumbling and tripping as soon as they left the paths. Tyra had to lead him by the hand like a child.

The glade in the dark was all but invisible to ordinary eyes. Only the dead branches of the tree itself showed against the sky, but life itself was everywhere. To those who could see, there was a cascade of light.

The three of them stood for a moment in the little glade, preparing themselves.

'Frey said she's starting to move on,' said Bea's dad anxiously.

'In that case she'll bring a lot of energy with her from the Underworld,' said Tyra. 'She ain't going to be happy.'

Jamie shook his head. 'I don't understand why Kelsey's so angry with Bea,' he complained.

'Bea has stolen spirits, committed murder and slept with the enemy,' said Tyra. She shrugged. What more was there to say?

The wind pushed at the trees and the cold air moved around them. Bea hated Tyra for making her commit yet another sin; but she trusted her too, for her ruthlessness, for her brutality, for her will to fight. If Tyra thought she needed to do this in order to face Lok, she'd do it. Perhaps the truth was that she had to learn to be as ruthless as Tyra herself.

'An angry mother is a powerful spirit,' said Tyra. 'She's gonna trash you. Here.' She handed Jamie the fetish. 'We stand our best chance if you have it. You're the one she's least likely to attack. OK, Bea. When you're ready.'

Bea nodded and lifted her arms as the others stepped back. She felt it coming to her at once, the power to call, as if it had been waiting in the ground for her – as if it knew that this was the right thing to do. From deep below, from far beneath her feet, it came rushing towards her. Nearer, nearer . . .

'Yes!' cried Tyra, and she ran back, away from the power of it.

'MOTHER OF MINE, I SUMMON YOU TO ME. I SUMMON AND COMMAND!'

Instantly, the tree exploded. Both Bea and Jamie were flung violently backwards. There was a light as deep and as red as blood; the spirit reared up before them, towering above the trees. Truly, it had become a demonic force.

'Send her to Jamie,' screamed Tyra. 'The fetish! The fetish!'

The ghost roared at Bea like a thunderstorm. She could see her mother in there, her features twisted out of shape into something like a Tibetan demon mask. It bellowed again, a blast of scalding air, in rage or pain, Bea had no idea. It was gathering a physical form to itself by sucking moss, soil, rocks, bits of old wood into the maw of the tornado it was generating. Bea shrieked at it. It shrieked back – then it went for her.

Bea prepared to command again, but her jaws were suddenly full of dirt from the ground. She was flung down. There was no sense of protection this time; this time she was going to die. A torrent of sticks, clods of earth, stones and branches began to rain down at her, battering her like a doll. A stone as big as a tennis ball slammed into her shoulder. She curled up, waiting for the fatal blow – but then another weight hit her back. Her dad had jumped on her, getting in between her and the spirit. The fusillade of missiles paused; the spirit moved back slightly. Somewhere, close as it was to the next world, it recognised one it had loved more simply than it had loved Bea.

'Command it,' bawled Tyra.

Bea spat out her mouthful. 'I SUMMON AND COMMAND YOU TO THE HOME WE MADE . . .' she called; but her mother's spirit did not want to be locked into this world. It shrieked at her again and thrashed at her; her father, crouched above her, groaned as he was beaten in her place. But it didn't kill him – not yet.

'I SUMMON AND COMMAND,' screamed Bea. With a shriek, the spirit, which seemed to tear itself almost in half as it did so, moved away from her and towards the fetish that was lying on the ground a short way off. 'I COMMAND!' screamed Bea one more time. And suddenly, in one crazy rush, the whole thing swooped down to the skull. There was a tornado of dust, insects, rotten wood, earth, twigs and leaves around it for a minute or more, but as the cloud of debris settled, the skull was revealed, the eyeholes glowing with a fierce white light.

Tyra came running out from behind the rocks she had hidden behind. 'I Grip you, you bitch!' she yelled, and thumped her fist down once on the skull's dome. 'Gotcha! We gotcha!' She picked the skull up and began to dance around, holding it up to the sky. 'Gotcha, gotcha!' she howled, while Bea and her dad cleared the debris off themselves and tried to clamber to their feet. Bea's dad was bleeding from several wounds, as was Bea herself. Both were bruised from head to foot. Tyra turned to look at them, grinning like a dog.

'You beauty, Bea!' she cried, clutching the skull like a treasure to her chest.

Limping, Bea made her way across to see the fetish, her dad behind her.

'I think she recognised me,' said her dad.

'Just about,' said Tyra. 'See, Bea? Depressed? – bah. You're still good for some serious action. You just caught yourself a mother.'

By the time they got back to Salem Row, the others were up – there had been a flash of light and an explosion that awoke half of Heptonstall.

'She did it! She did it!' crowed Tyra.

Odi and Frey had grim faces. 'You tore it out of the Underworld—' began Frey.

'Oh, shut it. It was only partway in. I put the Grip on it – it's not going nowhere,' said Tyra, holding the skull up in that great fist of hers. She capered about in front of the house, holding the skull above her head. 'She did it, she did it, she did it!' she yodelled. 'Now we celebrate.' She pushed past the others and ran into the house.

Silvis was furious. 'You went without me,' she said.

'It was dangerous,' said Bea.

'You could have died,' Odi said.

Bea rolled her eyes. Big deal.

'You could have wiped out the town,' said Frey.

'But I didn't, did I?' said Bea. She pushed past them and followed Tyra into the house.

43

The witches gathered in the kitchen, where Tyra had placed the skull fetish in the middle of the table as a centrepiece. She'd been to the cellar to pull out a bottle of Frey's apple brandy.

'Time to celebrate,' she said. She banged glasses on the table for everyone and began to pour.

Bea looked at the skull and the skull looked at Bea. She'd done it – captured her mother's spirit. She had no idea if it was the right thing. She wasn't even sure what was in there. All she knew was that if she hadn't got out of bed right then, she may never have moved at all.

Frey pointed a finger at it. 'That,' he said, 'is no longer your mother.'

Bea, her nose in her drink, peered at him over the lip of her glass and swallowed a mouthful. 'It's the nearest thing I've got,' she said.

'Is that all you can say?' He was genuinely furious. 'You're not planning on putting it back in her body, I hope.'

'I guess I am,' said Bea.

Frey turned to Tyra. 'What are you playing at, Tyra? You know how dangerous this is. God knows what it's brought with it from the Underworld. Don't you care about that?'

'We've got our girl back. Look! Here she is! More than you did with your lovey-dovey potions.'

Frey glared at her. 'You're an idiot,' he said. He turned on Jamie. 'You have no idea what you're playing with. She's as likely to hate you as love you, if she even knows who you are.'

Jamie looked as a pale as a ghost himself. 'I just wanted my wife back—' he began.

'You don't have your wife back!' yelled Frey. 'That thing in there could be anything. What if it doesn't want to be your wife? What if it hates you for what you've done?' He looked at the skull in disgust. 'The bloody thing could tear us all to pieces if it gets out. And you can bet it's trying right now.'

'It's got the Grip on it,' said Tyra.

Frey looked to Odi sitting quietly opposite him. 'You don't have much to say about this,' he said.

Odi shrugged. 'This has all passed out of my hands now,' he said.

'Oh, of course, you have half a billion other worlds to hang out in if this one gets blown to pieces. Why should you care?'

'It doesn't work like that, as you know,' said Odi quietly.

'What are we going to do with it? They can't put it back in its old body.'

'We don't know that,' said Odi.

Frey was visibly shocked. 'You're joking. You can't let that happen. You know how powerful these things can be.'

'Bea summoned her mother's spirit, so we can reasonably hope that it was her mother who came. She had begun to move across, and she may have lost some memories and yes, there may well be something from the Underworld in there with her – we'll have that to deal with when the time comes. But it may just be possible to get the same person back.'

Frey peered at him closely. 'What do you see, Odi?' he asked. 'How's this going to pan out?'

Odi scratched his face. 'The possibilities for this world are narrowing down very fast,' he said. 'Already I can see only twenty or thirty possible outcomes. And then . . .' He shrugged. 'To tell you the truth, it all goes dark on me fairly quickly.'

'It ends? Is that it? But what ends? This world? The witches? Or just us?'

'Could be any of them,' said Odi. 'Could be all of them. And there's another possibility; it could just be me.'

Frey looked at Tyra. 'Which one of those would you prefer?' he asked sarcastically.

'I prefer to go down fighting,' said Tyra. She lifted up her glass. 'To the future,' she said.

Silvis lifted her glass; so did Odi, Jamie and Bea. But Frey would not.

'This is wrong from top to bottom,' he said. 'I can't drink to it.'

'In that case, I'll have yours.' Tyra seized his glass and downed it in one. 'You're a fighter, Bea, and you're not afraid to break the rules. Just like me. Tomorrow, we go down and try to put your mum back in her bottle. How 'bout that!'

It was a simple plan. A visit to Bea's old house, exorcise the golem spirit from Kelsey's body, get her own spirit back in there – and then back up the hill to home. That was it. Simple – but so dangerous. Maybe they could pull it off, maybe not, but for the first time in a long, long time, the witches were fighting back.

To have any chance of success at all, they needed disguises. Half of Hebden would be watching out for them and they were going to need powerful fetishes to hide the appearance of both their spirits and themselves. Odi was going to need all his skill, but he was confident he could keep them hidden. Not for long, though.

'For every piece of magic, there is an opposition. It's a game of chess. They move so quickly these days. I can give us a few hours at most.'

'Time enough for what we have to do,' said Tyra.

While Odi locked himself away to work, Frey – refusing to change his routine in any way at all – sent Bea and Silvis to the storeroom to sort out some jam jars. He had frozen some fruit during the summer glut and now he wanted to make it into jam. But for the first time, the two girls were quarrelling. Silvis was at the sink rinsing out dusty jam jars while Bea stood behind her, nagging at her.

'You can't come,' she said.

Silvis seemed amused. 'So stop me,' she said.

'It's too dangerous.'

'Life's dangerous. So what? I'm coming.'

'You're being ridiculous,' snapped Bea. 'What can you do, anyway?'

Silvis paused her washing for a second, but enough for Bea to see how much that hurt. She regretted it as soon as she said it, but it was out now, and anyway – that was the point, wasn't it?

'Be fair, Silvis,' she said. 'You can't help. You'd be—'

'In the way?' said Silvis. 'Is that why you sneaked out without me when you went to get your mum? Because you didn't want me in the way?'

Bea groaned. It was coming out all wrong! She pulled at Silvis's arm and tried to turn her round to face her but Silvis shrugged her off.

'No! Because it's dangerous. Because I care for you.'

'Right.'

Bea shook her head. 'You know it's true, Silvis. I do care for you. But all right – yes, I don't want you in the way.' Suddenly she felt angry. 'What are you going to do anyway, open the oven door for us?'

Silvis stiffened. Bea could see how upset she was but she hardened her heart.

'Maybe it'll come one day,' she said, 'But it's not here yet. I'm sorry, Silvis. I won't let you come. You're just a kid . . .'

'What are you talking about?' snapped Silvis furiously over her shoulder. Her eyes glittered with tears. 'You can't tell me to do anything. You bloody try,' she said. She turned back and accidentally knocked a couple of jars onto the tiled floor, where they shattered.

'Now look!' Silvis pushed past her and ran out. Behind her, Bea cursed herself. She'd been crap, said all the wrong things. But Silvis would thank her one day.

She went off to talk to the others about it. Tyra, of course, was in favour of anyone who wanted to fight. Frey was on her side. A draw. She was sure of Odi, though, who adored his granddaughter above anyone else. But to her surprise he backed Silvis up.

'Who knows what use she'll be?' he said. Bea and Frey were furious with him but it was no good. As usual, Odi was immoveable in *not* putting his foot down. Bea would have argued for ever – she cared about this. She didn't want Silvis caught up in her crimes. But Frey shrugged and gave up. So Silvis got her way.

44

A slim grey-bearded man in a black suit and a felt hat was standing with a short fat woman in trousers at the top of Moss Lane. The man had a suitcase by his side in which he carried the decorated skull of a dead poet. With them was a young boy about fifteen or sixteen years old, also suited, and a younger girl, no more than ten, in a neat white blouse and pleated skirt.

Jehovah's Witnesses and other evangelists often made their way up and down Moss Lane to hand out leaflets and talk about God. The witches had come today disguised as Christians. Back at Salem Row, Bea's dad and Frey held fort. Her dad had wanted to come, but Odi said no. The problem was bringing him so close to Kelsey. No one knew how he would react – not even himself. Jamie had wept and raged but it was too unpredictable and that was it.

You could see most of Hebden laid out at your feet from up here. Bea had stopped here many times in the past herself, catching her breath after coming up the hill. Back then, she'd had no idea that such things as witches even existed, let alone the Second World. Now here she was with a bunch of crazies, trying to reunite her mother's body with her spirit.

She was terrified. Terrified of her mother's golem, terrified of her spirit – if it really was her mum's spirit. Even her old home scared her, waiting there so full of memories ready to ambush her. She was even frightened of seeing her baby brother Michael again. How would he have changed?

And really, what chance did they have? Odi had more or less said it was going to end badly – and yet here he was with her, going forward.

And this was just the start. After this she had to face the Hunt to retrieve the spirits she had stolen. And then, one day – Lok himself.

Bea had risked so much, committed so many crimes in the hope that she could save her family. Now it was all coming together here on her home turf amid a host of uncertainties and with barely any plan at all. The Hunt was so powerful – and Lok! How could you defeat such a powerful witch, who had no shape, who could swallow spirits whole?

Inside her, her heart failed her. She was actually in the act of looking up at Odi to ask him if he really thought they should be doing this, when he turned his head to her – and winked. Bea turned away, confused. What did that mean? That he actually had something up his sleeve after all? Or perhaps he just thought that life was one big joke anyway?

The latter, probably.

Next to her, Tyra patted the briefcase in which she'd packed Christian pamphlets and a couple of bibles. 'Ready?' she said.

'Ready,' said Bea.

'Ready,' said Silvis in a shaky voice.

'Everything's in place,' said Odi. Tyra glanced at him, but he was already off, striding down Moss Lane.

*　*　*

Left into Beech Road. Number one, number two, number three, number four . . . number *five*. Up the steps. At the door the roses were showing off their last blooms, red on one side for Yorkshire, white on the other for Lancashire. Bea took a deep breath to stop her trembling and suppressed the urge to reach past Odi, turn the handle and walk in.

Odi glanced round to check they were all ready. 'All OK?' he asked.

Bea glanced at Silvis, whose face was as grey as concrete. There was such fear in her eyes – but she'd made her choice. She nodded.

'Get on with it,' growled Tyra.

Odi knocked on the door. Inside, a big dog started barking ferociously and Bea bowed her head. In all of this, nothing had scared her so much as the time one of the Hunt's giant hounds had held her in its jaws in the wood.

Feet pounded along the hallway and a huge grey shape loomed behind the glass of the door. It jumped up, paws on the door, taller than a man. It let out another deep, loud bark.

More steps, lighter on the wooden floor. Her mum. Oh God, thought Bea. Just then, she would rather have been anywhere but here. A brief rattle; the handle turns, the door opens a fraction . . .

It was on the chain. Her mum never kept the door on a chain. She peered round Odi's broad shoulders – and yes. A slice of her mum's face peered out at her. She looked thinner. That would please her, if she only knew.

'Good morning. Thank you for seeing us. We've got some

good news,' said Odi in his gravelly voice. 'We were wondering if we could talk to you about it.'

Kelsey's eyes shifted from one to the other. Bea automatically shrank back. Despite the fetish, despite her disguise, in her bones she could not believe that her mum would fail to recognise her.

'Your boy doesn't look very happy to be here,' said Kelsey, eyes flicking from her to Odi and back. Her voice was odd – more nervous, higher? Bea wasn't sure. Odi gestured to Bea and she stepped forward obediently and smiled.

'We'd love to tell you why we're here,' she said.

Her mum's eyes narrowed as she looked closely at her.

'We're all very friendly,' said Tyra, leaning forward and twisting her face into the nearest thing she could manage to a big smile.

Behind the door, the dog barked again. Her mum nodded. 'I don't normally, but just this once,' she said. She shook the chain off the latch and opened the door to them, watching them curiously. If Bea ever imagined for a moment that this was still her mum, she knew now it never was. No way on this earth would Kelsey ever invite evangelists into the house.

Her mum stood to one side. Odi smiled, doffed his hat and stepped past her into the house. Bea paused on the threshold and tried to wave Silvis back, but Silvis tossed her head and stepped in front of her. Bea followed her with Tyra behind.

Her mum held the dog firmly by the collar as they trooped past. The bloody thing was built like a Shetland pony. A Shetland pony with predator's teeth, Bea thought.

'He's big but he's friendly. Aren't you, boy?' said her mum, banging his sides with her hand. She smiled at Bea. Not a shred of recognition, thought Bea. Despite herself, she was disappointed.

The small group gathered in the hallway while Kelsey closed the front door behind them. The dog padded up before them to the kitchen at the back of the house. As he arrived a small figure appeared, pushing past him. A boy about three years old.

Michael. Older now, but Bea recognised him at once. It took every bit of her strength not to run to him. He was staring at her intently, a frown on his face. She smiled at him. He twitched. Kelsey was still behind her, so she risked mouthing, 'Michael,' to him.

The boy, who had been half hiding behind the dog, stepped out, looking at her intently. Could he sense her spirit? He'd been so tiny when she last saw him.

Kelsey pushed her way past them. 'Come on, you,' she said, shooing Michael back into the kitchen diner. But as she reached him, he dodged past her and ran full pelt towards Bea. Bea caught him in her arms as he flung himself at her and she pulled him to her chest. Michael hugged her, hard, hard as he could and Bea hugged back, trying to look surprised and keep the tears out of her eyes at the same time. Up the hallway Kelsey stood, frowning at her from the kitchen door.

'He's so good with the little ones,' said Odi, but Bea hardly heard him. Her little brother had buried his face into her neck.

'That's not my mummy. That's not my mummy,' he whispered desperately to her. 'I don't like that lady.'

Bea held him tight and took deep breaths. She opened her mouth to speak, tried to stay calm, but her throat was so dry all she could manage was a croak. Odi stepped forward to hide her from Kelsey's view. He paused there for a moment, talking about the house, how nice it was, how well looked after. Then he went through into the kitchen. Bea followed, Michael still in her arms: her mother frowned as she passed. Odi had just gone through the door and Bea was peering past his bulky form into the house, when Tyra leaned past her and banged her fist neatly but forcibly in Odi's back, just under the ribs. The big man paused and bent his head.

'Ah,' he said in an odd little voice. 'This world.' He half turned to Bea and smiled at her as Tyra pulled back her hand. Bea saw the blade she held: serrated, hooked, wicked, red with blood; over twenty centimetres long.

Odi fell to his knees and put out an arm. 'Silvis,' he croaked; but he was looking at Bea. 'Silvis,' he said again. Silvis ran to him as he tipped forward onto the carpet. All Bea could do was stare and stumble backwards, with Michael in her arms. Of all things! Of all possible things, this she had not considered. She stared down at the stricken giant at her feet. Already, colours and shapes were forming around him – his memories, preparing to leave.

'Here's the darkness, old man,' Tyra said. She shoved Silvis aside, pushed Odi flat to the ground and finished him off by sinking the blade under the skull and pushing it in up to the brain.

Suddenly there was chaos. At the second of death, everything left him in a single pulse – memories, dreams, ideas going back goodness knows how long. The house, the ground, the town itself shook with the violence of it and for minutes on end all any of them could do was fall to the ground and clutch their heads, and wait for the confusion to stop.

By the time Bea got back to her feet, Michael and Kelsey were both screaming, Silvis was flat on her back, the dog was howling – but the enemy was already in control.

'Hide, little rat,' commanded Tyra, and obediently, gratefully almost, Kelsey dived under the table. She scuttled back behind the chairs and hid there, back to the wall, peering anxiously from behind the chair legs. Michael had buried his head as far as he could into Bea's shoulder, hiding his eyes from what was going on, whimpering. The dog still crouched, growling, his eyes going from Tyra to Bea, unsure who to attack. Tyra put out a hand towards it, and the dog lay obediently. Behind them both, Silvis started to scream.

'Run, you idiot,' Bea said – too late. Already she could hear the bikes roaring up the hill. She stepped quickly over the huge still body of Odi to put herself in between Silvis and Tyra, who was wiping her blade on the tablecloth.

'Take him!' she commanded, holding Michael out to Silvis. Her brother screamed and held tighter onto her. Silvis paused a moment, gathering her wits, then she dragged Michael off Bea and ducked down to hide with him under the table with Kelsey.

'Pathetic place to hide,' said Tyra.

Bea lifted up her chin to face him. 'Hello, Lars,' she said.

Tyra glanced at her and smirked. 'Fooled ya. I so fooled ya!'

Even as he spoke he began to change – taller, thinner; hair from grey to red. It only took a moment and there he stood – beautiful, laughing, just as he had been when she first saw him at the skateboard park. Bea realised three things: first, that she hated him with all her heart. Second, that despite that, she had missed him. Thirdly, that she would do everything she possibly could to kill him.

She was taken with an immense calm. She had to do this very carefully.

'When did you take Tyra?' she asked.

'Ah! We found her drunk in a ditch one night while you were busy being miserable. She always drank too much. I sniffed her out – one of my many new talents, thank you very much. Remember the witch-sniffer? No? Perhaps I lied to you about him,' he said. His bright eyes glittered at her, 'Man, she kicked and screamed until we ripped that hand off her. Then she went through the Rook easily enough. With her spirit inside me, the Spook thought I was her. Easy. Everything's easy, Bea, once you know how.' He smiled and dipped his head to one side. 'Oh, Bea, I know I was a bad boy. But we had fun, didn't we? Didn't we have the *best* fun!'

'You could have taken us in Salem Row.'

'Ooh, no, far too dangerous! You were there, Odi was there. Frey might look like a wimp but he has a few tricks up his sleeves. And of course my friends couldn't get there because of the Spook – which is a wonderful thing, don't you think? My first invention! Now, *this* way I have a few more bargaining chips. Your mum's spirit, which you so thoughtfully called up for me. Little Silvis, who so stupidly came along. Little Michael.

All at my mercy. Maybe we can do a deal. Hmm? Your spirit for theirs. You see, Bea, Bea – I very much want your spirit.'

As he spoke, the front door opened and footsteps came up the hall.

'And here come the troops. Back-up. Not that I need much back-up these days. I am an army unto myself – thanks to you, my beautiful Bea.' The door opened, and in came the Huntsman himself.

'You have her,' he said. He grinned; but he was not the boss there.

'Wait outside,' Lok commanded him. 'Surround the house. No one is to go in or out. This one's mine.'

The Huntsman scowled but nodded, and left. They could hear him repeat the orders in the yard. Outside the bikes revved, the dogs growled. Inside her, Bea's heart fluttered like a trapped bird.

'Quite a few of them out there,' said Lok. 'No escape. And now – well. I think we're done, don't you? You, my little sweetie, are the final thing. The summoner. The Rook is far too slow and clumsy. With your spirit inside me, sweet Bea, I can call up whatever I want, whenever I want.

'So, tell you what – how about you just submit? Look, Odi is dead. I can't tell you what a pest he was! He can mix up worlds. Did you know that? I never knew what was going on half the time.' He poked the old man with his feet. 'Dead, dead, dead. Pity. I'd have liked his spirit. But he was far too dangerous.' He smiled at her, as if killing was a normal thing.

'You must hate us all so much,' said Bea, buying time to calm her terror.

'No! I loved you, Bea. I still do. I fell in love with you when you first rode my board, and I loved you even more when I realised who you were. I know – I lied and lied and lied to you, but I never stopped loving you. Still do now.'

Horrified, Bea shook her head.

'Not that love makes much difference,' admitted Lok. 'So, come on – what do you say?' He bent down to pick up the suitcase at Odi's side, now stained in his pooling blood. He clicked it open and peered inside at the fetish containing Bea's mother. 'What a good job you did with it! I could do some very nasty things with her, you know. Frey was right when he said it didn't belong here.' He lifted up the skull out of the suitcase and shook it in his ear. 'She sounds *very* unhappy. But it doesn't have to be like that. We could put her into her body again. Your family, all together, just like you always wanted. Except for you, of course. And your little friend! Look – poor Silvis, with her pretty little voice. What shall we do with her, eh? Something nasty or something nice? Your call, Bea. And Michael. Sweet Michael. Nasty or nice? What do you say?' He stuck his face forward. 'You don't stand any chance against me, you know that, don't you? I have the Grip.'

All the time he was speaking, Bea was preparing herself. Odi was lying in a pool of his own blood – so much for her imagining he had any kind of handle on this. Silvis was crouching in the corner, shaking like a leaf. She was completely on her own and out of her depth – and she knew at once what Lok meant about the Grip; he could use it to keep his own spirit inside him. She was defeated before she'd even started – but she would try. Here in her own home, she would try. As Odi had said – trying is all we ever have.

She felt down into herself, and it was there waiting. She lifted her arms . . .

'Oh dear,' said Lok. 'The trouble is, it will hurt me. And I'm not going to be very happy about that.'

And then it arrived . . .

'I SUMMON AND COMMAND YOU, FATHER OF LIES, CREATURE OF GREED AND DECEIT, MAN WITH TWO FACES. I SUMMON AND COMMAND YOU HERE TO ME.'

Lok leaned forward and gritted his teeth. 'It won't leave me,' he hissed. 'Tyra's Grip holds it tight. My spirit is anchored.'

Bea reached right inside him and found his spirit easily enough; it lay inside his second face. She seized hold of it, and pulled . . . and pulled . . . and pulled.

It was rock-tight. It was like pulling at a mountain's root. Lok roared with the pain of feeling his spirit tugged like that, but they both knew it would not give. Bea had as much chance of lassoing the moon as of pulling the spirit of Lok out into the open air.

Even so, she heaved. She heaved and heaved and heaved.

'You feel it?' he roared. 'You feel how strong I am? Give it up, child. I am as old as the hills, as wicked as the Devil. You *cannot* defeat me.'

That was the truth of it; she was certain it was so. But Bea had one last trick up her sleeve. She still had the connection to his spirit and it had to obey her if it could. One more try . . .

'SPIRIT OF LOK, MAN OF TWO FACES, FATHER OF LIES, BROTHER-KILLER, TRAITOR – I SUMMON AND COMMAND; SHOW YOURSELF AND SPEAK.'

Lok hollered in rage, but he had to follow her command. He turned his back and from behind him his second face, the seat of his spirit, began to migrate forward to speak to Bea. It crept up his back – Bea could see it moving under the cloth of his jacket. It appeared on his neck and then travelled up to the back of his head, where she could see it watching her dolefully from amongst his hair.

It was old – so old! Old and hideous. Bea had no doubt that she was regarding the spirit of Lok – the one thing he was never able to look at himself.

The face looked sadly at her. 'It's true. He hates me. He will show you no mercy now. You are defeated.'

'I COMMAND,' said Bea.

'You know you can't get me out,' said the face. 'I am held by the Grip of Tyra.'

'I COMMAND YOU TO TELL ME, SPIRIT OF LOK, HOW YOU MAY BE DESTROYED.'

There was a brief silence. Bea was fully expecting the answer that she could not.

'Don't tell her,' Lok shouted over his shoulder. 'Don't you dare tell her!'

The face fell silent for a moment, eyes down, then it looked up at her again.

'I cannot say. I am the spirit of Lok, so I am unable to tell the truth,' it said. 'It's against my nature. I don't even know what the truth is.'

'You are commanded,' said Bea.

The face was silent a while longer. Then it said, 'It's a hard thing you ask of me, Bea, to give myself up now of all times, when I have so much.'

'But I do command it.'

'You have no time.'

As soon as it said that word, time, Bea felt a sword of fear inside her. Was that the truth? Was her spell weakening?

'I COMMAND YOU NOW!' she roared.

'I answer, Little Bea,' snarled the face back. '*You* cannot defeat me. Only the opener of doors, the breaker of gates, the destroyer of prisons and lids can do that. Only the shatterer of enclosures, the defeater of locks, the cracker of bolts and closures can defeat me. I am the prison of spirits. And that, Little Bea, is the last thing you will hear, because now you must die.'

As it spoke, the second face began to slide back down and Lok struggled to turn and face her. She could see him glaring round at her over his shoulder, black with rage.

The spirit had tried to speak in riddles, but Bea had understood. Odi had told her.

'Silvis,' he'd said.

'SPIRIT OF SILVIS, BREAKER OF LOCKS, OPENER OF PRISONS, SHATTERER OF ENCLOSURES – SING! SING, SILVIS. I SUMMON AND COMMAND.'

And at once the voice answered her. Silvis, still clutching Michael, had no choice; she was commanded. She turned to look at Bea, opened her mouth and from within came that pure shining note. No breath was needed for it – it was spirit itself. Lok seemed to freeze in the air. He bent over and clutched at his stomach. Silvis's voice rose, pure and perfect, rising on the air. Around them the stones in the walls, the floor beneath their feet, the glass in the windows, began to vibrate in tune to it. Louder and clearer than ever it rose, filling the valley with its music. Released from her body, in the form of pure spirit, Silvis's gift was perfected.

Lok fell back, staring in panic. 'Stop her,' he begged. 'Don't let her, Bea. Remember our love!'

'Louder, Silvis darling, louder,' called Bea. At once the voice rose higher – up, up, up into the air. Behind Bea, the windows to the house burst. The glass shattered, but there was no crash or clash, no noise at all. The air had ears only for Silvis.

The humane mousetraps in the next-door house but one all burst open at the same moment; out ran the mice. The doors to a stack of rabbit hutches a couple of streets down the hill swung open in unison. The rabbits peered out, trying to work out if it was too far down to jump. Front doors the length of Hebden jumped open, and from within the dogs of the town joyfully ran out.

Who would have thought after all that had happened it would end with a song? It hit the air perfectly and resonated around them in every direction for one, two, three full minutes. The trees, the stones, the earth underfoot, even the clouds in the air began to vibrate in tune to it. In the back garden, where rows of huntsmen and women had gathered, the spirits that animated them leaped out of them. Their bodies fell to the ground. Golems, every one.

In the house, Lok fought and clawed, but there was no escaping the gift of Silvis, now released. He began to swell up like a balloon, clawing soundlessly at his chest. His clothes ripped; fault lines appeared on his swollen belly and back, then cracks. You could see the light of life escaping from it. He roared with pain. Finally, his skin ruptured right down his back, like a pupa splitting. Out of that split poured an eruption of spirits, a flood, a fountain, a cascade of life, back into the world. By their hundreds the spirits poured out from the corrupting body of Lok. Some fled up to Heaven, some to the Underworld; some wandered the earth, confused. Many of them found their true homes right there, around the house – the men and women who had been hijacked to serve the Hunt.

Silvis came to Bea's side and opened her mouth even wider to let the noise grow. Michael, perched on her hip, tried to sing with her in a baby shout. Her song spread in circles out from Moss Lane over Hebden, across the surrounding valleys and hills, past Old Town, up to the moors, on to Edge and beyond. Hutches, prisons, locked sheds, goldfish bowls, any barrier that trapped any living thing, all burst open. Boxes buried underground with treasure a thousand years ago erupted and their precious contents burst to the surface in a shower of gold. Still Silvis sang, the purest note ever heard. It rose higher and higher, hit a plateau, then, finally, began to fade. It died quite quickly, although the echoes of it hung around for over a day, vibrating among the atoms of the air.

Amid a torrent of life, as a crowd of people slowly awoke around them, two girls and a small boy fell into each other's arms and a mother emerged from under the table to greet her children.

Acknowledgements

Writing books is such a ludicrously time-consuming pastime, I wonder if a real friend wouldn't do everything possible to stop me going anywhere near it. Perhaps they encourage me to keep me away from under their feet, but I remain very grateful to everyone who has helped me with this one.

First, thanks to Lee Hardman who got the ball rolling with this project by commissioning it as an online graphic novel. Alas, the idea never got beyond the drawing board – but here it is, Lee, several manifestations later. Thanks for trying. Nothing is ever wasted.

Special thanks go to Martin Riley, who is always ready to play with stories. That man has them coming out of his ears. Stuck as I am with books, I just wish I had his facility for telling them in so many forms and in so many ways.

Thanks too to Lucy Christopher, who got the whole MS while it was still a vast amorphous blob and went through it meticulously – a real help.

My agent, Caradoc, who always manages to read my stuff quickly, always gives me great notes and is such a pleasure to talk books with. Also to Millie from the same office, for her help as well.

Andersen Press have been really supportive. My thanks are to all of them – to Klaus Flugge, of course, for managing not to stab me to death with his letter opener over the past few years when I've been so slow; to my editors – Chloe, but in particular Charlie Sheppard, to whom this book is dedicated. My early books came out of me pretty well formed, apart from minor changes, but the longer and later ones would be simply impossible for me to execute without the help of a really good editor, which she most definitely is. Couldn't have done it without you, Charlie!

I'd like to thank Cora Linn and Mel Rogerson for providing their names and paying for it in charity auctions. I hope you like your characters, even if one of them turns out to not exist even fictionally!

And finally the lovely Anita, who I'd rather have even more than all the books in the world.

JUNK

MELVIN BURGESS

WINNER OF THE CARNEGIE MEDAL AND THE GUARDIAN CHILDREN'S FICTION PRIZE

With an introduction by Malorie Blackman

Tar loves Gemma, but Gemma doesn't want to be tied down – not to anyone or anything. Gemma wants to fly. But no one can fly forever. One day, somehow, finally, you have to come down.

Junk is a powerful novel about a group of teenagers caught in the grip of heroin addiction. Once you take a hit, you will never be the same again.

'Everyone should read *Junk*'
The Times

'Ground-breaking . . . remains
the best book about teenagers
and drugs to this day'
Guardian

9781783440627